"**I wish you well,** young man, and I honor your courage, but you have chosen only to die with your lady. No man has ever faced the King Bull barehanded and lived." The chief saluted him and returned to his seat.

Conan blinked, trying to see into the darkness of the passageway. Surely, no natural bull could be so huge! Then the animal trotted into the full sunlight, and Conan's heart sank somewhat at the task he had undertaken.

The bull saw Conan and spun to face him. Down went the head, leveling the fearsome horns. To the great amazement of all who watched, Conan did not prepare to dodge. Instead, he took a wide stance, with his left foot toward the beast, his right well to the rear. His left arm was stretched out full-length, fingers extended toward a point between the bull's eyes. The right hand was clenched into a great knotty fist, cocked beside his ear. He stood unmoving as a statue, awaiting the charge.

Again, the bull flexed back slightly, dug in its hooves, and shot forward with a speed that seemed unbelievable in so large an animal. Before the horn could begin its deadly hook, Conan's fist shot forward, too swift to see. In the seats the men heard a sound like an ax sinking into a hard tree. The bull's charge halted and it stood, trembling slightly. Then Conan's fist came up again and descended like a hammer, smashing into the bull's neck just behind the skull.

Look for all these Conan books

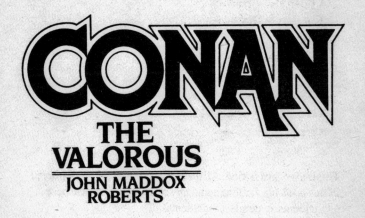

CONAN
THE
VALOROUS
JOHN MADDOX ROBERTS

A TOM DOHERTY ASSOCIATES BOOK

CONAN THE VALOROUS

Copyright © 1985 by Conan Properties Inc.

A TOR Book

Published by Tom Doherty Associates
8-10 West 36 Street
New York, N.Y. 10018

Cover art by Kirk Reinert

First TOR printing: September 1985

ISBN: 0-812-54244-4
CAN. ED.: 0-812-54245-2

Printed in the United States of America

$\mathfrak{To}$

The ChattaCon Committee, good people, good hosts. Thanks for your unfailing hospitality to Bethany and me.

In the time between the adventure of *The Bloodstained God* and the events of *The Frost Giant's Daughter,* there lies a vaguely documented period of which little is known except that, at that time, Conan made a journey to visit his Cimmerian homeland. This tale relates the events of that homefaring.

One

In the City of the Plain

Through the narrow window, with its pointed apex and ornate plaster molding, could be heard the sound of the huge drum that hung from poles of bronze above the Great Gate of Khorshemish. The deep reverberations were taken up by other, lesser drums above the city's eleven smaller gates, serving notice to all that the massive oaken doors were about to shut for the night. Any now outside who did not scurry within ere the gates closed must remain through the dark hours upon the grassy plain, and not seek to enter the city upon pain of death.

The woman who sat behind the massive table looked up from the fine parchment upon which she was writing in the tortuous hieroglyphs of Stygia. The last red rays of sunlight streaming through the lancet window glittered upon the serpent bracelets circling her bare arms and on the cobra-headed band of gold that rested above her straight black brows. At a slight beckoning of her hand a tall man strode from the corner of the room in which he had been standing. His dress was that of a desert man from east of Shem.

"Moulay," the woman said, "it is time. Go and find this man of whom we have been told, and bring him here. As you

1

go, tell our host to send up more lamps. I would see the man when he arrives."

The man called Moulay bowed with hand to breast. "As you command, my lady."

He descended the broad stairway to the tessellated floor of the small courtyard, which surrounded a marble pool. After delivering the order for lamps, he walked out through the pointed archway, which gave onto the narrow street.

At this time of evening the street was devoid of all except foot traffic. The animals of farmers and caravaneers were banished to pens and stables without the city walls during the night hours, and the small merchants of the marketplaces were folding up their mats and awnings.

Stopping occasionally to ask directions of local residents, Moulay made his way into the oldest part of the city, where the streets were even narrower, the buildings shabbier, and the noise much louder. If the rest of the city were shutting down for the night, this district was just beginning to open up. Heavily painted women in revealing dress called to him as he passed. Moulay ignored them, his carriage and stride bespeaking his heritage as a proud desert man, his swarthy, scarred face and fierce gaze discouraging any thoughts of violence from the minds of lurking footpads.

The inn he sought was a dilapidated place; great chunks of whitewashed plaster had fallen away from its walls, exposing the ugly brown mud brick beneath. Moulay stooped low as he passed through the doorway into the dim, smoky interior of the common room. A short fat man came up to him, wiping his hands upon his soiled apron.

"Welcome, sir," the innkeeper said above the sound of a few musicians' tuneless, wailing music. "Would you have food? Wine? Lodging? All is to be had at this house."

Moulay held up a silver coin and said a few words to the man, whose face took on a look of wonderment.

"The Cimmerian? Yes, he is here, but what use have you for that rogue?"

"My business with him is none of your concern. Just lead me to him." Moulay looked about the room for a man who answered the description his mistress had given him.

"These Cimmerians breed to type," she had said. "He will be tall, and dark-haired. His eyes will probably be blue. His skin will be pale or dark, depending upon how much he has been in the sun of late. He will almost certainly be stronger and quicker than most men. Like all northern barbarians, the Cimmerians are known for uncertain moods and quick tempers. Take care with him."

Moulay saw no man in this room who answered that description. A few tables held small parties of townsmen or foreigners, most of them caravaneers. The slow rattle of the dice bespoke the earliness of the hour. Later, after the wine had flowed freely, things might well get raucous, culminating in a brawl broken up by the city watch.

Seeing the direction of Moulay's gaze, the innkeeper said: "No, he is not here, although he has been making this room a living hell all month. Come with me."

Moulay strode across the common room and up a flight of rickety wooden stairs. The loft above had been divided by thin partitions into a multitude of tiny, dark cubicles. The innkeeper took a lantern from a wall hook, and going to the last and smallest room, held the lamp high. The doorway had not so much as a curtain, and Moulay looked inside.

The desert man's thin lips curved into a contemptuous smile. "*This* is the great Cimmerian warrior?" he demanded.

The occupant of the room, half-sitting, his back against the wall, was snoring faintly, his massive arms folded across his breast. The man's shaggy head was sunk upon his chest, and his only clothing was a ragged white loincloth. On his feet were sandals with holes worn in their soles. The room's only furnishing was a thin carpet.

"He calls himself Conan, and he arrived here a month ago looking like a Turanian general at the very least," the innkeeper explained. "He had a fine horse and saddle, a sword, armor, bow—everything. He had money, too, and he spent it freely. Every night he drank and gambled with his friends and bought them wine. When his money was gone he wagered his weapons and horse and his other belongings. What he has left is what you see now. I tried to throw him out this morning, but he threatened to break my neck. I was waiting for the watch to make their first rounds for the night to have them take him away."

"Then he is just a thief," Moulay said, "and a stupid one. He must have stolen those things he came here with. This can be no warrior. Well, I must bring him nevertheless. You may go, but leave the lantern." With an expressive shrug the innkeeper did as he was bidden.

Moulay hung the lantern on a peg, squatted by the sleeping Cimmerian, and reached out to shake his shoulder. The instant Moulay's fingers touched the bronzed skin a massive hand shot out and gripped him by the neck. Moulay reached for his dagger, but his fingers found a big-knuckled hand gripping its haft. The eyes that glared at him were bright and unclouded. An ordinary man woke slowly, bleary-eyed and befuddled. Yet Moulay knew that the man had not been shamming sleep.

"Do you think I'm that easy to rob, dog?" growled the Cimmerian. His voice was deep, and his accent grated upon the ear.

"Have I any use for your filthy loincloth or your foul sandals, fool?" Moulay managed to choke out.

The grip on his throat eased somewhat. "Then why do you disturb my sleep, dog?"

"I am here," Moulay said, "to bring you to my mistress. She has a commission to be performed for which she will pay you well."

The Cimmerian released Moulay and rose. He was taller than the desert man had expected. "What commission? I'll fight for pay, but I am neither assassin nor bravo. Nor a fool to be gulled."

Outraged at this cavalier handling, Moulay straightened his robes. "She will tell you what she wants. Come with me."

The Cimmerian stretched. "I haven't eaten in two days and I'm famished. Your mistress will get little from me if I drop from hunger before I see her."

Fuming, Moulay said, "I'll buy your dinner, barbarian. Come downstairs and feed until you can hold no more."

Conan grinned. "That takes more than you would think."

Moulay scratched at the door to his lady's chamber. True to his promise, Conan had eaten enough for three men and had lost much of his surliness, even though Moulay had refused him any wine prior to his interview.

As the two had entered the most expensive inn in Khorshemish, the innkeeper had regarded the towering, nearly-naked barbarian with a dismay that bordered on horror. Conan cared little about the thoughts of a mere townsman, but he knew that his appearance might not favorably impress a prospective patron.

At Moulay's signal a woman's voice called, "Enter."

The two men went inside. "My lady, this is the Cimmerian you wished to see. His name is Conan."

Moulay stepped aside and Conan stared at the woman. She was beautiful, with square-cut black hair, a dark complexion, and fine, aristocratic features. Her eyes were large and black, rimmed with heavy kohl. The kohl, her serpent-decorated jewelry, and her severe black robes proclaimed her a Stygian. He had no love for Stygia, nor for its ancient evils and sorceries.

"I am Hathor-Ka," she said. "Come closer."

Reluctantly, Conan obeyed. Starting at his toes, the woman

studied every inch of his body, pausing to take note of the powerful thighs, the lean waist and broad chest, his heavy arms and thick, swordsman's wrists.

"Turn around," she ordered. Not sure why he did so, Conan obeyed and she gave his back the same careful scrutiny. "You seem fit," she pronounced at length.

Conan turned to face her. She had the impassive Stygian countenance that made age difficult to judge. She might have been in late youth or early middle age; and although her beauty was great, it left him unstirred.

"You are a Cimmerian," she said. "I have need of a Cimmerian."

"Why a Cimmerian?" he asked. "I've been hired for my good sword arm before, and even for my skill as a thief, but never for the land of my birth."

She leaned back slightly and gazed up at him with unfathomable eyes. "I wish you to undertake a mission for me to your homeland. You must deliver something for me, to a certain mountain cave in Cimmeria. In return"—she reached beneath her robe and drew forth a leathern bag which she dropped to the table with a loud klink—"this shall be yours. Open it."

Conan picked up the bag and loosened its drawstrings. Fine gold Aquilonian coins sparkled in the candlelight. His heart exulted but he let nothing show in his face or voice. "What are the terms? Half now and half when I've made your delivery?"

"No. If you agree to undertake this mission, it is yours now."

"You are trusting," the Cimmerian said. "How do you know I won't toss your parcel into the nearest bush when I ride from here?"

"I am many things, Cimmerian," Hathor-Ka said, "but trusting I am not. You Cimmerians are said to be people who do not give their word lightly. Swear that you will do my bidding in this without fail.''

"So be it." Conan tossed up the bag and caught it as it fell. "I swear I will take whatever it is to Cimmeria, and deliver it to this mountain cave you speak of.''

"That is not enough!" she said.

"Why not?" he said, nettled. "I do not break my word.''

"You must swear by Crom!'' she demanded.

Rashly, wanting the gold and not pausing for thought, Conan said, "Very well, then. I swear by Crom to do your bidding." As soon as the words were off his tongue he would have given the whole bag of gold to have them back. What knew this woman of Crom, and what was her purpose?

Hathor-Ka leaned back again with a cruel smile upon her lips. "That word you must not break, Cimmerian. In Stygia we have knowledge of all the gods, and your pitiless Crom will not suffer his name to be used lightly.''

"You have the truth of it," Conan admitted.

The woman nodded to Moulay, and he went to a rich chest that stood in a corner. Taking a heavy key from within his sash, the desert man unlocked the chest. He threw back the lid, and from its depths withdrew a small flask of silver, sealed with lead. The seal was stamped with an oddly disturbing hieroglyph. Hathor-Ka accepted the flask from the hand of her servant and held it out to Conan. Reluctantly, he took it and felt its surprising lightness.

"It feels empty," Conan said.

"It is not," Hathor-Ka assured him. "Your duty is simple. When you enter the cave, you must build a fire. Then you must unseal the flask and pour its contents on the flames, calling my name three times in a loud voice. Is that clear?''

The hairs on the back of Conan's neck prickled. This was sorcery, and he wanted nothing to do with it, but he had given his word. Crom curse me for a fool! he thought. "And then?" he asked.

"Then your duty is discharged and you may do as you like," she said.

"Well," he growled, "it seems simple enough. Which mountain is this cave in? Cimmeria is full of mountains, and most of them have caves."

"This cave you should have no trouble finding," she assured him. "You are familiar with a mountain called Ben Morgh?"

Now Conan's heart sank into his worn-out sandals. "Ben Morgh?" he said in an awed whisper.

"Exactly. The flask must be emptied on a fire as the sun rises upon the morn of the autumnal equinox in the great cave in the east face of the mountain called Ben Morgh." She smiled at the dismay writ large on the face of the Cimmerian. "What ails you, Conan? You seem to fancy yourself a hero. Have you no stomach for a hard journey and a climb up a mountain?"

"You Stygian bitch!" Conan said, ignoring Moulay's hasty grab at his dagger, "Ben Morgh is the home of Crom! That cave is the home of my people's god!"

The man who dangled outside, just above the window, heard those words with much interest. He was supported only by a thin rope, one end of which was looped about the battlement surrounding the inn's flat roof, the other end terminating in a broad leather strap buckled about the man's ankle. When speech within the room concluded, he hoisted himself back to the roof, set about detaching his tackle, and looped it about his waist.

He was a small man, quick and deft in his movements. He sat atop a merlon as he performed his task and watched the street below. It was full dark now, but his eyes were as sensitive as a cat's; he recognized the Cimmerian, who emerged from the building and turned to walk dejectedly toward the poorer quarter of the city.

The little man crossed over several tight-packed rooftops until he reached a house near the goldsmith's quarter. Here he descended through a trap leading from the roof garden into the house proper. In a large room he found a corpulent man sitting cross-legged on a cushion, his hands folded limply in his lap, his eyes closed.

"Jaganath?" the small man said hesitantly. "I have returned." His speech was that of the highest caste of Vendhya.

The seated man's eyes opened, and he smiled benignly. "And did you learn anything of note, Gopal?" Quickly, the younger man described what he had heard outside the room of Hathor-Ka. The fat man's smile increased. "The Double-goer's Spell of Tuya! The Stygian woman is indeed clever. She has saved herself an arduous journey."

"Why did you not utilize that spell yourself, uncle?" the younger man asked.

Jaganath turned his gaze upon his inquisitive young kinsman with little favor. "Because, Gopal, it requires an extraordinarily trustworthy person to make the delivery certain, and I trust nobody but myself." He smiled benignly again. "Not even you."

He contemplated the parchment laid out before him. "Now, at least, there can be no doubt. Hathor-Ka has stumbled across the same lost text from the *Book of Skelos* as I did so many years ago. I wonder how many others are making the same journey at this very moment?"

"Uncle," said Gopal, "do you not think that it is now time for you to tell me the meaning of this journey we have undertaken? It has been so many long, weary leagues from Vendhya to this barbarous place. Surely, it is not only for the sake of knowledge that we have endured such hardships."

"Not knowledge," Jaganath said, "but power."

"Power?" said Gopal, his eyes alight.

"Exactly. When I was a very young man, little older than you are now, I studied in many strange lands. One day, in the library of a wise man of purple-towered Aghrapur, I found a book, a frivolous book of poetry. I was about to put it away when I noticed that the parchment lining the inside of the cover was peeling loose, and there was strange lettering on the inner surface. I cut it free carefully and returned the book to its place. This parchment before me is the very one I found that day. Can you read it?''

Gopal craned his neck to look, but the script was utterly alien to him. Even though the letters meant nothing they seemed to draw and twist his thoughts down paths unwelcome even to a Vendhyan apprentice wizard. "No, uncle, I cannot," he admitted.

"And neither could I in those days; yet, even as you feel it now, I felt this was a thing of unsurpassing importance. Years later, after much study under great masters, I gained knowledge of this language and remembered the parchment I had acquired. I found that this was a fragment from a lost chapter of *Skelos,* written in the original tongue. It is in the form of obscure quatrains, but the burden of the message from the ninth line to the twentieth is this: A new star shall appear between the horns of the Bull. Upon the morn of that year when day and night are of equal length, after the blaze of summer, before the chill of winter, a new Master shall arise to command all the wizards of the Earth. That one shall reign without peer or rival. On the morn of that year when day and night are of equal length, as the sun rises and casts its rays into the cave of the mountain of Ben Morgh, in the land of Cimmeria, the wizard who is to be master of all others will chant the Great Summoning of the Powers. That one shall gain the ultimate power of sorcery, and shall not die until struck down by an Arrow of Indra. So prophesieth Skelos.''

Gopal sat silent for a moment, jaw slack with awe. "What does it mean 'an Arrow of Indra'?" he asked.

"The Arrows of Indra are falling stars, which are seen to drop from the constellation called Indra's Chariot only once in every thousand years. There is a rumor that the palace of the King of Valusia was destroyed by such eight thousand years past. The Arrows of Indra were last seen to fall a mere hundred years ago. Thus he who reaches that cave on the appointed morn, and chants the Great Summoning, will rule as supreme wizard of the Earth for at least nine hundred years!" The assumed mantle of serenity fell from the Vendhyan, leaving the naked mask of power-lust.

"The text says 'master,' " Gopal said. "How can the Stygian woman hope to gain this power?"

"The ancient tongue makes no distinction between male and female," Jaganath answered. "And Hathor-Ka is among the elite of adepts who can chant the Great Summoning. No more than ten of us have mastery of that spell. Of those, how many have found this prophecy? Two I am certain of. If there are more than two others I shall be very much surprised."

"And what of this Cimmerian?" Gopal asked.

"The road to his homeland is a long one, fraught with perils. Something may happen to him. In fact, I am sure that some ill thing will befall him."

The younger man nodded understanding. "But, just suppose he should survive this something. What then?"

"He will travel overland," Jaganath explained patiently. "He must go through Ophir, then through Nemedia or Aquilonia and across Gunderland or the Border Kingdom before he can reach Cimmeria. Even then it will be a long journey from the border to Ben Morgh."

"But, uncle," Gopal persisted, "what is to keep the barbarian from going to the coast and taking ship?"

Jaganath smiled with pleasure. "That is most perceptive, nephew. In fact, that is exactly what I intend to do. We shall travel east until we reach the Tybor River in Argos, take a barge to the port of Messantia, and thence ship north. Thus shall we travel in relative comfort to Vanaheim, where we will find men to escort us to Ben Morgh. The Cimmerian cannot take this easy route, for to reach Cimmeria from the sea he must cross the Pictish Wilderness or Vanaheim, and both Pict and Van are deadly enemies of the Cimmerians.''

"Then," Gopal said, "if we win the race, as seems certain, you shall be the greatest sorcerer who has ever lived." He was awed and eager at the same time.

"I shall be as powerful as a god," Jaganath said, "and you shall be second only to me."

Conan sat brooding over his wine in a tavern, a much finer establishment than the one at which he had lodged. From a tall Aquilonian mercenary he had purchased a patched but clean tunic which would serve to keep him acceptable in better surroundings until the markets opened on the morrow. Glumly, he ignored the strains of wild music and the posturing of the dancers. He was not yet hungry, and he could not savor his wine. For lack of a purse or other personal furniture, the bag of gold hung from his neck on a thong, hidden in his tunic. He had paid the tavern keeper for three days lodging with one of the gold coins: a heap of copper and silver now lay on the table before him, brought by his host in change.

"Tell your fortune, master?" Conan looked up to see an ancient, ragged Khitan standing by the table.

Even in such a cosmopolitan caravan center as Khorshemish, men of the distant east were a rare sight. The man's shredded tunic did not even cover his skinny shanks, and he wore a bizarre headdress of feathers and bells. Strings of bones and shells and coral and other nameless things hung around his neck. He grinned ingratiatingly at the barbarian, nodding with senile glee that made his thin goat-beard flutter. "Tell you good fortune, very cheap."

"Is this what attracted you?" Conan said, gesturing toward a little pile of coins before him. He picked up the smallest—a thick, ill-stamped copper shekh from Shem—and tossed it to the ancient. "Here. Now, be gone with you." He turned his attention to his neglected wine.

The mountebank caught the coin and studied it. "You get no good fortune for this," he said. "For this, all you get is a quotation. Duke Li said: 'Each piece on the player's board thinks that it moves by its own sovereign will from one square to another.' "

"Eh?" Conan said, mystified. "What kind of fortune-teller are you?"

"Good one," the old man said. "Give me one piece silver, I tell you good fortune."

Reluctantly, Conan grinned. The crazy little old man was amusing, and right now he needed distraction. He hated sorcery, but he had no fear of the petty magics of mounte-banks. "Sit down," Conan said, gesturing hospitably. "Have some wine."

The ancient cackled gleefully and plunked his skinny back-side onto a stool opposite Conan. He snatched a cup from another table, and dumping the lees on the straw-covered floor, filled it from the pitcher that sat before the hulking Cimmerian. "You Northman, not so?" he asked.

"From Cimmeria, yes. Now you're drinking my wine, so I want a favorable fortune."

The old one dipped his fingers into the wine and spattered drops in the cardinal directions, drawing curses from tavern patrons who were struck by droplets. He drank all but a few drops from his cup and studied the lees swirling in the bottom while he muttered incomprehensibly. Grinning, he looked up. "Very good fortune! What you do, the gods direct. You think you decide your own actions, but in reality you do only the bidding of higher powers, like Duke Li's gaming pieces." Once again the old man switched from foolish chatter to sensible speech.

"You call that a fortune?" Conan said. "I always hear

that kind of nonsense from easterners. The gods don't direct me; I am my own master.''

"Yes, yes," said the Khitan, nodding and grinning furiously, "but sometimes you do something a little strange, not so? Something you do not understand?''

About to retort sharply, Conan remembered his ill-considered oath to Hathor-Ka earlier that evening. "Yes," he admitted at last, "sometimes I do.''

"See?" said the Khitan, as if that explained everything. "Soon you go on long trip, not so?''

"That takes a little gift of prophecy," Conan grumbled. "Of course I'm going on a journey. Nobody stays in Khorshemish if he can help it.''

"Well, you do things now, you do things soon, they are important. They seem like little things, unimportant things, but they are part of the gods' plans. Nothing you can do about it, all for good anyway." The old man poured himself another cup.

"Crom take you," Conan said, now bored with the mad old fool and disgusted as always with eastern fatalism.

"Soon enough," said the old man, laughing and nodding.

Two

The North Gate

In the great market of Khorshemish, as in markets everywhere, the people gathered in the morning to buy and sell, to trade the latest gossip, and to talk politics. Women waited in long lines at the central fountain with empty water jars to fill, taking the opportunity to socialize with their neighbors. In a corner of the market, the local astrologers were met to discuss the same phenomenon about which they had been heatedly arguing for months: the new star that had appeared between the horns of the Bull. No agreement was reached except that it was either significant or otherwise, and, if significant, it meant something either good or bad.

Conan entered the market at midmorning, having just come from the clothiers' quarter. He was now dressed in a decent tunic and trousers, with leather boots. None of his garments was of excellent quality except the boots, for he knew he would be trading the clothes for cold-weather gear as he traveled northward. He strode across the market, drawing admiring looks from the women who stood by the fountain. His mind was not on women, but on weapons. Khorshemish was not noted for its metal work, but many caravan routes met here and consequently there were weapons of many nations to be found among the wares of its merchants.

Conan examined the goods displayed before the shop of an arms merchant. He picked up each sword and hefted it, running a critical eye over each piece while the merchant supplied a continual commentary in praise of his stock.

"A Turanian sword, master? Curved like the crescent moon, its hilt rich with pearls and gold. The weapon of a prince, my lord."

"You don't kill with the hilt," Conan said. "You do it with the blade."

"Exactly, master," the merchant agreed. "Do but examine this pilouar of Vendhya. The blade is inlaid with potent spells in gold and silver."

"I don't believe in spells," Conan said. "I believe in a good sword arm. Have you any western or northern blades? I prefer a straight, broad blade to these curved slicers."

"Then this is exactly the sword my lord wishes," purred the merchant, pulling a cloth cover from a splendid straight sword with a short guard and heavy pommel of carved steel. "From Vanaheim, master."

Conan's eyes blazed with pleasure. The Vanir made fine swords, at least. He picked it up and tried its balance. The high polish flashed in the morning sun. That was wrong. The Vanir preferred the pearly gray luster of steel in the first polish, which displayed the fine grain and pattern of their intricately welded blades. They never polished a sword to mirror brightness. Suspiciously, he ran a thumbnail along one edge from hilt to point, then turned the blade over and tried the other edge. Halfway up he felt a slight unevenness in the steel. He held the blade close to his eye, out of the direct sunlight, where the polish could not hide a flaw. There was a hairline crack running from the edge almost to the central fuller. He tossed the sword to the table in disgust. "Worthless," he said. "Haven't you anything better?"

Fuming at the barbarian's obstinacy, the shopkeeper waved him toward the shop behind him. "There are some old blades in there, if you want to look at them."

Inside the shop Conan waited for a few minutes, letting his eyes adjust to the gloom, then examined a pile of swords and daggers on a table. He found a plain, heavy dirk, single-edged and broad-spined, and stuck it in his sash. None of the swords was to his liking. He was about to pay for the dirk and leave, when he saw a big pottery jar standing in a corner with a cluster of swords protruding from it. He pulled out several, but most of them were ancient, notched, and rusty, their grips broken or rotted away.

On the point of leaving to seek out another shop, he drew forth a sword that felt different from the others. In the dimness he could tell little except that the blade was broad and straight, and the grip had long since deteriorated, leaving only a stretch of thin tang between hilt and pommel. He took it outside for a better look. In the sunlight he saw that the blade had turned purple-black with age, but bore no trace of rust. The curiously wrought hilt and pommel were of bronze long since turned green.

To get a feel of its balance, Conan borrowed a strip of leather from a nearby stall, wrapped the tang, and swung the brand a few times. Even with the inadequate grip he knew that this sword had a balance as fine as any he had ever felt. He returned the leather strip to its owner and asked the merchant what he wanted for sword and dirk.

"A very rare old sword, sir," the merchant said, "no doubt possessing many hidden virtues."

"Well-hidden at that," the Cimmerian said. "You bought it from some tomb-robber for a trifle."

Conan's time in the eastern lands had taught him the art and entertainment of haggling. The argument continued occasionally threatening to escalate into open violence, and idlers passing by paused to contribute views and opinions. Eventually, Conan walked away with the sword wrapped in a length of cloth and the dirk tucked into his sash, certain that he had paid a pittance for so fine a blade. The merchant was equally sure that he had unloaded a worthless item on an ignorant outlander for an outrageous price.

In the jewelers' quarter Conan found a sword dresser sitting before his workshop, surrounded by polishing stones of varying grit, bowls of sand and other powders, and sheets of rough sharkskin. Conan handed the man his new purchase.

"Can you clean this up and sharpen it? It needs a grip as well. Plain wood will do, or staghorn or bone."

The sword dresser examined the weapon minutely, and the way he handled it told Conan he had come to the right man. This one knew weapons, if not with the arm of a warrior, at least with the eye of a craftsman.

"A fine weapon," the artisan pronounced at last. "Most unusual, but I think I can do something with it. It will look much handsomer than you'd think when it is cleaned, and it deserves an exceptional grip. I have something you will like."

"Nothing fancy," Conan said, "I prefer plain wood or bone." But the craftsman had already disappeared into his shop.

Conan fretted, suspecting that the man would try to sell him a handle of solid jade or crystal or other splendid, useless material.

When the man returned, though, he was holding a thin box of fragrant sandalwood. "I had this from a Hyrkanian trader two years ago," he explained. "I've been waiting to find a worthy sword." He opened the box, revealing a sheet of thin, parchmentlike material. It was as white as new ivory, and covered with tiny irregular bumps. Intrigued, Conan ran his fingertips over the knobbly surface. His experienced hand told him that this exotic stuff, beautiful as it was, would afford a fine grip.

"What is it?" Conan asked, mystified. "Some kind of shagreen?"

"It is the backskin of the giant rayfish, from the isles east of Khitai. It is said to make the finest swordgrips in the world. I will fashion you a handle of plain hardwood, then glue this rayskin over it. It's a long hilt, big enough even for both your hands, with a little crowding, but I think there will be enough left over to make a matching grip for your dirk."

"Then I'll have this stuff," Conan said, not even asking the price, which he knew would be steep. He was willing to pay well for fine weaponry, or take exceptional risks to steal the best. "Can you make sheaths as well?"

"My apprentices will see to that. What kind do you wish?"

"Plain leather for the dirk. For the sword, thin wood, the strongest you have, with oil-treated leather glued over it. Bronze chape and throat. I want the wood lined inside with close-sheared lamb fleece, and the bronze throat cut away lest the edge touch metal in drawing or sheathing."

The craftsman nodded. "You are a man who understands weapons, sir. It is always a pleasure to deal with such. Return in two days and all will be ready."

Conan continued on his way, this time to look at horses and saddles. Knowing that he faced a long journey, he ignored the splendid chargers and coursers the horse-traders tried to sell him, though at another time he might have spent days testing them all. He settled on a strong bay gelding, sound of wind and limb. Since he wanted to travel light, and make the last part of his journey on foot, he did not bother with a pack animal.

His last purchase was a voluminous cloak that would serve as garment and blanket, and in which he could keep his few belongings rolled up and tied across his saddle during the journey. He decided against purchasing armor and helm, both because he must travel light and because his fellow Cimmerian countrymen considered armor to be effeminate.

That evening he sat in the same tavern, this time in a far better mood. He had made his decisions, and he was not one to brood over mistakes or lost opportunities. Already he was looking forward to the northlands again. It had been too long since he had seen his kinsmen and breathed the free air of the mountains. Perhaps he would pay a visit to his old friends the Aesir, and go a-raiding with them for a while.

"Amulets, master?" Conan looked up to see the ancient Khitan holding forth a mass of indescribable pendants dangling from leather thongs. "Protect you from harm, from Evil Eye, from drowning, from snakebite." The old man grinned encouragingly.

"More gloomy predictions for me, old crow?" Conan said with a grudging smile. He would not let the elderly doommonger shake his mood of elation. "Here." He flipped the shaman a heavy silver coin from Koth. The old one caught the coin in his free hand and bit it. Cackling, he secreted the coin in his rags and held out a thong from which dangled an oddly carved bit of green stone.

"Take this," the old one urged. "Good protection."

"Against what?" Conan said dubiously. "Drowning, snakebite? I believe in my own strength."

"Sometime strength no good. Then need first-rate amulet and charm. This one save life when strength all gone."

Reluctantly, Conan took the thing and hung it from his neck, more to silence the old man than for any other reason. It would make a gift for some pretty girl along the way, at any rate.

The old man kept grinning and cackling. "Keep inside of shirt. Magic no good if too many people see." He started to walk away, then turned back and waggled an admonitory finger. "Remember, only playing pieces on board of gods."

"If we're moved about by other powers," Conan demanded, "what use are amulets?"

The old man cackled gleefully. "Sometimes even gods have need of amulets!"

Two days later Conan stood before the sword dresser's shop. In his hands he held the splendid sword. Its blade now shone bright, an odd pale blue color such as he had never seen in sword steel. The bronze guard and pommel had been polished to a warm luster, and were perfectly set off by the pearly-white rayskin grip. Best of all, though, was the marvelous balance and design which seemed to make the sword swing itself with little effort from the wielder.

In his enthusiasm Conan set the blade flashing through the air in a series of intricate maneuvers he had learned from a Turanian swordmaster. His impromptu display drew frightened squawks and curses from passersby who wandered too near. At last, satisfied, he sheathed the brand in its new scabbard. Balancing the sword on the other side of the belt was the refurbished dirk with its now-matching hilt.

"I needed twice the usual time to put an edge on it," the craftsman said, "so hard is the steel. But you can shave with either edge now. And the blue color—that I have seen only in a few very ancient blades. It is a style of steel making long lost. Look closely and you will see a slightly paler color along the edges. They were made of a different quality of steel welded in with the softer metal, and tempered separately." The man sighed. "Such secrets the ancients knew. The finest Turanian blades are trash compared to this. I hope it serves you well, my friend."

Conan paid the high price gladly; he would have paid more. Gold was nothing, and it always seemed to trickle through his fingers like water. Steel a man could trust. With the reassuring weight at his waist, making him feel lighter instead of heavier, he strode to the inn where Hathor-Ka stayed.

This time the keeper of the inn was obsequious. Conan

was not splendid in his plain clothing and boots, but he was every inch a warrior, and such men always command respect.

He climbed the stairs and rapped on the door. It was opened by Moulay, who ushered him inside. Conan saw Hathor-Ka seated at her table with a large chart spread out before her.

"I leave at dawn tomorrow," Conan announced without preamble. "Give me the flask and I'll be on my way."

"You are too hasty," Hathor-Ka chided him.

"Would you prefer a slow messenger?" Conan asked.

"Come here," she ordered. "Show me the route you plan to use."

Conan walked around the table to study the chart. He had seen maps before, but at the best of times he had difficulty relating these drawings on parchment to real land. "I can't read these scratchings," he said.

Hathor-Ka named the principal nations for him, and the most prominent rivers. Thus oriented, the map began to make sense. He could see that the central, civilized nations were clearly delineated, with many cities marked, while the barbaric nations of north and south were vaguely and sketchily indicated. With a blunt finger Conan traced the route he planned to take.

"I'll go straight north through Ophir, then up through Nemedia. I may stop in Belverus if nobody's besieging the place, then up to the Border Kingdom. They'll hang me there if they catch me; but it's only a narrow bit of land I have to cross. Then I'll be in Cimmeria."

"Why not go up through Aquilonia?" Hathor-Ka asked. "There are far more cities and settlements. You could travel north to Gunderland and the Bossonian Marches, and it would be civilized country most of the way."

Conan shook his head. "The eastern route is open plain most of the way. It's fairly well-watered, but with no big rivers to cross. It's the best way to travel by horse. In

Aquilonia the land's all cut up by rivers, and they all flow south, so boat travel would be slower than riding. All those settlements mean traveling by road, and the traffic and towns slow you down. Also, it would mean entering Cimmeria in Murrogh territory, and the Murrogh clan have been waging a blood feud with my own for five generations, ever since one of my ancestors stole all their horses.''

"Excellent," Hathor-Ka said. "I have no interest in your route, but I wished to be sure that you are a man who knows how to think ahead and plan." She turned to Moulay and nodded.

Once again he opened the chest and drew forth the flask. Hathor-Ka held it for a moment, then handed it to the Cimmerian.

"Upon your oath," the woman said, "let nothing happen to this vessel or its contents before the last step of your mission is carried out."

"You don't have to remind me," Conan grumbled. "I will get it done." Without further pleasantries the Cimmerian left.

Moulay watched Conan leave. "My lady, I have no wish to see the cold north, but I think the two of us should have undertaken this task."

She crossed to the narrow window and looked down into the street. The Cimmerian was walking away with his lengthy hillman's stride. "No, Moulay, you are wrong. Even if the two of us could endure the journey, we would never arrive by the autumnal equinox. I would have to employ my mightiest sorceries to speed our way, and would arrive too exhausted to face the struggle that might ensue. This man is perfect. He is strong and simple, and he will honor his word."

Moulay snorted through his beaked nose. "What does a savage know of honor?"

"More than you would think. Honor is a barbaric virtue, of which civilization retains only the empty forms. Besides, the greatest advantage of using this man is that he is a Cimmerian, and he will be in his own country." She turned for a last glimpse of Conan's broad back disappearing around a corner. "No, I could not have chosen better."

The next morning Conan rode out through the North Gate of Khorshemish. The rising sun was just staining the east wall of the city red, and here on the north side all was still in shadow, retaining the faint chill of night. Conan's horse was through the opening valves as soon as they were wide enough to pass its sturdy barrel. The guards atop the wall were yawning, yearning for their relief to arrive so they could collapse into their empty bunks at the barracks.

Early as the hour was, however, they were not alone atop the wall over the North Gate. Beside the green-flecked bronze poles which supported the gate's drum stood a skinny, ragged figure rattling his strings of bone and shell. As Conan rode away from the city of the plain, the ancient Khitan mountebank waved to his unseeing back.

Three

Five Riders

Conan had been on his journey for seven days. For six of those days he had known that he was being followed. It was very difficult to trail a man unseen on open plain, and even more difficult when the man in question was experienced, suspicious, and Cimmerian. From long habit, every few hours Conan would ride to the nearest rise of ground and scan all around, paying special attention to his back trail.

On his second day he had descried the five riders who followed. They were well behind, and could not close the gap quickly. At the same time, he knew that he would eventually have to turn and give battle. There was no way that a lone man could keep ahead of five indefinitely except on the most favorable ground. Clever pursuers would divide the chase, with some riding fast to make the quarry stay ahead, others catching up at a more leisurely pace, then taking the fast chase in their turn, gradually wearing out the mount of the pursued while keeping their own horses relatively fresh.

On the other hand, Conan knew that his horse was a good one. He also was not lacking in personal confidence, and had no doubt that his own stamina was greater than that of his pursuers. The fighting ground would be his choice. High ground was always best, but there was precious little of that hereabout.

On the eve of the seventh day he found a mound several paces high and settled on that as a good place to conquer or die. He picketed his horse by a small stream a quarter mile away from the mound, where the grass was good. First he watered the beast, then curried its glossy hide. He made sure that the picket cords were such that the horse would take no more than a few hours to gnaw them through. Should he and all his enemies be slain today, he did not wish the beast to be left to a lingering death on the empty plain.

When all was ready he ate a handful of dried fruit and jerked meat, and walked to the mound. From its crest he could see that the five horsemen were still an hour away. He sat down to await them.

He did not want to signal his presence from afar, lest they pause and approach him slowly, catching their breath and regaining their full strength. At five-to-one odds even Conan knew that he needed every advantage he could wrest from the situation. As the men neared, he drew his sword and admired its beauty. Since the fight could not be avoided, it cheered him to have a chance to try out his new blade, and such a fight as was coming would surely test it to the full.

When the five were no more than a hundred paces away, he stood, brandished the sword above his head, and shouted: "I am Conan of Cimmeria! If you would slay me, here I am! Come and try me, lowland swine!"

The horsemen reined in and stared up the mound in wonderment. Of all things, this was the last they had expected. Such challenges rightly belonged to the age of heroes, and everyone knew that that age was long gone. After a hurried conference as to who should go first, they very sensibly decided to charge all at once.

Conan grinned when he saw five horses spring forth as

one. This was just what he had hoped for. Only in a well-disciplined army could five men fight as a well-drilled team, and these men showed no sign of such training. They were clearly of different nations, each armed and armored in his own fashion.

As the ragged line approached him, Conan darted to his left to engage the last man on that side, putting the rider between himself and the others. While to his opponents he seemed bent on suicide by dismounting thus to fight, in reality he had gained an advantage. Without a horse to manage he could concentrate on killing, and this suited his headlong style of combat.

The lefthand rider was a man of Shem, with curly beard and billowing trousers. He wore no armor and rode without stirrups, a slender lance held low at his right side and a small buckler on his left forearm. With a gobbling war cry he lowered his point, intent upon skewering the Cimmerian.

Conan ran down the mound and reached his range just as the horse changed gait to negotiate the rise in ground. The sudden change in motion threw the rider slightly off balance for a moment, and that was all the time Conan needed. As the point wavered he slapped it aside with his blade and leaped upward, holding his sword at full extension and turning his whole body into a spear. The Shemite tried to bring his buckler across, but with so much weight and momentum behind the sword, the act was futile. The point caught the man beneath the jaw and he all but flew backward over his cantle, spraying blood in a crimson arc.

Immediately, Conan ran back to the crest of the mound. The others circled in confusion, trying to decide just what had happened. First to see Conan was a Turanian in spired helm, and that one set spurs to his mount, waving a heavy, curved talwar as he sought to ride the Cimmerian down. Conan darted to the man's shield side at the last possible instant and swung his sword as he did so, hewing the Turanian's left leg off. The man toppled screaming from his saddle.

Before Conan could regain his balance after the mighty blow, two more horses were upon him, and he was knocked sprawling to the ground. As he tried to scramble up, a Zamoran leaped onto Conan's shoulders and sought to wrestle him to the ground while stabbing at him with a long, curved dagger. Conan dropped his sword to deal with the man, and managed to seize the Zamoran with both hands just as he felt the dagger burn like a hot iron across his shoulder.

From the corner of his eye Conan saw a sword swinging at his back, and with a speed and strength unknown among civilized men, he swung the Zamoran around, using him as a shield to intercept the whistling blade. The Zamoran screamed thinly as the sword cleft his spine, and Conan heaved the body into the face of the Argossian swordsman, whose visage still bore a look of confusion. Both bodies thudded to the ground as Conan darted to the Argossian, seized him by his wide helmet, and twisted until a faint snap informed him that further effort was unnecessary. Quickly, he looked for the fifth.

The man was perhaps twenty paces away, sitting his horse with grim patience. The rider wore a cuirass of hardened leather straps, studded with iron, and on both forearms bracers of stiff leather. The sword at his waist was straight, its handle long enough for both hands. Beneath his nasaled black helmet spilled locks of tawny hair, and his eyes were as blue as Conan's own. Except for his clean-shaven face, the man might have been Aesir, but Conan knew that he was from farther south.

"You've had a good morning's sport, Cimmerian dog," the man said as he dismounted. "But the men of Gunderland are harder to kill than these eastern weaklings."

Conan found his sword and picked it up, first making sure that its grip was not slippery with dew or blood. "Gundermen die as easily as other men. I slew many at Venarium, and I was only fifteen then."

"Venarium!" spat the Gunderman. "I've sworn to kill a dozen Cimmerians for every kinsman I lost in that slaughter. Their blood calls out for appeasement. I will send them another black-haired servant this day!"

The two northerners met atop the mound. They fought without art or subtlety, swinging their broad blades two-handed. Blue sword and gray met and rang, shedding sparks with each terrific impact. Boasting and challenge were over now, and the only sounds they made were snarls of rage and grunts of effort wrenched from their bodies with each massive chop. It was swing and block without pause, but the fight was not slow nor ponderous despite the size of the men and the weight of their weapons. The swords licked out to cut or block too swiftly for any but the most experienced eye to see.

Conan broke into a profuse sweat and breathed like a blacksmith's bellows. It had been years since he had tested himself against a fellow northerner, and the hard-living men of Aquilonia's Gunderland frontier grew up every bit as swift and powerful as any Nordheimer or Cimmerian. But Conan was mighty even for a Cimmerian. Preparing a terrible over-hand slash, the Gunderman swung the blade a fingersbreadth too far back, giving Conan an instant in which to step aside. As his blade met no resistance, the Gunderman leaned forward, fighting to regain his balance, but it was too late for that. The Cimmerian's sword came across horizontally, biting into the man's side through the hard leather. Yanking his blade free, Conan raised it and sent it in a great half-circle, splitting cuirass and flesh from shoulder to waist, shearing bones and entrails relentlessly.

Sheer animal unwillingness to die kept the Gunderman standing for a moment; then he toppled like a falling tree. Conan, panting like a winded horse, ripped a scrap of cloth from one of the bodies and began carefully cleaning his sword. The others were all dead, the man he had unlegged having bled to death during his fight with the northerner. Conan walked back to the Gunderman, who was still breathing faintly.

"Who hired you, Gunderman?" the Cimmerian asked when he once again had breath to speak.

"Are we friends that I owe you such a favor?" the man gasped. "I do not betray those who hire me."

"Well, what is your name, then?" Conan asked.

"Is it not enough you have slain me, but you want power over my spirit as well?"

"You know Cimmerians better than that!" Conan said angrily. "We slay our foes in fair battle and leave the demons of Hell to any further vengeance. I want your name for the song I shall make when my wanderings are at an end. That was a good fight, and it will be remembered in the song my women shall sing around my funeral pyre."

"I am Hagen," the man wheezed. "Now ask me no more. What little breath I have left I wish to expend in cursing you."

Not wishing to deny the man this final pleasure, Conan examined his sword, and was gratified to see that it bore no slightest nick, and the edges were still shaving-keen. Resheathing the blade, he rounded up the five mounts, then bound up the knife wound on his shoulder. In searching the bodies he found on each of them three heavy, square coins of gold stamped with strange script. He had seen such coins before; they came from Vendhya. He chuckled to think that what had been intended as the price of his life would instead enrich his purse.

The five horses he took with him to sell in Belverus. He left the rest with the bodies. Any man might sell five horses, but the personal effects of five men would arouse unwelcome official attention. Behind him he left the bloody mound. In a year's time the gnawed bones would be scattered abroad, cloth and leather would have rotted, and there would be nothing to mark the battle except some rusting bits of iron and a slightly greener patch of grass. Later, even those would be gone, leaving only the limitless plain, which had drunk the blood of uncounted thousands.

Conan was feverish and reeling in his saddle as he arrived within sight of the walls of Belverus. Happily, he noted that there was no besieging army encamped outside its walls. Just now he had no time for such things. It was midday, and the gates of the city stood wide. A guard held up a restraining hand as Conan rode through the gate. The guard held a wooden tablet bearing a panel of wax, and a bronze stylus was tucked behind his ear.

"What is your name and your business, stranger?" the guard demanded.

"I am Conan of Cimmeria, and I need lodging for the night, and a horse market to sell my stock." His face was flushed and his voice unsteady.

"What ails you?" the guard asked suspiciously. "You may not enter the city if you bear any contagion."

Wordlessly, Conan let his cloak fall, exposing the raw and angry cut which festered upon his shoulder. Fierce streaks of red and black radiated from the puckered, swollen wound, and it seeped an unhealthy fluid.

"Mitra!" swore the guard. "You need a leech, man, else you'll lose that arm, if not your life. Leave your beasts here the nonce, I'll give you a receipt for them, then get you to the house of Doctor Romallo. It is but two streets distant."

It galled Conan to have to seek the aid of a leech. In normal times he preferred to let his body heal itself. On the few occasions that he had sought such professional services, it had been to have a bad wound stitched. He harbored a suspicion that leeches did far more harm than good. This time, though, he knew he had no choice.

An oversized bleeding knife over the entrance proclaimed the house of Romallo. Conan pounded on the door and an elderly, bearded man opened it. "You desire treatment?" he asked.

"I need something, by Crom!" Conan said, baring his wound once more.

"Hmm. A most interesting injury. Come in, young man, and we'll see what's to be done." The leech's house was full of strange objects. Stuffed beasts dangled on cords from the rafters, and vaguely obscene marine creatures were preserved in jars of spirits. Instruments of bronze and glass abounded, and the air smelled of herbs. Strange as the place was, Conan at least felt no sorcery here. The leech directed him to a bench near a window, and Conan sat, bearing his pain in stoic silence as the man poked and prodded.

"I can lance and clean this wound," the leech announced at last, "bind it with a stitch or two, and put a healing poultice on it, but I fear that these things might not prove to be sufficient."

"Why not?" Conan groused. "Is that not your art?"

"It is. However, this infection is not of natural origin. I can tell by the tone of your flesh how rugged is your constitution, and such a gash as this should not be causing you such agony."

"True," Conan agreed, "I've been wounded far worse without trouble. Have I been wounded with an envenomed weapon?"

"No, in that case the characteristics of the inflammation would be quite different. I think you lie under the influence of some baleful spell, and I can only wonder that it has not killed you long since."

Chills ran through Conan's powerful frame, chills that were not part of his fever. Who had cursed him? And what was protecting him? Then he understood. In spite of his ills, he began to laugh.

"Odd time for mirth," the leech said, frowning.

"I've just realized that I'm paying for my own greed. Do what you can, and leave the rest to me. I'll need a moneychanger when you are through."

Mystified, the leech set to his task. Despite his pain, Conan wore a grim smile. How subtle was his enemy! Not content merely to set five killers on his trail, the man had paid them with cursed money, knowing that should Conan survive the attack, he would surely take their gold and doom himself.

What had protected him? From beneath his tunic he fished the talisman the ancient Khitan had given him. He was not sure, but the color seemed subtly altered. In stony silence he sat enduring the doctor's painful ministrations. More and more he felt like the playing-piece of the game board of a god the old Khitan had spoken of.

By the time he had exchanged the unclean gold for other money and sold the five horses, the day was almost over. Conan stabled his mount and, exhausted, collapsed into a bed at an inn. His wound was less virulent, but he was still in a weakened condition. He knew that he would have to wait for several days in Belverus until his full strength returned. The delay did not fret him. After all, he would still be able to reach Ben Morgh by the equinox. It was a mission he had undertaken, not a race.

The waterfront tavern was filled with voices speaking boisterously in many languages. Most of one wall was open, revealing the serried masts crowding the great harbor of Messantia. Through the huge window blew a salt-scented offshore breeze, causing the torches to flicker.

Messantia sprawled along the mouth of the Khorotas River, where it joined the Western Sea. It lay on the Zingaran side of the river, but it was as international as most seaports. The fact that Argos claimed this piece of land concerned the inhabitants not at all. Hemmed in by the bulk of the Rabirian Mountains to the north and the river to the south, the bulk of the city lay on a wide floodplain that constituted a minor nation in itself. At any given time, at least half the population was transient, consisting mainly of sailors from the multitude of nations and islands that drew a living from the sea.

The occupants of the tavern were a cross-section of the maritime life of the area: besides the local Zingarans and Argossians, there were Shemites with hooked noses and curling beards; quiet Stygians, who wore black silk; sinister Barachans, whose belts were festooned with the daggers and short swords favored for combat at sea. One table held a party of Kushites, feathers woven into their elaborate hairdos, their black skins glossy with the scented palm oil which they prized. Two red-haired Vanir seamen had already passed out in a corner. The torchlight glittered on earrings, nose rings, and other ornaments favored by seagoing men.

On a small platform in the center of the room a Zamoran girl was performing one of the lascivious dances of her nation to the music of a flute and a tabour. Her clothing consisted of a great many bangles and a single small veil. Many of the sailors clapped in time to the music and shouted their appreciation of her performance.

"I had thought," Gopal said, "that we had reached the nadir of civilization in Khorshemish. I see now that it was the epitome of culture compared to this place." The young man and his uncle sat at a tiny table as near as they could get to the window.

"You must enjoy this cosmopolitan atmosphere while you can, nephew," said Jaganath with his usual complacent smile. "Where we are going, there has never even been a word for civilization. After all, there are booksellers in this town. There are some scholars of small repute and even a few second-rate sorcerers. Our destination is a howling wilderness of barbarians and savages as primitive as those Kushites over there.''

"The very thought fills me with dismay," Gopal said. He took a sip of the wine which he had watered heavily. A platter of spicy meats wrapped in vine leaves lay before them, but the tedious, inactive journey by barge down the river had left him with little appetite.

"If you would be a mage," said Jaganath, "you must tread some very strange paths indeed. No man who quails at hardship or danger can succeed in the quest for knowledge and power." He picked up a tidbit and popped it into his mouth. "At least their cooking is tolerable here. A port like this affords access to spices of variety and high quality." Like most Vendhyans of high caste, Jaganath and Gopal ate meat but rarely, and then only in small quantities, highly spiced.

A newcomer entered the tavern and scanned the room for a moment. Spotting the two Vendhyans, he crossed to their table. His boots and short tarry breeks identified him as a seaman, and his arrogant stride bespoke authority. His features were scarred and badly pockmarked, but they bore an aristocratic cast. Jaganath quickly typed him as the scion of decayed Zingaran nobility.

"You are the two who seek passage northward?" asked the newcomer.

"We are," said Jaganath. "Please join us."

The man sat and poured himself a cup of wine from the pitcher on the table. He ignored the pitcher of water that stood beside it. After draining the cup he refilled it and picked up a handful of the stuffed vine leaves. He stuffed three into his mouth and said around the mouthful: "I am Kasavo, from the Barachan Isles, captain of the *Songbird*. I heard on the wharf today that two Vendhyans sought passage north, and that they were to be contacted here at the *Sailor's Delight*."

"We must travel in haste to Vanaheim," Jaganath said. "Do you go so far north?"

Kasavo laughed. "To Vanaheim? Nobody sails that far from here. In any case, it is late in the year to be traveling north. I can take you to Kordava, the last civilized port before the Pictish Wilderness. From there, if luck is with you, you may find a Vanir merchant who has stayed until the very end of the season, braving the storms for the sake of picking up late-season goods at bargain prices. I warn you, though, that a northern passage at this time of year can be very dangerous. Best to winter in Kordava. It is a very wicked port. Most diverting." He grinned and toyed nervously with a large, fiery, teardrop-shaped ruby that dangled from his earlobe on a short chain.

"I do not fear storms," Jaganath said. "When do you sail?"

"With the morning tide, about an hour after sunrise to take advantage of the inland winds. Have your belongings aboard by sunrise. I have a cabin you can use. There is the matter of payment for your passage."

Jaganath waved a pudgy hand in dismissal. "We can settle that during the voyage. I have abundant funds."

The man's eyes sparkled for a moment with greed, which he tried to cover with a feigned curiosity. "Why do you wish to go to a place like Vanaheim? From the look of you, you've little love for cold climes."

"We are scholars," Jaganath told him. "I am writing a book about far lands for the king of Vendhya."

"Vanaheim should satisfy you, then," Kasavo assured him. "It is about as far as you can go. You are with the court of Vendhya, then?"

"Yes. While not a true ambassador, I have a certain semi-official standing and I bear gifts from my liege to the great men of that land. He wishes to establish cordial relations with all nations, however remote." Once again, at the mention of gifts, Kasavo's eyes glittered. As always when dealing with outsiders, Gopal remained silent and kept his ears open, ready to back his uncle's story.

"Then I shall expect you at sunrise tomorrow. I must return to my ship now, and I'll have my men prepare your quarters. The *Songbird* lies alongside the Lesser Wharf. Her hull is painted red, with green eyes at the prow, just above the waterline." He drained his cup and left, not weaving despite the considerable amount of wine he had drunk in so short a time.

"Unless I am much mistaken, uncle," Gopal said when the man was gone, "this fellow is no more than a common pirate. Did you see the way his face changed at every mention of gain to be had?"

"Exactly. And these Barachan Isles of which he speaks form a notorious nest of cutthroats, so I am told. That is why I stressed that we travel with valuable goods. Several masters have already told us that they will not sail north at this time of year, but a pirate will take on passengers of wealth, to rob or to hold for ransom."

"Surely, uncle, they will seek to murder us and give our bodies to the sea gods?"

Jaganath smiled broadly and picked up another snack. "Are you not happy, Gopal, that our voyage north shall not be as dull as our barge journey hither?"

Despite her lyrical name, the *Songbird* had the predatory lines of a shark. Low, lean, and sleek, she was built for speed, with a shallow draft and sides that rose no more than two cubits from the waterline. She had no capacious hold for transporting bulk cargoes, and the men working or idling on her deck were far more numerous than would ever be needed to sail her. They wore few clothes and many weapons. The single mast bore a long, slanting yard which would support an enormous lateen sail. With that sail spread in a following wind she would speedily overtake any vessel built for utility, say, a fat, lumbering merchantman. Along her sides were tholes for a dozen long oars, handy for working into position around a crippled victim or rowing up shallow creeks and rivers to raid or unload contraband.

Jaganath was most pleased with what he saw. They would be able to make good time in this vessel. He took a deep breath and enjoyed the multitudinous smells of the waterfront. From the hold of one ship rose the aroma of sweet spices, from another the reek of the slaver. Over all were the odors of tarred cordage and the sea. The timbers beneath his feet creaked as the wharf shifted to the receding tide.

Jaganath turned to the porters who stood behind them. "Take our belongings aboard that ship," he said, pointing to the *Songbird*. The men looked at the ship, looked back at him in amazement, shrugged, and shouldered the few chests and bales. Precariously, they made their way down the steeply pitched gangplank to the deck.

Kasavo emerged from a tent set on the fantail and grinned up at them. "Come aboard, my friends. Your cabin is ready and the tide is running." His tone was faintly mocking and his men looked up from their work or their idling and grinned as well. Gopal negotiated the gangplank with effortless grace and Jaganath descended with magisterial dignity and an astonishing sense of balance for so fat a man.

"Haul in the gangplank and cast off!" Kasavo bellowed. "We sail!" The porters scrambled back up the plank and cast the mooring lines loose from their bollards. The ship began to drift away from the pier and men clambered aloft to begin loosing the great sail.

Satisfied that preparations were well started, Kasavo turned to his passengers. "Come, let me show you your cabin. I moved out two of my mates to make room for you. No matter, they can bed down on the deck with the rest. The weather should be fair for this voyage."

"You are most kind," said Jaganath. Their "cabin" turned out to be little more than a lean-to set up near the stern, with a thatched roof and canvas sides. The interior was barely adequate to accommodate both men and their belongings.

"It will be a bit cramped," Kasavo said with mock apology. "If you wish, we can store some of your belongings in the hold, where they will be out of your way."

"We shall keep them here," Jaganath said. "From what I can see, you have little enough cargo space as it is."

"Yes, this is not a bulk carrier. As you have noticed, the *Songbird* is built to transport small luxury cargoes. Spices, for instance. Speed is of the essence when transporting spices. From the time they are picked and dried they begin to deteriorate. A fast ship like this can get them to the market early in the season and turn a good profit."

"Say you so?" said Jaganath, feigning both credulity and interest. As if a westerner could teach a learned Vendhyan anything about the spice trade. "Is condition more important than bulk?"

"Very much so," said Kasavo, enjoying the sport of taking in an ignorant foreigner. "The spice merchants of the North will pay far more for a chest of spices still fresh than for one spoiled by weeks at sea."

"Yet I smell no spices aboard," Jaganath said in seeming puzzlement.

"The spice season is over," Kasavo assured him smoothly. "Now we sail to Kordava in ballast, there to take on a cargo of fine glassware for shipment south. That is another low-volume, high-profit cargo. The black nobles of the southern coasts pay handsomely for it in ivory and fine skins and feathers."

"This is most fascinating," Jaganath said. "My king will be most interested in these matters. We must speak of these things during the voyage. His majesty wishes me to withhold nothing concerning travel and commerce from my book."

"I shall be at your service," said Kasavo with a friendly smile. "And now I must see to my ship. You may wish to secure your goods with rope. When we pass the seawall, the water will be far rougher. If you begin to feel ill, remember to use the lee rail. That is the one where the wind does not blow in your face." With an insolent grin he left the shanty.

"Spices!" Gopal said in their own tongue. "As if anyone with a nose could not tell that this ship has never carried more than their cook's pepperpot! I yearn to tread upon that arrogant fool's insolent mouth."

"Peace, nephew," Jaganath soothed. "What matter the slights of ignorant foreigners? For now, we are no more than silly scholars who believe everything we hear. Smile at them, laugh at their jokes on you. Let them have their sport." He smiled serenely. "Soon we shall have a great deal of sport with them."

By the next morning Gopal was very seasick, to the merriment of the sailors. Jaganath borrowed the cook's tiny stove and brewed a potion of herbs that quickly restored the younger man's health. The sailors were a little disappointed that their sport had been so short-lived. In the ensuing days they continued to bait the passengers, at first with the mild jokes traditional at sea when landlubbers take passage, then with rougher, more malicious jests. Soon Kasavo dropped his mask of affability and treated his passengers with barely veiled contempt. It was clear that soon the corsairs would tire of their sport and consign two Vendhyan bodies to the sharks prior to dividing up their belongings. The voyage turned out to be longer than expected, with much tacking and wearing against contrary winds. Tempers were not improved by this, but the Vendhyans continued to smile obsequiously and made no protest at being the butt of the crew's rough jests.

At last the *Songbird* weathered the dangerous Baracha Strait between the islands and the mainland, and fair weather and winds prevailed. No more than two days remained before they reached Kordava. The sun was lowering sedately over the yardarm after a leisurely half day of sailing when Jaganath addressed his nephew: "Gopal, it is no longer necessary to abide the insolence of these subhumans. Do as your spirit bids you." With these mild words the great mage loosed the bonds of his young kinsman.

"As you say, uncle." Gopal grinned ferociously, then calmed himself and exited the little cabin. Despite the advancing season, the weather was very mild, even balmy, and Gopal wore only his turban and a clean linen loincloth. Tucked into the loincloth he carried a short, curved dagger with a jeweled hilt. He went to the rail, where a bucket was tethered by a long rope to a belaying pin. He cast the tarred leather bucket into the sea and drew it forth brimming with seawater. Squatting by the bucket, Gopal began his ablutions, splashing the water into his face, under his arms, and over his chest and shoulders.

Nearby, a knot of sailors lounged. They were typical of the crew of this or any other pirate vessel, a polyglot pack of sea sweepings united only in viciousness. A shaven-headed black of some Kushite tribe stood next to a hooknosed Shemite. At their feet sat a quiet, deadly Stygian next to a yellow-haired Gunderman, somehow strayed from his landlocked frontier district. Several others made up the group, most prominent among them a tall, lean Poitainian who wore knee-length breeks of red silk and a wide sash of Kothian cloth-of-gold. The group watched Gopal with broad grins until Kasavo emerged from his quarters with a predatory gleam in his eye. The Poitainian caught the look and Kasavo nodded, jerking his head toward the squatting Vendhyan. With a vicious grin the Poitainian strode on bare feet toward Gopal.

Gopal, still squatting, was drying his hands on a scrap of cloth when a pair of silk-draped knees appeared at his eye level. Before he could stand, a bare foot kicked over his bucket, drenching his legs and loincloth. Slowly, Gopal stood, smiling as obsequiously as ever. "Was my pail in your way? I am so sorry, my friend. I must be more careful."

The Poitainian grinned as Gopal stood and he poked a grimy forefinger into the Vendhyan's hairless chest. "Sorry, are you? Well, sorry isn't good enough. Vendhyan, how would you like to play a game?" He turned toward his friends and smiled viciously, happy to be the center of attention.

"A game, master?" Gopal said with a toothy smile. "A game like king-is-dead? I can play that. We can make a playing board here on the deck, and use fishing sinkers for men."

"No, no," said the Poitainian, shaking his head and speaking with broad mock gravity. "What I have in mind is a more active game."

"Active, master?" Gopal said with a look of mystification.

"Yes. Can you dance, foreigner?"

"Dance, master?"

"Yes, dance, you fool!" the Poitainian shouted impatiently. From his sash he drew a broad-bladed poiniard of Zamoran design, etched upon the blade with prayers to Mitra, but with an edge of irreligious keenness. Playfully, he poked the point toward Gopal's bare belly.

"Master, what does this mean?" Gopal pleaded.

"It means I want you to dance!" The Poitainian lunged and Gopal saved himself only by a nimble leap backward. Jaganath emerged from the cabin and surveyed the proceedings serenely. By now everyone except the steersman had gathered around the main deck to watch the fun.

"Oh, I see!" said Gopal. "You mean to dance like this?" He drew his small dagger and held it as if he were about to hand it to the Poitainian. It was thin and slightly curved, keen on both edges.

"Like what?" said the Poitainian, slightly disconcerted. Then, seeing the smallness of the Vendhyan's dagger: "Very well, landlubber, if you'd like to match blades, let us dance!"

He crouched slightly, belly sucked in and dagger held out before him, with his thumb on the crossguard against the flat of the blade. This was the guard position taught by Poitainian weaponmasters, and his left hand was raised slightly above the position of the right, ready to block or grip his enemy's weapon hand. This, too, was in accordance with the Poitainian theory of dagger fighting.

Gopal, still smiling, held his little knife so tentatively that he seemed almost on the point of dropping it. "I am most ignorant of your dances, master," Gopal said. "Please, of your goodness, give me a lesson."

The Poitainian, suddenly aware that he was in mortal danger, was more than a little nonplused. Still, the eyes of his comrades were upon him, and he did not want to appear intimidated by this little eastern book scholar. "Well, first, you must look to your throat!" Abruptly, he lunged, the blade licking out toward Gopal's neck, but the Vendhyan was no longer there.

Delicately, Gopal stepped in under the blade. To the other crewmen the Poitainian's lunge had been blindingly swift. In any other shipboard brawl it would have spelled the end to the fight. To Gopal, trained by the best of Vendhya's master assassins, the lunge was impossibly slow and clumsy. He evaded it so easily that he felt a keen sense of disappointment, then he slipped in and swept his blade across the exposed belly before him. Then he stepped back.

The Poitainian looked down stupidly as the thin red line at his waist widened and his intestines began to emerge. Gopal reached out delicately and grasped a handful of entrails. "Now we can dance, my friend!" Gopal pulled, and a ghastly coil of bowels tumbled to the deck. The Poitainian, as if in a trance, tried to follow Gopal and dropped his dagger, trying to use both hands to stuff his entrails back into his belly. Gopal laughed and continued to lead him around the deck, laughing and encouraging him. In the end, Gopal stood by the rail and cast the huge loop of intestines into the sea. The Poitainian, now totally mindless, dived in, as if by that expedient he might repair his destroyed body.

Gopal laughed loud and long. "I like these games!" He looked around the deck, to be met with the bleak stares of the crew. "Will no one else play with me? Surely, someone else must wish to teach the foolish outlander a lesson!"

The shaven-headed Kushite sprang forth, holding the short-handled spear of his nation. "You slew my shipmate! Die, landsman!" He thrust mightily, but Gopal stepped lightly around the broad spearpoint and thrust delicately. The curved blade went in just below the Kushite's ear, cutting in no more than an inch, but it was sufficient. From the small cut emerged a fountaining torrent of blood. The black tried to cover the fount with his hand, but it was futile. Within seconds he collapsed onto the deck, with his blood staining the wood in a widening stream.

Others now rushed in. An ugly Argossian blundered in, swinging a short club. Gopal sidestepped nimbly and slit the man's throat in passing. A Zingaran thrust with a long, narrow sword of curious design. Gopal avoided it adroitly by turning slightly and sucking in his belly. A swift stab beneath the chin and into the brain killed the Zingaran instantly.

Now the pirates were drawing back toward the rails, leaving as much distance as possible between themselves and Gopal. The only one to stand his ground was Kasavo himself. The captain drew his short sword and advanced warily, balanced on the balls of his feet. "Try your eastern tricks on me, little man," he hissed. "See how much good they do you!" He feinted toward Gopal's face, then lowered his point to plunge his steel into the Vendhyan's bowels.

Gopal ignored the feint and stepped forward, twisting his body slightly, allowing the point to pass through empty air. His blade swept delicately across the captain's wrist and the sword clattered to the deck. Kasavo jumped back, gripping his wrist to stop the bleeding. His fingers would not move. Gopal had severed the tendons. "No one man can fight a whole crew!" Kasavo snarled. "Kill them both!"

With a howl all of his men drew steel and began to close in. Gopal stood where he was, unafraid.

"Hold!" The order crackled through the air with immense authority. Helplessly, the men stopped their advance and stared with fear-widened eyes at Jaganath, who now stood upon the fantail. He seemed to have gained a cubit in height, and an aura of sorcerous light shone around him. From his mouth emerged a stream of low, guttural words, oddly cadenced. The faces of the men grew slack, and their weapons fell clattering to the deck.

"Bind them, nephew," Jaganath instructed. "Leave four or five free to handle the ship."

While the crew stood apathetically, Gopal collected short lengths of rope and trussed them up securely. The five who were to handle the ship received special attention from the mage. With the blood of the fallen he traced certain symbols upon their brows, muttering incantations the while. He then freed the others of his spell. Immediately, they began howling in demented fear, tugging at their unyielding bonds. To no avail, for Gopal was as clever with ropes as he was with his dagger.

"Peace, gentlemen, peace," said Jaganath, his beatific smile restored. "I have selected you for a signal honor. This very night you are to make the acquaintance of certain very powerful beings. I know that you must look forward to this with keen anticipation, for men in your profession seldom have the opportunity to mix with the great ones of this world. Or any other, for that matter." At this he laughed until his huge belly shook.

Throughout the rest of the day Jaganath made his preparations, assisted by Gopal. The crew sat stupefied by horror as

the Vendhyans took one of their number and cut his still-
living body into several pieces, using the selected portions of
his anatomy for rites conducted at various parts of the ship,
where Jaganath had drawn complicated designs upon the
deck with fresh blood. All was in readiness by the setting of
the sun.

"It annoys me to have to do this, nephew," said Jaganath.
"These complicated rites and the calling up of the powers of
the deep are trivial things, suited to a novice sorcerer. I had
thought that I had done with these things many years ago,
when my studies advanced into the truly great realm of wizardry. However, we must have fair winds and calm seas for
the next step of our journey. To be sure of those, I must
summon He Who Dwells in the City Beneath the Sea." He
pronounced this title in the secret tongue of the highest order
of wizards, and the timbers of the ship shuddered to the
reverberations of the name.

As the gibbous moon rose above the waves, Jaganath stood
in the prow of the ship, arms raised and voice chanting
horribly in a language never meant for human tongue. The
captain and crew of the *Songbird* huddled wretchedly amidships as the sea all around the hull began to glow an unearthly green.

From time to time immense humped forms broke the surface within a few yards of the ship, then sank beneath the
water once more, leaving behind only a hideous stench, the
essence of all the foulness and corruption upon the ocean
floor. Great tentacles, slimy and iridescent, coiled and looped
over the waves, slapping the surface before slithering below.
Once, a long, serpentlike form swam around the ship, half a
league of serrated back rising and plunging before it disappeared. Its head and tail never became visible.

Although the sea was turbulent and foamy as far as vision
could reach, the ship floated placidly in an unnatural patch of
calm water. Gradually, the green glow of the water was

transformed to a lurid blood red. The lesser beings of the deep ceased to appear and the waves became quiet.

A shadow darkened the glowing water, shapeless and vast. Slowly, it grew larger, as if some unthinkably huge creature were arising from the farthest depths of the sea. The shadow widened until it seemed impossible that it could be made by any living thing.

Then it broke surface. A titanic, humped shape arose from the water, and the sea cascaded from its sides in foaming torrents. Big as an island, it continued to rise until its crest was far higher than the tip of the mast. The rounded bulk was corrugated like an eroded hill, and it was splotched and rough, with dense growths of barnacle and coral. Smaller creatures crawled or scuttled amid its growths and protuberances.

A cluster of insanely glaring eyes appeared, and below them a wide, toothless mouth that slobbered a foaming green scum. Last of all appeared a cluster of hundreds of tentacles that seemed to completely encircle the thing's horrid bulk. Coming from it was a stench so awful that all that had gone before was trivial by comparison. The prisoners who had not yet passed out from fear retched helplessly upon the deck.

Jaganath's chanting continued, and after a few minutes the thing from the bottom of the sea began to respond, its flabby lips working in an obscene parody of human speech, its voice a rumble so deep that it did not register upon the human ear as sound but rather was felt in the flesh and bones. In its horrible fashion it was speaking the same words as Jaganath. This unnatural communication continued until the moon was high, then it stopped abruptly.

In silence the thing came closer to the ship until its cluster of eyes stared down into the knot of insanely gibbering men who writhed helplessly against their bonds in a futile effort to get away from this horror.

"You now have the privilege," Jaganath said, "of entertaining my guest at dinner."

A tentacle slipped over the rail and wrapped itself about the waist of a shrieking man. It raised him high, holding him close to the eyes, like a man examining some exotic delicacy before tasting it. Other tentacles took him by the limbs and, one at a time, tore them off, thrusting them into its gaping mouth. Last of all it twisted his head off, ending his sufferings, and held up the limbless carcass like an obscene wineskin, squeezing it dry of blood and then popping it, too, into its mouth.

One by one it consumed the rest of the crew in the same fashion, last of all taking the unfortunate Kasavo. Gopal had given the man a drug to ensure that he would not pass out from the horror of the proceedings, but his face was perfectly mad even before the creature began to dismember him.

When all was done, the thing from the deep spoke a single word to Jaganath, then slowly sank beneath the surface. A broad, churning whirlpool marked its passing, then the red glow faded as the shadow shrank in its descent. Soon all was calm again, and the moon shone down placidly upon the ship that sailed the calm waters. Mindlessly, the spared ones continued to work the vessel, having taken no notice of the past hours.

"I had never thought to see the great god of the deep," said Gopal when he felt he could trust his voice to be steady. Never before had his uncle allowed him to witness such a thing.

"That was not the great one," Jaganath corrected. "This was one of his minions. The great god sleeps in his city beneath the sea. Even I, as I am now, could not bear the sight of him! Soon, though, I may be able to speak to him as an equal. Surely, the events which lie before us shall rouse him from his age-long slumber."

"If this was, as you say, a trivial matter for such as you,"

Gopal said in wonderment, "then my mind reels at the thought of the power you command already."

"Yes," Jaganath said complacently, "I am already one of the greatest of mages. Soon I shall be greatest of all, and infinitely more powerful than I am now. I am somewhat fatigued, nephew. Let us sleep now. These slaves will sail the ship safely. Tomorrow we shall be near Kordava."

The next morning, within sight of the city, the mage and his nephew lowered a ship's boat into the water and deposited their belongings into it. As they rowed away from the ship, the automatons hauled the yard around and set sail to the west.

"What will they do now?" Gopal asked.

"They will sail until they are far from sight of land. Then, in obedience to my instructions, they will fire the ship and burn or drown with her."

Gopal set himself to the oars and began pulling strongly for shore. "What shall be our story when we reach the port?"

"We need none. I shall simply render us invisible as we enter. Kordava is a large port, and there will be much shipping there. All will assume that we have come in on one of the vessels. That way we do not need to make up a story of a disaster at sea to explain our arriving in a small boat. After all, we wish to take passage on another ship, and we do not want to arrive with a reputation for bad luck at sea, do we?" At this both men laughed loud and long.

In the great hall of Starkad, the Vanir chieftain was holding revel for his fighting men. Along the benches the Vanir warriors sang and drank ale or mead from silver-mounted oxhorns and ripped great dripping hunks of half-raw meat from the bones of boar and stag with their strong teeth. They were big men, and their hair and beards ranged in color from bright orange to reddish-brown, but always the red tint proclaimed their Vanir ancestry, just as gold hair identified their kinsmen and deadly foes, the Aesir. Behind each man's place on the bench hung his round shield, his horned helm and shirt of scales or mail, and his sword, spear, and bow.

At the head of the long trestle table, elevated on a dais, sat Starkad and his guests. The Van was studying the two arrivals who had come off the ship that had put into the fiord of Starkadsgarth this very morning. They were as odd a pair as he had laid eyes on in many a year. Dark they were, and beardless. One was large and fat, the other small and delicate. They were from some far eastern land he had never heard of, and there was something strange about the fat one that proclaimed him a wizard. More to the point, the man was rich and seemed to desire some service of the Van.

"That is a most interesting cup you drink from, King Starkad," said Jaganath.

"I'm not a king," Starkad grumbled. "I'm a chief. If my men hear you name me a king, they will wax angry and kill you." He raised his cup and looked at it. It was a human skull, the top of which had been removed and the braincase lined with gold. The eye sockets had likewise been filled with gleaming gold, and it had a stem and base of the same precious metal. "Yes, it is fine, is it not? This was Hagmund of the Aesir, and he slew my father, wherefore I was obliged to put him to death in a leisurely fashion. Whenever I drink from it, my father's spirit is comforted. Somehow, wine is always sweeter when drunk from the skull of an enemy."

"So I presume," Jaganath said.

Starkad was a little disappointed that the Vendhyan was not more impressed or intimidated. The reason, though, was simple: Jaganath's sorcerous studies had led him into practices compared to which the simple brutalities of the Vanir were the merest child's play. Although Starkad knew naught of this, the easterners made the chieftain uncomfortable in some obscure fashion. He thought of simply killing them and taking their gold, but he wanted no curse laid on him and his house.

The Vendhyans sat picking daintily at their food, now and then tugging loose a small morsel of bread or piece of fruit while ignoring the steaming slabs of meat laid before them on trenchers of flat, twice-baked bread. Their eyes were reddened from the abundant smoke of the fire that burned in a long trench down the center of the hall. Chimneys were unknown in Nordheim, and the smoke was left to find its own way out through the holes left in the gables at either end of the longhouse. Despite the presence of the fire, both men were bundled in heavy woolens and furs, being unaccustomed to the biting weather of the northern autumn.

At the far end of the hall two Vanir were having some sport, tugging at a wet sheepskin stretched over the fire pit at a spot where the flames had burned down to glowing coals. With a shout of dismay the slightly drunker loser was tugged into the pit. The victor, in traditional fashion, then threw the sheepskin over the loser and jumped up and down on the unfortunate man before allowing him to scramble out, scorched and singed. All around the board the men roared with laughter at this sport.

"I'll wager you have no such amusements down in the soft lands of the South," Starkad said when his laughter had subsided.

"I fear not," said Jaganath. The stench of singed hair and burning fleece was overpowering. "But then, you have probably never seen a losing army of some ten thousand staked out and stamped to death by elephants."

"Hmm," Starkad said, "I've never even seen an elephant, for that matter." He thought of sending south for an elephant so he could have his enemy prisoners trampled.

"You have spoken of your Aesir enemies," Jaganath said, "but do you not also raid among the Cimmerians?"

"Yes, by Ymir, we do! It's a trading of hard swordstrokes with them too."

"Do you raid them to take wealth?" Jaganath queried further.

"Wealth, no. The Cimmerians are a poor folk, with little silver or gold. The poorest As or Van is a chieftain compared to the richest Cimmerian."

"Then what is the advantage of warring with such redoubtable foes when they have nothing worth taking?"

"Did I say they had nothing? We raid their villages to take their children! A grown Cimmerian is useless as a slave. Men and women, they fight to the death or kill themselves rather than be enslaved. But Cimmerian children bring a high price in the South. Properly brought up, they make the best of slaves. Work them as hard as you like, on short rations, and beat them to your heart's content. Nothing seems to kill them. Why, I've seen a Cimmerian householder, with his hut surrounded, slay his wife and children before running out to meet us with his bloody sword. Yes, they're a hard people." He sat back in his great chair and took a long drink from his skull goblet. "But we Vanir are harder."

"Then," Jaganath said, "you will not fear to make a little expedition into Cimmeria?"

"Fear?" roared Starkad, outraged. "We Vanir fear nothing!" Then, more quietly: "However, we venture nowhere if there's no profit to be had, especially this late in the year. This is the feasting time, when we hold revel in our halls. Soon, I will take the hospitality of my fellow chieftains, and they mine, until the great feast of midwinter. We shall need strong persuasion to leave the warmth and the hall joys and go death harvesting among the Cimmerians."

At this unsubtle cajolery Jaganath opened the bag at his side and let Starkad see the massive golden coins therein. Idly, Jaganath's fingers wandered among the shining, clinking pieces. "Is this not a splendid bag?" he said.

Starkad's mouth went dry, and his palms began to itch. He was already rich in gold, but greed was as much a part of him as blood lust, and as the glittering metal he could never have enough of. "What is the nature of this journey which you wish to undertake?"

"A mere trek to a certain mountain. It need not involve the shedding of Vanir blood. We must have an escort, and we must be upon this mountain by the coming equinox."

Starkad chuckled mirthlessly. "We'll not walk on Cimmerian soil without a fight. What mountain is it you wish to find?"

"In the Cimmerian tongue, it is called Ben Morgh."

Starkad went pale beneath his windburn. "Ben Morgh," he half-whispered. "Why in the name of Ymir do you want to go there?"

"My business there is my own concern. Is it so fearsome a place?"

"It is the Cimmerian's sacred mount, where dwells Crom, their god. I care nothing for Crom; Ymir is my god. But to get to the foot of Ben Morgh we must go up Conall's Valley and cross the Field of the Dead. All the great war-chiefs of Cimmeria are buried in the Field of the Dead. If they know that we are coming, there could be a gathering of the clans. To protect the bones of their ancestors they will put aside the feuds of generations, as they did when they put Venarium to the sack."

"But," Jaganath protested, "we will do their graves no injury. We will just pass between them."

"The ground itself is sacred to them," Starkad told him. "Besides, once we were there I could never prevent my men from toppling the cairns of the Cimmerians any more than the Cimmerians will spare our sacred groves when they invade our land. The hatred is bred too deep."

"Well," Jaganath said, closing his bag, "if you cannot do this thing, I will not impose further on your generous hospitality. I have heard of a chieftain, farther up the coast, named

Wulfstan. Perhaps he will have more stomach for a little adventuring among the mountains.''

"Be not so hasty," Starkad said as he saw the bright glimmer of gold disappear. "Perhaps a few of my bolder lads would not mind a bit of brisk work among the blackhairs." He looked down at the paunch that was beginning to bulge over his broad belt. Slapping the hill of flesh, he said, "I myself could use a little exercise. I have not plied my ax this year. Let us see.''

Starkad roared for silence, and gradually the noise in the hall abated. "Our honored guests," he bawled, "have come from afar. They have heard that we Vanir are the mightiest and bravest people in all the world!" His statement was greeted with a roar of approval and agreement. "They have a journey to make, and for an escort of fearless Vanir, they are willing to pay rich golden treasure!" This time the roar was even louder. "Who is with me for a little tramp inland and perhaps a bit of ax play?" There was much cheering and many volunteers, but then a broad-bearded warrior stood and addressed the chief.

"Where do these outlanders want to go?"

"To Cimmeria," answered Starkad. The cheering abated somewhat.

"Who would go into those misty hills this time of year?" demanded the standing warrior. "The snows will be coming soon, the blackhairs will be down out of their mountain pastures and all together in their villages. Nothing there but hard fighting and no captives." Others nodded and muttered that these were true words.

Starkad leaned forward. "Gurth," he said, his voice dangerously quiet and low-pitched, "this is an escort I propose, not a raid. Every man here is free to have his say, but if you would rather be sitting in this chair, my ax is here." He gestured toward a magnificent silver-inlaid weapon propped against his seat. "And there is yours." He pointed to a similar weapon hanging from a peg behind Gurth. "This chair is always open to a man bold enough to take it."

Among the fierce Vanir, a chieftain held his position so long as he could defend it with the strength of his arm. Abashed, the man named Gurth resumed his seat on the bench. Starkad smiled with amusement but no humor.

By ones and twos and in small groups men came forward to volunteer for the undertaking. Mostly, they were younger men, eager to seek adventure and prove their courage. The chief praised them and promised them gold and gifts. When all had finished giving their oath of service, he said to Jaganath, "Tomorrow I will send to the outlying holdings, and we'll get more men. I wouldn't set foot in Cimmeria without at least a hundred."

"Very well," Jaganath said, "but we have little time if we are to be there by the equinox." Then, after a little thought: "I will pay you well, but you will pay your own men. Even this much gold will not go far when spread among a hundred men."

Starkad slapped his knee and roared with renewed mirth. "Fear not, stranger. There will not be a hundred when we return!"

Four

In the Border Kingdom

Belverus lay far behind Conan. He was fully recovered from his injury and rode effortlessly through the last hot days of early autumn. His bronzed skin shone glossily in the full sunlight, for he rode clad only in boots, loincloth, and swordbelt. A headband of scarlet leather kept his unshorn mane out of his eyes as he scanned the horizon restlessly. At any moment the nearby ridges could be aswarm with strangers of unclear intent.

Ten days' riding had taken him from the plain surrounding Belverus into the hilly land that would eventually rise into the great mountain ranges of the northern lands. The grasslands of the south lay behind him, and the hills all about him were clad in a verdure of open forest, most of it hardwood, that would give way to pine as he journeyed northward. Already, leaves were changing color and beginning to fall, presaging an early winter.

This was the Border Kingdom, an area bordered by Nemedia, Brythunia, Hyperborea and Cimmeria, with a finger of land thrust into Gunderland and the Bossonian Marches. It was a land too diffuse and primitive for the strong kingship of the south, and although it was termed a kingdom, it could seldom be determined just who was king of the place. Frequently, there were several claimants to the title, leading to inevitable warfare. The eastern sector through which he now rode was the domain of petty chieftains and he hoped to avoid their squabbles if he could.

The sun of noon looked down upon him as he came to the ruins of a village. Its wooden stockade was little but a circle of charred stumps, and all the huts within had been burned to the ground. There was no smoke, but Conan's nose informed him that the burning had taken place no more than two days past. His mount shied at the smell of blood-soaked ground. A litter of broken arrows and several sword-hacked shields told him that this place had put up a fight. He cursed silently. This was just the kind of thing he had hoped to avoid. His comfortable lead on the solstice was already narrowing, and he wanted no more delays.

Whoever the people of this place had been, they were now dead, scattered, or led away into captivity. And what of the attackers? He made a circuit of the ruined stockade, but could make nothing of a hash of old tracks further obscured by a recent rain. A trail of droppings told him that the village's livestock had been led away to the northeast, but the savagery of the destruction showed that this had been no mere cattle-raid. This was the work of warring clans or a foreign invader. He determined to proceed with utmost caution.

Unfortunately, it is not easy for a man on horseback to avoid detection when riding through strange hills, especially when those he seeks to avoid are keen-eyed men who know the land intimately. A few miles from the village he heard the blast of a horn. Immediately, he saw the mounted picket who was stationed on a nearby hillcrest, keeping watch on the small valley through which Conan was riding. Within minutes the horn blast was followed by the drumming of horsemen.

Conan leaned upon his pommel and waited patiently. He

could flee, but that would mean selecting another route and losing far too much time. Best to allow the riders to examine him and to state his business honestly. If the worst happened, he would cut a way through them and bolt for Cimmeria. If he had to flee, best to flee in the direction of his mission.

The file of horsemen heaved over a ridge and poured into the little valley. There were a score of them, hard-faced men in helms and short cuirasses of mail or scale. By the look of them he judged them to be cousins of the Gundermen to the west. The majority were fair-haired and blue-eyed. He noted one peculiarity about them: Each wore the horns of a bull upon his helm. There was no individual variation in the ornamentation of their headgear. Their shields likewise were decorated with the heads of bulls, and one rider bore a tall standard upon which were the skull and several tails of the same beast.

He kept his hands well away from his weapons as the riders circled him. Their manner was wary but not overtly hostile. His eyes widened as one of the riders rode toward him. This was not a man, but a woman dressed for war. He studied her with open admiration, for she was well worth looking at.

Her face was obscured by a horned helmet which left only a Y-shaped slot for vision and breath, but her body was as splendid as that of a warrior-goddess of Vendhya. Her full breasts were protected by cups of polished bronze, and her wide, powerful shoulders tapered to a small waist cinched by a broad belt covered with silvered scale. Bronze greaves covered her shins and knees, leaving her thighs bare except for a dagger strapped to the right. Except for her armor and the straps that held it in place, she wore nothing except for a narrow loincloth of black silk, not even sandals.

The woman loosened her chin strap and lifted the heavy helm from her head. A mane of tan hair spilled from the helm and hung as low as the woman's elbows, and Conan was pleased to see that her face was as beautiful as her form. It was a strong face, with a brow that was low and wide, and cheekbones that were wider still. Her jaw was square and firm, her nose straight. Many would have considered her features too strong and heavy for true beauty, but the hard planes and angles of the face were softened by a wide mouth with full, sensual lips. In any case, Conan thought the face perfect for her woman-warrior's body. The exceptional development of her neck and shoulders proved that this was no king's daughter dressed up as a soldier for play, but a woman who was accustomed to wearing armor, probably from childhood. He judged her age at somewhere in the mid-twenties.

Meanwhile, the woman was studying him as frankly. Her cool blue eyes registered approval as they took in Conan's powerful, heavily muscled frame, his big, scarred hands with their calluses from his years of weapon work.

"I am Aelfrith, chieftainess of Cragsfell," the woman said. Her voice was low, almost husky. "You are a Cimmerian, by your look. What is your business in my land?" As Conan had expected, she spoke a dialect of the Gunder tongue, which he understood.

"My name is Conan. I go to my home in Cimmeria, which I have not visited in many years. I travel alone and I mean no harm to you or your people. May I pass through your land unhindered?"

"That may not be easy to grant. I would not interfere with your homefaring, but there is war here."

"So I have noticed," Conan said. "Earlier I passed through a village, or rather a place where a village had been. There was not enough left of it for the crows to fight over."

"That was Atzel's work," the woman said, her face paling with rage. "Many of the folk escaped to my fortress at Cragsfell. We reached the place yesterday, in time to carry off the dead for burial, though there was naught else we could do. Atzel's men left nothing but the bodies of the dead.

He slew all the men he could catch, and carried off the women and children to sell to Nemedian traders."

"Who is this Atzel?" Conan asked. "Is he a bandit or an enemy chief?"

Aelfrith spat upon the ground with a short curse Conan had never heard before. "There are no good words for what he is." She gazed for a moment at the sword at Conan's waist, with its long white handle. "Since you are a stranger here, and mean no harm, I offer my hospitality. We ride for Cragsfell now, so ride with us. You must pass it on your way, so you may as well get a night's lodging and a good dinner before moving on. You can hear all about Atzel and my woes over a pot of ale."

Conan would have been content to sleep beneath the stars again, but it was a deadly insult to refuse hospitality that had been offered. Besides, this regal warrior-woman intrigued him. "I accept, and gladly."

"Good. We shall be there before nightfall. It may be that we shall be attacked on the way, but you are now under my protection. That is something you would not get from Atzel. He would have killed you by now for your horse and sword, and whatever else you have."

"He might have tried," Conan said grimly. "Many men have tried ere now. They keep one another company in Hell now, plotting what they would do to me when I join them."

Aelfrith regarded him with a measuring gaze. "Yes, I think you would take many with you before setting out on that road yourself. Come, let us ride." She rehelmed and wheeled her horse. Conan kept close behind, admiring the view thus afforded. He strove to hide his broad grin from Aelfrith's men. The rear of her loincloth was no more than half a handsbreadth wide, and rendered this view very nearly as interesting as the front had been. Such scantiness of garb was common enough in Zamora or Nemedia, but it was not at all common among northern women. He guessed shrewdly that this was a way she chose to emphasize her difference from the common run of women. She rode as expertly as any cavalryman, her supple body moving as one with her mount. Conan found himself regretting that his mission would not allow him to stay in this place and get to know her much better.

A long afternoon's ride through the wooden hills brought them within sight of a craggy tor surmounted by crude battlements of heaped stone. Aelfrith pointed to the hill fort. "Cragsfell," she said. By the time the sun was a handsbreadth lower in the sky, they were riding through cultivated land where the harvest was being taken in and swineherds were driving their beasts into the woods to fatten upon the fallen acorns. Conan noted that every man kept a spear handy even at these rustic labors, and many had sword or bow.

The road rose to wind around the tor like a serpent, circling so that approachers must always keep the unshielded side toward the fort. Archers and crossbowmen studded the battlement, casting speculative glances toward the black-haired stranger who rode behind their chieftainess. A dozen men worked a great windlass which raised a bronze-strapped gate of thick timber, and the small cavalcade rode inside.

The fort was small by southern standards, no more than a village surrounded by a drystone wall. At its center was a long, timber hall, elaborately carved and painted. The whole place swarmed with people, most of them women and children sent there by their menfolk to be out of harm's way in these troubled times. They smiled and waved as Aelfrith rode in. She seemed to be popular with her people.

They dismounted, and boys took their horses. Most of the men stretched, their bodies stiff from riding, but Aelfrith merely unhelmed and strode gracefully toward the great hall. Conan stayed close behind her.

Inside the hall she tossed her helm to a boy and an

nounced: "We have a guest!" She pointed at two tow-headed boys. "You and you, see to his needs. Show him to the bathhouse and find him clean clothes. He is to receive the courtesies due a visiting thane." Suspiciously, Conan wondered why a mere wandering warman such as he should warrant this kind of courtesy.

A tousle-haired girl of no more than five years ran from a curtained alcove at the rear of the hall, and Aelfrith gathered her up in her arms. She turned to Conan. "This is Aelfgifa, my only child." The little girl looked at Conan with distrust. Young as she was, she knew that this black-haired stranger was no kinsman or friend of hers.

"She will be the mother of fine warriors," Conan said. It was a customary way to praise a host's girl children in the northern lands, but Aelfrith seemed to take exception.

"She'll be a warrior herself if I live long enough to raise her properly." She smiled at the child in great pride. "Already she can ride and use a little bow I have had made for her. When she has enough strength of arm, she shall learn the sword and spear."

Conan wondered what had become of the child's father, but he knew better than to ask questions of a ruler, even a ruler of a small realm such as this chieftainess. If she thought fit, she would tell him in the course of the evening. If not, he was riding out in the morning in any case, and curiosity would not kill him.

"Bathe and rest," Aelfrith advised him. "When darkness falls you shall sit beside me at table. I have matters to discuss with you, but not until you have rested and eaten and cut the road dust with some ale." She turned to one of the boys she had designated as his attendants and rapped him on the skull with her knuckles. "Why have not not brought our guest a horn? He thirsts." The boy ran off, rubbing his scalp. She turned back to Conan. "The lads will take you to the men's bathhouse. I go now to wash and find out what new bad habits my daughter has learned. We shall speak at dinner." She walked toward the curtained alcove. A pair of young women came out and began to unbuckle her harness before she was through the curtain.

"I shall lead you to the bath, sir," said one of the boys with great self-importance. The other ran in with a horn of foaming ale. Conan noted that it was a common oxhorn, before he emptied half of it at a single swallow.

"Are you really a Cimmerian, sir?" asked the boy who had brought the horn. "Cimmerians sometimes come down out of their mountains to steal our cattle." The boys led him outside and toward a wooden building that was larger than the dwelling houses.

"That would be the Murrogh," Conan said. "They are the enemies of my clan. I am your friend. My clan never raided in the Border Kingdom that I ever heard of. We do most of our fighting with the Picts and the Vanir. And, of course, with our fellow Cimmerians." This seemed to reassure the boys.

They entered a single large room, most of which was taken up by a huge wooden tub, in which several of the men he had ridden with that day were already splashing. The room was filled with steam, and water slopped all over the flagstoned floor. Conan unbelted his sword and dirk and bade one of the boys take it outside, away from the damp. The other helped pull off his boots. He stepped from his loincloth and climbed into the great tub.

The hot, steaming water soothed the aches from his mighty but tired muscles, and he luxuriated in its caress. He greeted his fellow bathers and sought to engage them in conversation. They were courteous but curt in their speech. Clearly, they would remain cautious with this stranger until their chieftain-ess's intentions toward him became clear.

A boy brought him a full horn of ale and Conan sat back,

blissfully relaxing from the rigors of his trip. One small doubt gnawed at his contentment: Obviously, the chieftainess had a proposal to make, and she wanted him to be in a receptive mood before she broached it. He might find himself in the delicate, dangerous position of having to say no to a woman who was accustomed to being obeyed, and who had scores of tough fighting men at her command.

His musings were interrupted by a cry of "Hot stone!" A stout woman came in through a back entrance. In her hands she held a pair of tongs which gripped a glowing-hot stone the size of a man's head. The men in the tub pulled hastily back as she cast the stone into the water. It sank with a loud hiss and a burst of steam, and the water bubbled furiously over the spot where the stone disappeared.

He stepped from the tub and the boys scrubbed him down with stiff brushes and crude soap. He felt as if a layer of his skin were being peeled off before the boys doused him with a bucket of water. He climbed back into the tub to soak and had almost dozed off when one of the boys brought him a clean tunic. He climbed from the tub and dried himself with a coarse towel, then put the tunic on and went outside to don his weapons. He felt rested and refreshed and ready for a fight against stiff odds.

Mostly, though, he was ready for dinner. The long day's ride, the rough fare he had been living on, and the relaxation of the bath had brought on a ravening hunger. Good food and strong drink were always high on Conan's list of the important things in life, and the more of both he got the better he liked it.

In the hall he found preparation for the meal almost complete. Trestle tables had been erected down both sides of the hall, and platters of bread and fruits were laid at intervals, with pitchers of ale and mead plentifully supplied. He could smell meats roasting in a nearby cookhouse. His mouth watered and he put aside his doubts in anticipation of the feast. First things first.

The hall began to fill as the more important inhabitants of Cragsfell took their places at the benches. At the head of the two long tables was a small dais upon which stood a smaller table and a tall, richly carved chair. Ranking warriors and their wives sat nearest the dais, lesser people sat farther down. A steward took charge of Conan and led him to the dais, where a second chair was being placed next to the high seat of Aelfrith.

When Aelfrith entered the hall the diners stood respectfully, then resumed their seats at her signal. She had exchanged her armor for an ankle-length robe of thin green silk that was slit to the waist at both sides and had a neckline that plunged to her belt in front. Conan noted that she still wore the dagger strapped to her thigh.

Aelfrith sat and Conan sat beside her as the first platters of meats were brought in. He decided to let her speak first. He tore loose a chicken leg and cleaned it within seconds.

"You have seen much of war, have you not, Cimmerian?" she asked.

"Aye, since my fifteenth year I've fought, from clan squabbles to great wars. In recent years I've earned my bread in the armies of the great nations of the South, first as a common footman, then as a cavalry trooper, then as an officer of cavalry."

"That is good to know," she said. She cut into a slab of beef and began to eat almost as ravenously as Conan. "I said that I would tell you of my troubles with Atzel, and why my country is at war."

"Yes, I would like to hear about that." As long as she was feasting him like this, Conan was content to listen. He pulled a meat pie toward him and smashed in its top crust with the butt of his dirk. As Aelfrith spoke he scooped up meat with bits of crust and devoured them, washing the food down with drafts from his horn. The boys stood behind his chair at a respectful distance to see to it that his horn was never emptied and to fetch any viands he might call for. He intended to eat as mightily as possible, for there would be lean pickings in Cimmeria unless his nation had changed greatly in his absence.

"Atzel is a chieftain to the north of here who likes to style himself a king. He would like to take my lands in order to look like something greater than a robber-chief. He plunders other neighbors as well, but his grudge against me is personal. I slew his son."

"By your own hand?" Conan asked.

"I had no help," she confirmed. "Three years ago I was the wife of Rulf, who was chieftain of Cragsfell. He was young and handsome, and a mighty warrior. He was much like you, although his coloring was fair. We had loved each other from childhood.

"In the fall of that year we went to the Great Festival, where we pay honor to the King Bull, the most sacred of our holy symbols. At that time all the peoples are supposed to be at peace, and any may travel to the festival unmolested. My husband and I, as persons of highest birth, took part in the customary rituals. Atzel and his son, Rorik, also took part.

"There is a certain ritual performed on the second evening of the Festival by a small group of highborn women. I am forbidden to describe it to any man, or to any other who is not initiate, but I may tell you that it is performed naked and that it is forbidden by ancient law for any man to look upon this rite upon pain of execution."

Conan was sure he knew what was coming next, and her words proved him right. "Rorik, a very depraved young man, concealed himself in the grove where the ritual is performed and spied upon us. When he saw me unclothed he was smitten with an unquenchable lust to possess me."

"That is understandable," Conan said by way of compliment.

She went on as if he had not spoken. "That evening I lay down to rest in our tent, and my husband went out to drink with friends. Soon Rorik came and entered my tent unbidden. He babbled on about the great love he had conceived for me, and how he had spied upon the women's rite and that now he must possess me. I was more horrified at his sacrilege than frightened at his threatened outrage. My father had trained me as a warrior from childhood, saying that being born female was no excuse to allow my honor to be impugned, and that a woman had more need than a man to be able to defend herself. I had no doubt that I could handle Rorik, although he was a sturdy youth and armed with a sword.

"In my rage I ordered Rorik from my tent, telling him that I would inform all the chiefs of his violation of sacred law. He said that if I would not yield to him willingly, he would take me by force. I laughed in his face.

"At that moment my husband returned to our tent. Whether he had forgotten something or decided not to carouse with his friends I never learned. Not understanding, hearing only my laughter as he entered, he began to greet Rorik peaceably. Rorik spun around and when he faced my husband there was a dagger in his hand. In a fair fight Rorik would have had no chance against such a warrior as Rulf, but Rulf was taken completely unawares. Before he could so much as blink in amazement, the dagger of Rorik pierced his heart.

"I saw my husband lying dead upon the ground and his murderer standing over him. My hot anger was transformed to a cold rage. When Rorik approached me once more I pretended submission to him. In his haste to tear my garments off he neglected to remove his sword. I grasped it in one hand and shoved him from me with the other. Before he could comprehend what had happened, I hewed his head from his shoulders. It was poor compensation for the loss of my husband, but I took satisfaction in a task of vengeance accomplished so swiftly.''

''Most commendable,'' Conan said. ''So now this Atzel wants his own vengeance?''

''He does. He could do nothing at the time. He charged me with committing a crime of violence within the sacred precincts, but the chiefs judged that Rorik had already committed a sacrilege meriting death, and in any case he had murdered my husband and was the instigator of the bloodshed. Atzel tried to charge that Rulf and I had tried to murder his son, and that he had slain Rulf in self-defense. This the chiefs would not credit, for Rulf was loved by many of them, and they knew that he was no murderer. Besides, none would believe that the likes of Rorik could have killed Rulf when my husband was prepared for a fight. In the end I swore the truth of my story in the very presence of the King Bull. None doubted me after that.

''Since that day there has been unceasing war between my people and Atzel's. He has more men than I, but he does not dare open battle. Instead, he attacks villages such as the one you saw.''

''Yours is a sad tale,'' Conan commiserated. ''I wish you well in your struggle with Atzel, for you are clearly in the right.'' He cut a slab of bread and laid a slab of steaming venison upon it.

''I would like to have more than your good wishes, warrior, welcome as those are.'' She signaled to a boy to refill Conan's ale horn.

''How so, lady?'' Conan asked warily.

''I know warriors when I see them, having been raised as one and married to the greatest in the Border Kingdom. I can see that you are a fighter better than any I have in my following, experienced at command as well. You live by hiring out your sword. Let me hire it. I would give you a place at the head of my warriors, second only to me. My final struggle with Atzel must come soon. He has whittled and gnawed at my strength until he has now almost nerved himself for an all-out attack. I know that he wants to take me alive, to put me to death in some public and humiliating fashion. I shall not allow that, of course. I shall kill myself and my child before I would allow such a thing. But with you leading my men, I may still prevail. My men would follow one such as you into battle as a natural leader. Much as they love me,'' she said ruefully, ''my warriors have never fully accepted the idea of a woman leading them in battle.''

Conan stared moodily into his ale, his appetite suddenly fled. At any other time he would have accepted gladly. The woman had been wronged, and it is never unpleasant to take up a just cause, especially for a beautiful woman. War was his trade, and he did not doubt that he could fight her enemies to a standstill, or even gain a victory. He just did not have the time. He sought a face-saving way out.

''I am an outlander, lady,'' he demurred. ''Would your men accept a foreigner as their war leader?''

''Certainly. As a foreigner you could have no ambitions of installing yourself as chieftain in my place, so that suspicion would be at rest. It is customary here for women whose menfolk are dead to appoint a champion to take care of whatever violence must be performed on their behalf. They would accept you naturally.''

''I cannot accept,'' Conan said. ''Believe me, it would delight me to take up your fight, but I am on a journey which I may not interrupt.''

''Stay the fall and winter, at least,'' she urged. ''Cimmeria will still be there in the spring.''

''My journey is not merely a homefaring. I have a mission to perform, undertaken upon my most solemn oath. I must be in the very depths of Cimmeria by the autumnal equinox upon forfeit of my honor.'' It galled him to say this, but he felt that he owed the woman an explanation at the very least.

Her warm gaze turned cold. "Perhaps I was wrong. Perhaps you are not the warrior that I thought."

Conan refused to be drawn. "Judge as you will, lady. I have told you the truth. I give you this promise: When my mission is accomplished, I shall immediately return here and take up your standard."

"If you did not leave until after the equinox," she said bitterly, "you would not be here until early winter, at least. Atzel is on the move now. It shall all be over by then, one way or the other. But go your way, Cimmerian, I'll not stand in your path." She turned from him and sipped her wine, glaring toward the far wall of the hall and seeing nothing.

Conan sat sullenly, mortified at having to appear the coward. He continued to eat and drink, fortifying himself against the hardships to come, but the food and the ale had lost their savor.

Aelfrith's manner was remote, but she took her duties as hostess seriously. In the morning she saw Conan on his way, after making sure that he had a good store of preserved food to sustain him. Once again she was dressed in her armor and little else. "Your path will take you north," she said, pointing to a distant notch in the nearest range of mountains. "That is Ymir's Pass, and through it you must go if you would see your homeland before midwinter. Once you leave my land, you leave my protection."

"I have protected myself for many years now, lady," Conan said.

"You may well have need of your skill. Ymir's Pass lies in Atzel's land. He has built a fortress directly across it, from cliff to cliff."

"I was born to the mountains," Conan maintained. "I'll have no trouble avoiding him."

"Afoot, perhaps," she said, "but it may not be so easy mounted. Take care."

"I shall. Good day, lady, and I thank you for your hospitality. I shall not forget it."

All day he rode through the little mountain vales. He saw no people and very few animals. It appeared that Atzel had been busy in this area, for he passed several burned-down villages and many overgrown fields and unpruned orchards. This had once been a prosperous, productive land, and it was being turned into a wilderness.

Well, it was not his problem. At least, so he kept trying to tell himself. He rode befogged in sour thoughts, but he did not let his vigilance relax. Once, a small troop of horsemen appeared on the road, far ahead of him. Conan pulled off the road and led his horse well into the woods, where its sounds could not betray him. Cautiously, he made his way back to the road to observe the riders. He wanted to know whom he shared the road with, and he was mystified that they had not noticed him as soon as he had spotted them.

He found a substantial tree overlooking the road and climbed it. He lay along a great branch that would shield his form from observation and he waited. One passing below would have to look directly upward and be searching for watchers in order to notice him. Conan lay perfectly still, barely breathing. An ordinary man could not have held this pose more than a few minutes. Conan could maintain it for hours.

He heard the faint jingle of harness and clopping of hooves, and soon the first rider was passing beneath him. His eyes widened in wonderment, but he made no other motion. These were not local people, but Zamorans. He recognized them by their dress and by their horse-trappings. They were small, furtive men with dark faces and beards. What were a party of Zamorans doing here? There were five of them, and they were headed in the direction from which he had come, toward Aelfrith's land. He did not like that, but there was little he could do about it. At least, now he knew why they had not seen him. Men bred to the plains and the bare rocky hills of Zamora, they were alien to the wood-clothed foothills of the Border Kingdom. When they were gone, Conan climbed carefully down and went to fetch his horse. He did not like the look of the Zamorans. They had the aspect of thieves. Almost, he turned to follow them. Then, remembering his oath and his mission, he turned back toward Ymir's Pass.

The sun of late afternoon found Conan within a short distance of Atzel's fortress. The crude stone pile stretched across the valley as Aelfrith had described, and he was faced with the problem of finding a way around it. On foot he could have scaled the cliffs easily, but he could not be sure of finding a good horse on the other side. If he was to keep to his timetable, he would have to stay with the beast as long as possible. Darkness was coming on apace and he would have to stop and camp soon. He decided to find a good place to hide his mount and go on a reconnaissance of the fortress. He knew that it is never amiss for a man in danger to learn as much as possible about the nature and circumstances of his enemy.

With his horse picketed inside the forest, well away from any villages, Conan set out for the fortress. He stayed off the road but paralleled it within the cover of the second-growth brush flanking it. He found the ashes of an old campfire and rubbed soot in patches and streaks over his face and body, breaking up its outline and dulling the bronzen sheen of his flesh, the better to avoid detection. As for sound, he made none at all. Dressed only in loincloth and weapon belt, he glided through the woods as silently as a ghost.

It was fully dark when he reached the fortress. His eyes had adjusted to the dimming of the light, and the half-moon overhead cast plentiful light for a man with Conan's sharp senses. Most men would have floundered about near-blind in the forest obscurity, but Conan was as woodwise as a Pict, a people among whom he had lived, despite his nation's historic antipathy to that race.

Like Aelfrith's fort, this one was crudely constructed of roughly hewn stones, piled without benefit of mortar. The wall provided adequate finger and toe purchase for Conan, who had climbed walls that would have been rejected as too smooth by a Zamoran housebreaker. A childhood spent among rugged cliffs came in handy to a man like Conan, whose life had been devoted largely to breaking into or escaping from places specifically designed to discourage such activities.

Inside the fort, Atzel sat with his cronies, drinking ale by the light of a small fire built upon a stone hearth in the center of the arms room. The light glinted on the heads of spears ranked about the walls, each spear alternating with a short wooden bow and its attendant quiver of arrows. Higher on the walls were hung axes and cheap swords, of the type bought by small rulers by the hundreds to arm their common soldiery. Such blades, sold in bundles by the merchants of Nemedia and Turan, though plain of design and ornament, would kill a man quite as sufficiently dead as the finest champion's sword made by a master smith.

Atzel was a huge man wrapped in a bearskin robe despite the warmth of the evening. His once-golden beard was shot with gray, and his face was deeply lined. Features formerly handsome were marred with purple blotches, and dark bags hung beneath his pale-blue eyes, their whites turned red and yellow. He was the ruined hulk of what had been a stalwart warrior, broken down by age and excesses of every kind. As his body had been destroyed by immoderation, his mind was bent by greed, hatred, and lust for self-aggrandizement and vengeance.

Just now he was in a jubilant mood, swigging his ale with a gusto he had not felt in many years and laughing with his comrades. "We'll have that haughty bitch now!" the self-styled king proclaimed. "My bought Zamoran kidnappers will see to it. She'll pay for the murder of my Rorik at last! I'll have her stripped of every stitch and sacrificed to the King Bull for all to see. Then who will deny that Atzel is the greatest ruler of the North?"

"None, lord," said a follower with sycophantic zeal. The man grinned lasciviously at the mental picture of the chieftainess of Cragsfell stripped and bound for sacrifice.

"A masterstroke, my king," said another. "If we merely defeated her in warfare and slew her, as is our right in just vengeance for our beloved prince, still many would take up arms against us. But when the King Bull accepts her as a proper sacrifice, who can dispute with his divine will?"

"Who, indeed," Atzel chuckled. He turned to a cadaverous man who wore no weapons, his cattle master. "Are you sure that your Bossonians truly have the King Bull penned in that little valley?"

"It is he, lord," the man answered. "All has been done according to your wishes. The Bossonians are all master cattlemen, and to them he is merely another bull. None of them speaks our tongue, so no word will leak out that you now control the divine beast." Atzel was uncommonly astute in hiring foreigners to perform tasks his countrymen would have balked at.

"But will he attack?" Atzel urged. "He will attack another bull, as any bull will. He will attack a man trespassing into his herd. But it is important that the beast will gore and trample a tethered woman in front of the assembled people."

"All has been taken care of," the man assured him. "Each day a captive woman has been stripped and tied to a stake, and the bull has been tormented by men standing behind her. He has learned to attack them. Now he will attack such a woman on sight."

"My lord," said a grizzled warrior uncomfortably, "is this right? Your demand for vengeance is just, but I mislike this handling of the sacred beast. All the folk hold him to be a god upon earth, and the embodiment of our luck, and the fertility of our flocks and herds.''

Atzel snorted past his moustache. ''He is just a bull like any other. In time, the King Bull is always killed by a younger bull, or by the worshippers at the Festival when his virility flags. Then there is a new King Bull. Is this any different? So what if I decide to use the King Bull for my own purposes? Am I not a king, and may I not do as I wish? Besides, it may take a divine beast to kill this witch.'' His eyes grew wild and his voice strident as spittle flecked his lips. ''For that is what she is, mark me. She cast her spell upon my Rorik and caused him to conceive an unnatural lust for her. She bewitched the council of chiefs to find against Rorik after his murder! Surely the gods themselves must crave vengeance against the sorceress! It is only justice that the King Bull should execute her, since she defiled his Festival with her plot to destroy my son!'' His voice had risen to a shriek.

''As you say, lord,'' said the grizzled warrior, who now regretted having brought up the subject.

''That will all be set aright soon, master,'' soothed a courtier. ''The witch will die with the great bull's horn buried in her belly, and his hoofs trampling upon her face. The Zamoran woman-stealers will bring her to you. Soon your son's spirit will be at rest, lord.''

''I trust so,'' said Atzel, his good humor restored somewhat. He sat back in his chair and drank from a beaker of southern wine. ''Sometimes, his spirit appears to me, in dreams. He is all covered with blood, as he was when the witch murdered him. Sometimes, he carries his head beneath his arm. He demands vengeance, and by Ymir, he shall have it! He was my only legitimate son.'' His followers affected not to notice the great tears that rolled down the drink-blotched cheeks. In a life of utmost depravity, Atzel had experienced only one of the redeeming virtues common to most men: the great love which he had borne for his unworthy son. They all considered it to be his only weakness.

"I shall have her!" he went on triumphantly, the tears still streaking his cheeks. "As this first moon of autumn moves into its waxing phase, it is proper for any chief to call for a sacrifice to the King Bull. Already, my messengers have summoned my fellow chiefs from all over the west of the Border Kingdom. All of them shall witness the humiliation and death of Aelfrith, and who among them shall protest?"

"Her men might pursue," said a senior warrior. "There might be a rescue attempt."

Atzel snorted laughter through his nose. "Ancient custom forbids that any man shall raise weapon against the King Bull. After proper tedious ceremony, an old King Bull may have his throat cut with the old flint knife, but what man will face the current King Bull with no weapon? He is in his prime, and fierce beyond all measure. If a few of Aelfrith's men decide to try the task out of misguided loyalty, what of it? He will make short work of them and whet all our appetites for the main event, which shall be the death of Aelfrith!" He laughed uproariously at the prospect, and his men joined him in chorus.

High above them all, Conan perched motionlessly in the rafters. He had heard enough. Carefully, he began to make his way out of the fortress. His thoughts were in turmoil as he exited the stone pile. He had been tempted to simply cast his dirk into the heart of Atzel and end matters right there. However, the angle and distance would have made such a cast difficult. In any case, by now Conan was wise enough in the ways of men to realize that wars and other great matters were seldom averted by the mere killing of a single man. Atzel was surrounded by men whose importance was linked to his, and who would undoubtedly carry out his plans in order to legitimize their own succession to his power.

In addition to all this, he wanted to get to Cimmeria as

soon as possible. His honor was at stake. He trekked through the woods in silence, watching for enemies, making no sound but carrying on a furious, internal argument.

He found his horse placidly munching grass where he had left it. As he reached for the picket rope, a voice spoke behind him: "What kind of painted savage has blundered into our trap, Ulf?"

Conan whirled to see two armored men advancing upon him.

"When a thrall told us that he had found an unattended horse," said the one called Ulf, "we had hoped to catch a sneak-thief. I think that we have found one of Aelfrith's spies instead."

"Tell us who sent you, fellow," said the first. He held his sword extended, its point leveled at Conan's belly. "If you spill all you know, we may be merciful and kill you swiftly."

"Aye," said Ulf, "you would not like to be turned over to our master. He has never questioned a prisoner who did not talk in time, be he never so hardy."

Conan grinned with genuine delight. His internal debate had been a torment. This was something he could handle. "You are Atzel's men, are you not?" he said.

"That is *King* Atzel to you, oaf," said Ulf. He looked at Conan in puzzlement. "What kind of outlander are you? You're too big for a Pict, for all your paint and strange manner of speech."

"This is a Cimmerian," growled the other. "I have seen his like before, in many a cattle-raid. Be careful, they are dangerous, and do not be deceived just because he can speak almost like a man. Cimmerians are half-demon and half-wolf." The man held his sword well extended, as if to keep the maximum of space between himself and Conan.

"I am happy to hear that my people have not lost their good reputation," Conan said. "Am I to understand that you two intend to hinder me on my way?"

"We intend to take you to our liege," said Ulf.

"Then," Conan said, drawing his sword, "let us see who shall walk from this place, and who shall feed the crows. Come, dogs, taste Cimmerian steel!"

With a howl the two slashed at Conan simultaneously. One swung high from the left, the other low from the right. Most men would have been stymied by the well-timed double attack. Conan ignored both blades and simply waded in. His sword flashed up and then down in a huge half-circle. It took Ulf beside the throat, shearing through collarbone, ribs, and beastbone, ripping from his flank and catching the other man across the waist, gutting him in its course past his hipbone, tearing free of his body to scratch the earth with its point. The men made strangling noises as they fell, their weapons flying across the little glade. They lay drumming their heels upon the sward for a few moments, then they stiffened in death.

Conan grunted a satisfied chuckle as he cleaned and then sheathed his sword. It was not the first time he had slain two men with a single blow, but there was always a certain contentment in carrying out a dangerous move well planned and perfectly executed.

He was satisfied in more ways than one. At some point during the brief, brutal fight, his internal argument had been settled. He untied his horse and mounted. Before he rode from the glade, he addressed the corpses: "You were no match for the great Gunderman I fought and slew a few weeks agone, but you helped me with a decision. For that, I thank you, and I will pray that the devils of Hell torment you a little more gently for that assistance."

He wheeled his horse and trotted through the moonlight to the road. When he reached the road he turned south, away from Cimmeria and toward the land of Aelfrith.

*   *   *

"A horseman coming from the north!" shouted the lookout who stood in the tower that stood on the north wall of Cragsfell.

Aelfrith came out of the long house, wrapping her robe around her against the chill of early morning. Her face was grim. "Is it some parlayer from Atzel?" she demanded.

"No, lady," said the watchman. "I think it is the foreigner come back."

In spite of her circumstances, Aelfrith almost smiled. "Open the gate, then."

Conan rode through the gate and great was his relief when he saw Aelfrith still safe and unharmed. "I rejoice to see you, Aelfrith," Conan said. "I had not expected to. It seems that I have arrived in time. You must take care. I spied upon Atzel last night. He has brought up a pack of Zamoran woman-stealers to bring you to him. The old degenerate is not brave enough to try you in battle, but must hire these slavers to deliver you. I passed them on the road and they look competent." He dismounted and handed his reins to a boy. "Double your guards. I have reconsidered. I am still bound by my oath, but I cannot let this befall one who has behaved so fairly toward me. I have a few days to devote to other matters before I must be on my way. Perhaps we may settle things here in that time." He was alarmed by the paleness and haggardness of her appearance. Something had put years upon her face.

"I am pleased that you have reconsidered, Conan," said Aelfrith. "But you are already too late. The Zamorans have already struck. It was not me that Atzel sent them after. It was my daughter. They have taken my little Aelfgifa!"

Five

The King Bull

Conan sat in Aelfrith's hall, absently stroking the edge of his blade with a barber's fine whetstone. It was already keen, but he wanted it sharper. Around him sat Aelfrith's senior warriors, and they waited in respectful silence for their instructions. Aelfrith had told them to follow the Cimmerian's lead, and they were ready to obey their chieftainess. Men of the north did not follow blindly, but these could see that the Cimmerian was no common warrior.

For the moment Conan was preoccupied with his own thoughts. Primarily, he cursed himself for not following his first instinct and taking up Aelfrith's cause as soon as it was offered. He might have blamed Hathor-Ka's baleful sorcery, or the Khitan's game-playing gods, but Conan was not accustomed to blaming others for his actions. He held himself responsible. Had he followed the dictates of his heart, there would be five Zamorans lying dead in the courtyard now instead of a terrified child out there somewhere.

As he brooded, his rage grew. The Cimmerian's code of ethics was rough by civilized standards, but it was uncompromising and it was fair, by his lights. A man who faced his enemies in fair fight, be he never so evil, deserved to be slain in fair fight. One who brutalized or exploited women, or the old or the weak, was contemptible. For those who made war upon children was reserved Conan's deadliest hate. His Cimmerian kin fought their enemies with incredible ferocity, but never would they slay children, or women or those too old to raise a weapon in defense. They took no slaves and held effeminate a man who would order others to do work too dirty for his own hands. Conan would kill Atzel, and save Aelfgifa if the child still lived. If this stole too much of his time, and brought down upon him the vengeance of Crom, then so be it.

His belief in the terrible and remote old god of his ancestors held none of the complicated theology of the South. He could not believe that Crom would punish a man for doing what a warrior must do in good conscience. Up to the north were men who must die. Conan would not rest if he had to breathe the same air as they. He sighted along the edges of his blade and found them to be perfect.

"This is what we must do," he announced. The others sat forward eagerly, hoping to hear words which would send them into action, to defend the life and honor of their liege-lady. Conan did not disappoint them.

"It is no good crouching behind stone walls," he said. "You may beat off an attack that way, but you cannot win a war. I have studied under some of the great war masters of Nemedia. Man for man, they may not be warriors as great as we of the North, but they have devoted much time and thought to this business of winning wars. One thing they all agree on: To win a war, you must carry the fight to the enemy. That is what we shall do."

The men growled their eagerness. This was what they had been waiting to hear. Their lady was a true warrior, and a brave and skillful defensive fighter, but she had no knack for taking the offense, at which Atzel excelled, although he avoided open battle. Aelfrith, wise in the ways of warriors, recognized this limitation in herself. The moment she had laid eyes upon the Cimmerian she had known that he was the man who could lead her forces against her enemy. Now he was ready to take up the task.

"Atzel sends small detachments out unceasingly to raid against his neighbors' villages," Conan said. "We will go out today and meet them. They'll not be expecting fighting men to come against them. We'll make Atzel hurt and then he will come out against us."

"He is powerful," said a warrior whose chin was cleft by a livid scar. "He has more men than we have."

"I've seen the man close," Conan said. "He makes war on unarmed peasants, on women and children. True warriors cannot fear him."

The warriors mumbled assent. To a southern strategist his reasoning would have made no sense at all. To these northern warriors it was eminently sagacious. They gathered up gear and weapons and prepared to ride out. Conan went to find Aelfrith.

The chieftainess was in the hall, directing the storage of food in anticipation of a siege. Conan paused a moment to admire her cool deliberation, then announced himself: "I go to slay your enemies, my lady."

She glanced up at him, her eyes dark-circled from care. "I care not if you kill anyone, champion," she said. "Just bring my daughter back whole, and I'll reward you with land and titles and a place in my bed if you want that."

Conan bristled. "I want only one thing: to honor my given word. I have taken your service because my heart cries out that it is the right thing to do. I ask no reward."

The steel seemed to melt out of Aelfrith, and she laid a hand upon his rocklike arm. "Forgive me, friend. My care for my child makes me forget who are my true companions." She looked up at him and took his face between her palms, turning it slightly, as if to discern some imperfection. "No, I can see here no greed for land or fame. You will do as your heart bids. As for a place in my bed"—she paused, eyeing the Cimmerian with the same speculation she had used when judging him as a warrior—"I have wanted no man since Rulf died. I have seen no man his equal. It may be that you are that equal." She let her hands drop and she turned from him. "These things lie in the future. Now my only thoughts are taken up by my child and what might happen to her."

"My lady," Conan said, "do not give up hope. The swine cannot kill her without losing his lever against you. He will want to keep her whole for a while, and I will bring her back to you. I ride out today against your enemies. Stay you here and hold this fort. Above all"—he leaned close to emphasize his point—"do not move from this place. Atzel's emissaries may come to you with a proposal. Do not listen to them! If you wish, pole their heads above the gate, but do not believe their words. Do not budge from this place until I get back, do you understand?"

She nodded, but then said: "I know in my heart what is right, but whether the warrior or the mother in me shall prevail, I know not."

Conan nodded. "Just stay here. That is all I ask. If this matter can be brought to a conclusion satisfactory to you, I can do it."

"I believe you, warrior," she said. "Ymir watch over you."

"Crom is my god," Conan said. "I've had trouble with him lately, but I think he still watches over me. He may not help, but he is a warrior's god, and he'll punish unwarriorly conduct."

"I shall guard this place," she said. "Come back victorious."

Conan needed no further instruction. He found his men assembled in the courtyard and ordered them to mount. There were not quite one hundred of them, but he deemed the number sufficient for his purposes. He would not destroy

Atzel with a single blow, but he would make him hurt this day. They rode out through the gate and went in search of prey. Conan had a good notion of where they would find some. He had quizzed Aelfrith and the men about districts as yet unplundered. By comparing them with the areas which had already been struck, he was able to predict those most likely to be struck next. He was proven right when one of his pickets rode into camp to announce a pack of Atzel's men descending upon an undefended village.

"Let's give these swine a surprise," Conan said, donning a borrowed bull-horned helm. His followers growled a rabidly eager assent.

They mounted and went in search of the raiders. Scarcely had Atzel's men chance to set fire to a few huts when Conan and his followers were upon them. A screaming rogue turned to face Conan, swinging a torch. His face disappeared in a crimson mist as Conan swung his great sword. Others went down beneath the savage fury of Aelfrith's men. They were repaying years of uncompensated raiding and brutality, and the payment was not easy.

"Let us go," Conan said, wiping his sword when all the attackers were dead. The villagers were streaming in from the nearby forests, crying their praises of the warriors who had saved them, but Conan was in no mood for such praise. "There are many bands such as this harrying your lands. They must be dealt with."

"Lead us!" said an eager young warrior. "Show us where they are, lord, and we shall take care of the rest."

Conan smiled grimly at the young man's eagerness. "You'll have bloodshed aplenty where I lead."

For two more days they caught and ambushed raiding parties of Atzel's men. Conan was looking forward to the glowing progress report he would tender when he reported to Aelfrith. By surprise and clever tactics they had slain many times their own number. Atzel would be more determined than ever to avoid an open fight, and more inclined to negotiate a settlement.

On the eve of the third day they returned to Cragsfell. They would catch no more prey, for by now Atzel would have called in all his men, lest he lose more. His men had taken the left ear of each man they had slain, and now they were arranging these souvenirs on strings for the admiration of their families and friends.

He sensed there was something wrong before they were within bowshot of the gate of Cragsfell. A few paces nearer, and he knew that Aelfrith was not there. Always before, she had been the first out the gate to greet arrivals. Spurring his horse to a gallop, he dashed for the gate. Worried faces turned to face him as he rode in.

"Where is Aelfrith?" he demanded of a woman whom he recognized as one of her attendants.

"She left last night, lord," said the woman, wringing her hands. "From the time you left with the warriors, she sat and brooded. She was distracted with fear for little Aelfgifa. We tried to comfort her, but to no avail. In the darkest hour of the night she donned her warrior's gear and rode away through the postern."

Conan ripped out a curse that made his mount's ears twitch. "Did no one ride forth to fetch her back?" he demanded.

"Those men who did not ride out with you saddled their mounts and pursued her, but they have not returned, lord."

"We must find her before Atzel has her, Conan," said a young rider beside him.

"Aye," Conan agreed, "but I doubt we shall be in time. Still, we must try. I know that he does not plan to slay her swiftly. We might get her back, if not all in one piece. Damn the woman for a fool! Why could she not have waited?" He fumed and gripped his saddle pommel hard enough to tear the leather from the wood.

"You cannot expect a mother to reason coolly when her child's life is in danger," said the woman. "By now she has made herself believe that she can trade her life for Aelfgifa's."

"We solve nothing by jabbering here," Conan said. He turned to his following. "To the stables and saddle fresh mounts. We ride within the hour!"

Atzel sat in his throne room with the child seated upon his knee. From time to time he idly stroked her hair. She cringed at each touch of his hand. His chin rested on the knobby knuckles of his other hand as he considered his woes. His followers were silent, waiting for him to speak first.

"Where is Aelfrith?" the chieftain grumbled. "She should have been here within the first day. What kind of mother is she? Has she no love for her daughter? And how is it that she has suddenly taken the offensive against me? And, most of all, who is this black-haired foreigner who leads her men in battle?"

He tore at his beard in distraction. The ambushes had wiped out scores of his men. He had lost plunder and horses into the bargain. Worst of all, he was being made to look like a fool, and people might cease to fear him. That was intolerable.

"Aelfrith is a witch, lord," said his steward. "It may be that she has found some spell which has rendered her forces invincible."

"Yes," said another. "The foreigner may be a sorcerer from Hyperborea."

"The Hyperboreans are not black-haired, you dolt!" said a rival for royal favor.

"A Stygian, then." The speaker glared daggers at his rival. "In any case, it is clear that no natural force is at work here." It was always safe to remind the king of Aelfrith's supposed sorcerous proclivities.

There was a commotion at the entrance to the chamber and

a warrior came striding in, beaming immoderately. "See what we have brought you, my king!" he shouted importantly. Two more warriors entered. Between them, in chains, walked Aelfrith.

Beneath his hand, Atzel felt the child's spine stiffen in horror. Aelfrith was still in her warrior's garb, but a spearshaft had been placed across her lower back and her arms and her hands bound before her so that the spearshaft lay in the crook of her elbows, arching her spine and throwing her breasts into prominence. A bronzen ring was locked about her neck, and from it depended two chains fastened to fetters which bound her ankles. She could move only awkwardly and with difficulty, but her head was held erect.

Atzel's mouth sagged with the intensity of his satisfaction, so long delayed. "Greeting, Aelfrith," he said at last. "It has been too long since we have seen each other. Now you shall be my guest. Have you any idea what I will do to you?"

"You will do as you wish, Atzel," she said. "I ask only that my daughter not be made to witness it." Her voice was angry and undefeated.

"A just request, lord," murmured a counselor who stood at his elbow. "You do not want a reputation for unreasonable cruelty."

"Very well," Atzel said. "It was the mother I wanted all along, in any case. Take the child away and keep her under guard." The child broke away from him and ran to her mother, but a guardsman snatched her up as she kicked and squalled.

"Hush, Aelfgifa," said Aelfrith gently. "Remember that your mother died like a queen and avenge me."

Atzel saw many dark looks directed his way and he grew wroth at this spoiling of his moment of triumph. He wanted no sympathy shown for this woman. She was too queenly, and it was time to put an end to that.

"Be not so haughty, you murdering slut! It is time to

display you for what you truly are." He signaled to the guards and they grasped the spearshaft, forcing Aelfrith to her knees. Atzel rose from his throne and strode to her. He drew his dirk and began cutting the straps of her harness. Savagely, he jerked free her breastplates and cast them across the room. Armored belt, greaves, and underpadding went next, leaving her only her narrow hip belt and loincloth. Atzel twisted the belt in his fist until it snapped, leaving red weals on the fair skin. He placed a foot against her back and thrust her to the floor, now wearing only her bonds. "That is better. Now everyone can see what you used to ensorcel my son Rorik. Behold, my people, that the chieftainess of Cragsfell is nothing but a common harlot with a talent for witchcraft."

Her cheek was pressed against the floor, but Aelfrith's words were clear: "Do you think you humiliate me? Naked as I am, I am still ten times the chieftain you are, you degenerate swine. How long do you think you will last, when it is seen how you treat royal blood?"

"Royal blood?" shouted Atzel. "Is that what flows in your veins? Well, let us see some of it!" He strode to his throne and came back with a long lash of cunningly plaited black leather. With a swift motion of his arm it hissed through the air and slashed across Aelfrith's back. Her muscles jerked but she did not scream. With a demented howl Atzel laid two more stripes beside the first, then he was seized by his counselors.

"Restrain your just wrath, my king," shouted one so all could hear. "Let her death be according to ritual and carried out before the assembled chiefs." He leaned close and whispered: "If the King Bull kills her, you are safe, Atzel. If you flog her to death here, all your neighbors will unite to destroy you."

Atzel needed several minutes to calm himself. His courtiers saw with relief that his color gradually faded from apoplectic crimson to its usual unhealthy pallor. "Very well.

That is how it must be." He looked down at the bare, bleeding chieftainess and nudged her with his toe. "Chain her to my dais. I need a footwarmer. Prepare the holy enclosure. She shall be sacrificed upon the morrow."

They had been riding hard for half the day when Conan and his men came upon a small group of warriors sitting despondently by the side of the road. He recognized them as the men who had been left behind to guard Cragsfell while he rode forth with the others. He reined in near them, knowing that they would have ill news.

"We almost had her," said one mournfully. "We rode so hard, half our horses are foundered. We were almost within bowshot of her when she rode into a party of Atzel's guards. We charged them, but they were on fresh horses and outdistanced us easily. What is to become of our chieftainess?"

"I'll not bend the knee to that ancient swine!" swore a young warrior of no more than seventeen years. "I'll turn outlaw first, and I'll know no rest until Atzel's head decorates our standard!" The others shouted assent. Despite the desperate situation, Conan had to smile his approval of this show of spirit.

"That's for later," he said. "For now, all is not yet lost. First we must try to get Aelfrith out of that place. I've been in there already, and it is not too difficult for a skilled climber. Who among you is clever in the woods, and good at climbing, and game for a little raid and some dirty dirk-play?" Several limber young men strode forward, their faces wreathed in broad grins. The prospect of action and vengeance was bringing the men out of their despair.

"We go in at nightfall," Conan said. "Atzel's men will be out in force on the roads, but they'll not be patrolling the woods. Get some rest in the meantime. Let us find a good camp well away from the road and set up guard. Tonight we make Atzel bleed."

They found a favorable spot within an hour, and Conan dismounted to lie on the ground. He was asleep almost immediately. He woke as the moon rose and went to where a small, smokeless fire was burning. The volunteers were already assembled and smearing one another with soot. Conan did the same.

"No swords," Conan directed. "Just dirks or short-handled axes. It's cramped inside that fort. If we need swords on our way out, we will take them from dead men." He saw teeth flash white in the darkened faces at the prospect of killing Atzel's men. "Is all ready?" he asked. He was answered by curt nods. "Then let's go."

They moved swiftly and quietly through the woods. Although, to Conan's keen ear, the men rustled noisily, he knew that most men would not hear them if they were to pass within ten feet. The moon was high by the time they reached the fort. He could just make out the shapes of two guards above them on the battlement. He tapped the youth who had vowed outlawry and vengeance rather than submission. They drew their knives and placed them carefully between their teeth. Warily, they began to climb.

On Conan's last entry to this fortress he had easily evaded the guards. This time they would have to be eliminated. The guards seemed to be scanning the approaching road rather than the walls below them. So much the better. Conan and the young warrior climbed to within five feet of the top of the battlement; then they waited. The guards were directly above them, talking in low voices. Soon the sound of shuffling footsteps and the fading of the voices told them that the guards had turned and were walking toward the opposite side of the roof.

Swiftly, the two raiders swarmed over the battlement. Their bare feet made no sound upon the timber roof. Their loincloths, belts, and dagger sheaths could make no rustle or click. Silent as ghosts, the two fell upon the guards. It was the quick, brutal work of a moment to jerk the two heads back and plunge steel into the exposed throats. In the supposed safety of the fort, neither man had bothered to come on duty with helm or gorget. Now they paid for their complacency with their blood.

The bloody dirks were quickly cleaned, and Conan went to the battlement to signal the others. Soon they were joined by the rest. Conan detailed two men to impersonate the guards and to deal with any guard relief that might appear, thus keeping their principal line of retreat open.

Conan led the way into the bowels of the fortress, feeling his way carefully in the dimness. Only the main rooms of the fort would have torches or candles at night. This upper floor was divided into rooms by timber walls, and a system of trusses supported the roof over all of them. It was possible, by crawling along the trusses, to go from room to room without having to touch the floor.

Like rats, the men progressed from one place to another, seeing little and hearing nothing but snores. A faint glow against the ceiling told Conan of a room in which a fire burned, so he crawled toward it. He found a system of beams above a very large room, and guessed that he had found the main hall of the fort. His guess was confirmed when he looked down upon the throne of Atzel. He heard a strangled noise beside him and he clamped a hand hard on the man's shoulder to keep him silent.

Below them, Atzel was contentedly resting his feet on Aelfrith's bloody back. Her hands and feet were bound to bronze rings sunk into the stone of the dais, and her luxuriant tan hair was so tumbled about her face that it was impossible to tell whether she was conscious. At least, she was still breathing. Of the child there was no sign.

Conan examined the room carefully. There were two guards at the door. He could hear voices from without that door which meant that at least five more guards waited there. It was probably a guardroom, which meant that there might be as many as a score more of the guardsmen within easy call. Surprise might make up for bad odds, but there was a more difficult matter: How to get Aelfrith out. She appeared to be in seriously weakened condition, and it might be impossible to get her up to the roof. She was a substantial woman for a man to carry while fighting. That meant fighting their way downward through the fort to freedom. He tapped the men nearest him and began to belly-crawl backward into the next room. It galled him to admit it, but there was no way to rescue her without putting her in even greater danger.

They were making their way back the way they had come when the youth who had first ascended with Conan came crawling along a beam, signaling frantically for the others to follow him. Silently, they went with him until they were looking down into a smaller room.

By the light of a candle two men were dicing desultorily to pass the time. In a corner of the room, upon a heap of straw, slept Aelfgifa. A ferocious grin split Conan's countenance, and he could see the same expression on other faces. This, at least, they could do something about. They crawled along carefully until they were directly above the two men.

The guardsmen did not even glance up as death dropped upon them from above. Conan landed upon his man like a thunderbolt. Seizing him by a shoulder with one hand and by the jaw with the other, he broke the man's neck with a single, savage wrench. Two of Aelfrith's men landed upon the other and sank their dirks into his body. All was over in an instant. The child did not even waken. Conan picked her up gently and mounted a table, handing her up to the out-stretched arms above.

The raiders crawled back along the beams and out onto the roof, where their two comrades still patrolled the parapet. Descending the wall was a trickier business than climbing it had been, especially while carrying a child who might wake up at any moment and give them away. They made it down safely in time, and the moon was still well above the horizon, lighting their way conveniently as they trotted through the woods, back to their camp.

There were sounds of joy when those at the camp saw that they had rescued Aelfgifa, and sounds of rage when word spread of the indignity being inflicted upon Aelfrith. Conan went down to a little stream to wash off the soot he had rubbed over himself. He was full of a seething rage, unable to wipe from his mind the picture of Aelfrith, stripped and bound, flogged and forced to grovel at the feet of a pig like Atzel.

He vowed silently but sincerely that he would rescue Aelfrith if that were in any way possible, and if it were not, he would slay Atzel, as the man deserved to die.

Aelfrith returned to consciousness slowly, and discovered herself to be inhabiting a world of pain when she was fully aware. Her wrists and ankles were bound tightly, the ropes biting into her flesh, her shoulders and hips stretched to near-dislocation. Worst of all was her back. From neck to buttocks it felt as if molten iron had been poured over it. She was stretched facedown against the rough stone, and her cheek rested in a puddle of her own blood. Her mental torment was, if possible, even worse. What were these swine doing to her daughter? Had they killed her already, since she had served her purpose as bait?

There was a sudden increase in the agony of her back and she knew that Atzel was, indeed, using her as a footstool. The pain increased as he dug in his toes. She would not satisfy him by screaming, but burning tears of rage flowed down her cheeks.

"Are you awake, Aelfrith?" Atzel crooned. "Good. How can you suffer properly when you are asleep. Let us see— what shall we try next? My counselors insist that I should not damage you further. We must keep you beautiful for your sacrifice, you know. Can't have my fellow chiefs thinking that I mistreat noble ladies. On the other hand, it is truly amazing how much pain may be inflicted without leaving a mark on the body. For instance, with a simple cow's horn, open at both ends, and a hot iron, one may cause incredible agony, and the body must be cut open in order to see the damage.''

Aelfrith shut her eyes tightly and gritted her teeth as the insane litany went on, Atzel detailing with relish the obscene torments he planned to inflict upon her. A child of the North, she was accustomed to lust for vengeance, but this went beyond even the most excessive of ancient legends. When he began on his plans for Aelfgifa, she was sure she would go mad before a merciful death could overtake her.

The demented voice ceased when there was a commotion from without. There was a moment of superlative agony when Atzel trod upon her to cross to the door, then she had a few seconds of relative peace.

Atzel's voice came sharp and incredulous. ''The child gone? Four of my guard dead? Fools! How did you let this happen?'' There was a sound of slapping and kicking, then Atzel stormed back into the throne room. Aelfrith laughed into the puddle of blood full and heartily. ''Thank you, Conan! If I were to live, I would make you a king, but now at least I shall die happy, no matter how great the pain. Thank you for my daughter's life!'' She laughed once more, happier than she could remember ever having been. Then Atzel's whip descended and she drowned in a scarlet tide of pain.

With break of day Conan and his followers rode down to the path which led to Atzel's fort. There was a good deal of traffic on the road, all of it headed for the fort. At first Conan thought it might be Atzel's men searching for them, but he soon saw by the designs on their shields that the men of numerous tribes were assembling, mostly petty chieftains with small entourages. Conan and the others fell in with them casually. Conan reined in beside a chief in fine armor. "Pardon me," he asked, "but I am a stranger here. Why do so many of you great folk journey thither?"

The chief eyed the big outlander curiously. "Our fellow chieftain, Atzel, has summoned us to witness a great sacrifice to the King Bull. For the life of me, I cannot imagine why, though. It is early for the Great Festival. But it is his right, and so we come."

"What kind of sacrifice will it be?" Conan asked innocently.

The chief shrugged. "Ordinarily, it would be firstfruits of the harvest, but it is too early for that. Sometimes it is fine cattle or horses. Perhaps the old man has finally gone mad. That would not surprise me. He has been behaving as if he were a king for years, and there is not a chief among us who does not have better blood, or command a following as large or larger."

They passed a row of adler poles surmounted by the skulls of bulls, and Conan asked the significance of this. "Those are the skulls of King Bulls of years past. It means that this is sacred ground for the duration of the ceremony, and no man may raise weapon to another without committing sacrilege."

That, thought Conan, was very convenient for Atzel. Should Aelfrith's men make a desperate attempt to rescue her and cut their way free, they would bring down upon themselves the wrath of the gods and the armed fury of all the neighboring tribes. He would have to come up with a plausible scheme, and he knew that time was growing short.

He spoke in a low voice to two of Aelfrith's men who rode near him. "Pass the word: disperse among this throng. Do not stand all together when we reach the sacrifice ground; give Atzel and his men no target to aim for. Make sure you stay in clear view of these chiefs. As I understand it, Atzel dare make no armed move against us within the sacred ground. Be sure that the horses are held by trusty men, ready to bring them to us at an instant's notice. We may have to run without a proper leavetaking.'' The men nodded and dropped back to pass Conan's instructions.

They were within sight of Atzel's fortress when the cavalcade turned from the main road onto a small path which led into a grove of gigantic trees. From most of the branches dangled figures of plaited straw, and around the trunks were tied ropes of various colors. In the center of the grove was a wide natural amphitheater. Around its periphery stood poles bearing more skulls of bulls, facing inward, into the arena. A gateway had been cut into one side of the amphitheater and closed by a wooden gate. In the center of the arena stood a fresh-cut stake, eight feet high and with a stout bronze ring fastened near its top.

The ground around the arena was filling up with the chiefs and their followers, muttering among themselves in their mystification. Many pointed at the stake, which was obviously never intended for tethering a sacrificial ox or horse. As Conan gathered from eavesdropped conversations, human sacrifice was extremely rare, undertaken only in times of famine or other natural disaster. Recent years had been fair, though.

Conan looked for Atzel, but there was no sign of him, nor of any of his men. He did not doubt that they were nearby. In all likelihood they were scattered throughout the woods, ready to fend off attack or prevent escape on the part of Aelfrith's men. He turned at the sound of a hunting horn being winded. The members of the throng were descending the sides of the amphitheater and taking seats on the grassy slopes surrounding it.

Conan went down the slope as well, finding himself a place as near to the arena as he could get. Here nature had been improved upon. Around the oval arena the ground had been excavated so that a sheer wall ten feet high surrounded it, lined with cut stone. The only way in or out was through the single gate, or by climbing down from the seating area.

In the distance Conan heard a monstrous bellow, and the conversation around him stilled for a second, then resumed. He did not like the sound of that bellow. If it was a bull, then it was one that exceeded ordinary bulls as a dragon exceeds a crocodile.

Then conversation stilled again as the gate opened and Atzel strode into the arena. Most of the chiefs sat at the farther end, and when Atzel passed the upright stake he paused to pat and stroke it gloatingly. Then he continued until he stood a few yards from his audience. He looked up at them and grinned, savoring the moment.

"Three years ago," he began in a bellowing voice, "I petitioned this assemblage for my just vengeance and the punishment of an act of bloody sacrilege, and I was refused. My own outrage is a small thing, but the offense to our sacred King Bull was intolerable. I have called you here to witness this great wrong set aright." The chiefs talked excitedly among themselves as he turned to face the gate. "Bring in the sacrifice!" shouted Atzel.

The great gate creaked open once more, and a small, naked figure was led forth by a halter around her neck. The crowd was silent as she neared the center of the arena, then a great shout of rage went up as Aelfrith was recognized. The guardsmen passed the rope that bound her wrists through the ring at the top of the stake and hoisted her until she was almost forced to her toes. Then they bound her ankles likewise.

The chief who had spoken to Conan on the road leaped to his feet and jabbed an accusing finger at Atzel. "Explain yourself, Atzel! What cause have you to treat a noble lady in such a fashion? Make your explanation a good one or, by Ymir, as soon as we are off this sacred ground I'll have your head hanging from my saddlebow!" A savage collective growl of assent showed that these sentiments were widely held.

"Aye," shouted another. "If vengeance for your son was in your heart, why have you not attacked her in force these three years past? Even then, had you prevailed, you owed her a clean and quick death. This is an outrage against all custom!"

Atzel made a calming gesture with both palms held outward. "I come here not for my own vengeance, although it is just, but to defend the honor of our totem beast, the King Bull." The others calmed and resumed their seats, curious to hear his proposal. "Although Aelfrith was slightly injured in her capture, I swear that neither I nor any other man shall raise a hand to slay her. She shall be sacrificed to the King Bull, yet her throat shall not be cut by the ancient stone blade, nor her heart pierced." He had their full attention now, and a great silence had fallen between his words.

"Instead," he went on, "the King Bull himself shall perform the rite. He shall come in through yonder gate"—he turned and pointed dramatically toward the wooden valve— "and he shall plunge his great horns into that witch in his righteous wrath!" Now he was pointing to Aelfrith, who hung in her bonds, her chin regally high, but tightly gagged.

Another chief rose and spoke, his harsh face framed by the cheek-plates of his silver-gilt helm. "Ungag her and let her speak. It is not right that a chieftainess should be unable to speak in her own defense."

"No, my lords!" shouted Atzel. "This woman is a vicious sorceress! Would you have me free her tongue so that she can deceive your minds once more with her spells?" There were voices in the audience agreeing that this was a valid objection.

"The King Bull lives in the deep woods and comes here only at the time of his great Festival," said the first chief. "How shall he be here to accomplish this feat which you predict, Atzel?"

"Already, he comes," Atzel said. "Did you not hear his

mighty bellow a few moments ago? He knows that the witch is here, and he comes apace to slay her!'' As if in answer to his words, the great bellow was heard once more, this time much closer. "You hear? He comes scenting revenge for the wrong done him, for the profaning of his Festival, for what man among us has ever dared to drive the King Bull like a common animal?''

Several of the chiefs put their heads together and conferred. Then the chief in the silver helm stepped to the edge of the arena. "Very well, Atzel. We shall let the King Bull decide. After all, he would not attack an unoffending woman, only a man who would intrude among his harem. But, if he stands so much as ten heartbeats without attacking Aelfrith, then by Ymir's icy beard you shall die this day.''

"That is all I ask, my lords, a chance for long-overdue justice to be done.''

Conan would stand for no more. He rose to his full, towering height and stretched his arms wide for attention. "My lords!'' he bellowed. "This man is a liar and a cowardly swine! He plans to murder this innocent woman before your eyes and hold the beast to blame! This is a plot as foul as any I have ever known. Do not allow him to hoodwink you!''

"He lies!'' screamed Atzel, foam flecking his lips in his rage. "Will you listen to the words of this foreign dog?''

The silver-helmed one turned to Conan. "Who are you, fellow, to speak to the assembled chiefs?''

"I am Conan of Cimmeria, and I am this lady's champion.'' Now Aelfrith's head turned in the direction of the familiar voice. Her eyes locked with Conan's, and her face, formerly a stoic mask, began to show a faint glimmer of hope.

"You are too late to do her any good,'' said the chief. "We have already taken counsel and have agreed to let the King Bull decide her fate or Atzel's.''

"I'll fight your sacred beast," Conan challenged. "This pig has brought in Bossonian cattlemen to train the bull to attack women. Let me fight in her defense."

The chief turned an icy glare upon Atzel. "Is this true, what the stranger says?"

"Lies! All lies concocted by the witch! Would you take the word of a foreigner against that of a chief of your own blood?"

"I might," the chief said, "when the chief is you. However, we have made our decision." He turned to Conan. "In any case, young man, it is forbidden for any man to raise weapon against the King Bull."

"Then I'll fight him barehanded, by Crom!" Conan shouted. "And if you would slay me, do it now, for I go into that arena now!"

Atzel heard the many shouts of admiration and knew he must change his tack. "My lords, I am perfectly content to let this fool impale himself on the horns of the King Bull. How can it happen otherwise, when divine justice is at stake? By all means, let this black-haired rogue try his puny strength against the mightiest beast of the North!" He whirled and stalked toward the gate, pausing to spit upon Aelfrith one last time. Then the arena was empty except for the suffering woman. The great bellow sounded again, now only a few yards outside the enclosure.

Conan unbelted his sword and dirk and tossed them to one of Aelfrith's men who stood nearby. He pulled off his boots for better footing and then yanked his tunic over his head. Naked except for his loincloth, he stood balanced upon the wall of the arena. There were murmurs of admiration at the sight of his steely, hard-chiseled body covered with its many scars. The silver-helmed chief came to him.

"I wish you well, young man, and I honor your courage, but you have chosen only to die with your lady. No man has ever faced the King Bull barehanded and lived. Even when an old one is taken to be sacrificed when his time has come, many are slain in the capturing of him.''

"If that is how I am to die, then so be it," Conan said. "I'll not see this woman further shamed with none to defend her.''

The chief saluted him and returned to his seat. Conan stood balanced on the balls of his feet for a moment, then he sprang lightly into the arena. He took the shock of landing on slightly bent knees and showed no more effort in taking the ten-foot drop than a man stepping off a low stair. There were cheers as he strode to the center of the arena.

Gently, he untied the gag which confined Aelfrith's mouth painfully. In spite of her great pain, she smiled warmly at him. "I thought it would be impossible for me to feel more gratitude toward you than when I learned that you had saved my daughter. Now I feel it even more keenly. No woman ever had a more splendid champion. But, I regret that you have done this thing. The bull shall kill us both.''

"Do not borrow trouble, Aelfrith," Conan said. "I have fought many a battle with man and beast, and I live yet. And I feel certain that I have a destiny to fulfill. I will meet your beast and we shall test which of us is stronger.''

"Then kiss me, Conan, and I will give to you what little strength I have left.''

Conan took her face between his palms and kissed her fiercely, and it seemed to him that an even greater strength flowed through his limbs than before. Then he turned away from her and faced the gate, folding his mighty arms across his chest. He was ready for a fight, be the enemy man, demon, god, or wild beast. Then the terrific bellow sounded once more, and an immense black shadow filled the gateway.

Conan blinked, trying to see into the darkness of the passageway. Surely, no natural bull could be so huge! Then the animal trotted into the full sunlight, and Conan's heart sank somewhat at the task he had undertaken. This was no domestic beast. It was not even one of the fierce fighting-bulls such as were raised for the bullrings of Zingara. This was one of the rare wild bulls of the northern forests, the ancient ancestor of common cattle. Conan had once killed a Cimmerian wild bull barehanded. That bull had been a relative of this one, but where the Cimmerian bull had stood perhaps five feet at the shoulder, this one stood at least seven.

It stood for a moment, blinking its reddened eyes in the sudden sunlight, surveying its surroundings. Its head was low-slung, and the back of its neck was a towering hump of muscle that looked iron-hard. The great muscles stood out in sleek lumps over every part of its body, and its astounding virility was apparent even at a considerable distance. Most terrifying of all was its head. There was a space as wide as a tall man's forearm between its eyes, and a great, shaggy beard depended from its chin, and over all stretched the tremendous horns. Gleaming like ivory, they spread in a complex, symmetrical curve like that of a Nemedian bow. Fully five feet separated the needle tips.

Even in this extremity, Conan, characteristically, was filled with admiration for so magnificent a creature. Its glossy black hide was scarred all over from a thousand battles fought in defense of its pastures, of its harem, of its god-hood. Truly, Conan thought, if cattle had a god, this must be it.

The bull caught sight of Conan and Aelfrith and its nostrils flared. It began to snort thunderously, and it lowered its head as it began to paw the ground with a forehoof. Great clods of earth with grass and roots attached tore from the ground and showered the beast's back.

Abruptly, the great head raised. It began to walk, going in an arc perhaps fifty feet from the two humans, staring at them with one reddened eye. Then it turned and circled the other way, this time studying them with the other eye. Conan realized that with such wide-spaced eyes the creature had to use one at a time to get a good idea of what these two-legged things were. As it circled, Conan unfolded his arms and sidestepped steadily, always keeping his body between Aelfrith and the bull.

A deathly silence had descended upon the amphitheater. This was the stuff of legends: a battle between god and hero, with the life of a beautiful and brave queen at stake. The bards in the audience were already composing their verses. Only one among them was frantic: Atzel chewed at his moustache in frustration. He longed to see Aelfrith's body rent to bloody fragments by the terrible horns, and this Cimmerian bravo was delaying his pleasure.

Now the bull stopped its circling and turned to face them again. It lowered its head and pawed the earth, this time more fiercely. The clods flew many yards behind the bull. It tensed and prepared to charge. Then it was hurtling like a black stone from a catapult.

Every instinct told Conan to sidestep, but that would leave Aelfrith's body unprotected against the horns. The bulk grew with unbelievable speed, and he knew that this was the moment of his greatest danger. He had spent his youth herding cattle in Cimmeria, and he knew the ways of bulls. A bull will favor one horn over the other, and always seek to gore with that horn first. Would this one hook right or left? If he dodged the wrong way at the last possible second, he would end his life impaled upon that horn.

Then he felt the bull's hot breath, and the right horn was lancing at his left side swifter than an arrow. Conan pivoted on the ball of his left foot and stepped forward into the gap between the horns. The wide brow slammed into his hard belly with a force that seemed impossible, but he managed to lean far forward and wrap his long arms around the neck at its narrowest point, just behind the head. He squeezed with all his might, seeking to cut off the beast's wind. It roared and shook its head from side to side, trying to dislodge the maddening creature that blinded and choked it.

The bull dug in its forelegs and tried to press the man against the ground, but the points of its horns created enough space to prevent Conan from being crushed between brow and earth. Then, with a mighty flex of its immense neck muscle, the bull flung its head back. Conan's grip broke and he flew through the air, turning end-for-end twice before slamming down hard on his back upon the solid earth. He was breathless and half-stunned, but he dared not let that keep him down for a moment. He arched his back, kicked out, and was on his feet in an instant. A mighty cheer greeted this seeming return from death, and he was relieved to see the bull turning this way and that in search of him. At least he had accomplished his primary goal: He had distracted the bull's attention from Aelfrith.

The bull saw Conan and spun to face him. Down went the head, leveling the fearsome horns. To the great amazement of all who watched, Conan did not prepare to dodge. Instead, he took a wide stance, with his left foot toward the beast, his right well to the rear. His left arm was stretched out full-length, fingers extended toward a point between the bull's eyes. The right hand was clenched into a great knotty fist, cocked beside his ear. He stood unmoving as a statue, awaiting the charge.

Again, the bull flexed back slightly, dug in its hooves, and shot forward with a speed that seemed unbelievable in so large an animal. Before the horn could begin its deadly hook, Conan's fist shot forward, too swift to see. In the seats the men heard a sound like an ax sinking into a hard tree. The bull's charge halted and it stood, trembling slightly. Then Conan's fist came up again and descended like a hammer, smashing into the bull's neck just behind the skull. The animal's knees buckled and it went down. In the past Conan had won many tankards of ale from army companions with those two blows. When bullocks were brought in for slaughter, he had bet that using only his fist he could smash the beast's skull and break its neck before it fell. An ordinary bull would have keeled over dead. The King Bull lurched back to its feet and swept its head sideways. Conan was just swift enough to keep from getting the point in his side, but the horn hit him like a mace swung two-handed by a powerful man. He staggered back twenty paces, managing to keep his feet beneath him, knowing that above all he must not fall.

The bull continued to shake its head from side to side, no doubt trying to clear its vision after the two incredible blows. It gave Conan time to catch his breath and plan his next move. The cheering was frantic now. Aelfrith watched him raptly, filled with fear for him but equally full of pride. Conan, her champion, a mere human, had survived two deadly encounters with the King Bull. Each time he had received blows that would have killed most men, yet he was on his feet and ready to renew the fray.

In the stands Atzel was beginning to experience doubt along with his frustration. Why was the man still alive? Had he truly hurt the bull with those blows? No man could be that strong! Then he sat back. Surely, the next encounter must see the Cimmerian slain, and then the death of Aelfrith.

Now Conan was eyeing the beast warily, and it was regarding him with equal caution. After the usual pawing it drew itself up and charged toward Conan once more.

And Conan turned and ran.

A loud groan went up from the spectators. The Cimmerian's great courage had cracked. He was just a mortal man after all. He ran until he was stopped by the wall, and there he whirled and spread his arms, pressing backward as if trying to burrow into the solid stone, eyes wide and staring, the picture of terror.

Atzel barked out a raucous laugh. "Ha! See the coward run like a whipped dog! It shall not be long now."

The silver-helmed chief turned and stared down his nose at Atzel. When he spoke there was limitless contempt in his voice. "Show me the man who has tried the King Bull even once, much less twice. My own courage would have snapped at the first charge. So what if this man's nerve has fled at the third pass? Speak not to me of courage and cowardice you foul *nithing*!" Atzel chewed his gall and kept his silence at receiving the greatest spoken insult in the northlands. One vengeance at a time. First he would see Aelfrith dead, then there would be time to settle accounts with his rivals.

Aelfrith was in despair when she saw Conan run, and as the horns neared him she shut her eyes tightly.

The bull was almost upon the Cimmerian. At the last possible instant, when the horns were almost upon him, he moved. He did not dodge, but instead rose onto his toes and spun just as the right horn was lancing for his belly. Instead of taking him squarely, the tip whistled past his narrow profile, missing his abdomen by less than an inch. The horn struck the stone wall and there was a crack like that made by a bow snapping from being overdrawn. When the bull staggered back from the wall, a full three inches of the horn was broken clean away.

Conan backed slowly toward the center of the arena, always facing the animal. The cheering was truly thunderous as the watchers understood his sham and the incredible calculated gamble he had taken. Aelfrith opened her eyes at the cheer, and great was her joy when she saw Conan alive and seemingly in control of the situation. She would have collapsed with relief if she could have moved at all.

The bull began to trot toward Conan, its legs a little shaky now, its movements no longer so swift and sure. In all its life it had never known defeat, nor even been resisted for very long. Its dim, savage brain could not comprehend how this little creature could cause it so much pain and difficulty.

This time Conan did not wait for a charge. With a light,

springy step he trotted toward the animal. There was a gasp of anticipation from the watchers. They were past all amazement. The bull, startled, just stood still as Conan reached out and grasped the horns. He placed a foot on the bull's forehead and leaped as the creature instinctively tossed its head. Conan curled himself into a tumbler's ball and did a triple somersault, landing on his feet and trotting toward Aelfrith.

"I still live," he said when he reached her.

"As do I," she said warmly. "Perhaps we shall both see sunset this day."

"Perhaps," he said. "But make no bets." Now he turned and strode toward the bull. It was time to try conclusions. The bull was weakening, but so was he. The next encounter would be the last. Then he stood and awaited the bull.

The beast seemed to understand as well. It stood breathing heavily, its sides heaving, trying to store up its remaining strength for one final effort. It snorted and pawed, then it charged. Down upon the tiny, seemingly frail man-figure it bore. Then they were together in the final embrace of death from which only one would escape alive.

As the right horn hooked in, Conan sidestepped again, but this time he did not lean away as far. A bull cannot see the tips of its horns. It only knows where they are by constantly gouging the ground, the trees, or other objects. As the King Bull hooked its right horn toward Conan, it automatically timed the move from the habit of years. But, three inches had been broken from the horn tip, and the hook that should have gutted Conan missed his belly by a hair. Swiftly, it hooked back with the left, but the tiny advantage which had allowed the Cimmerian to work closer to the horns had been the chance he needed. Seizing a horn in each hand, Conan took an iron grip and dug in with his feet.

There were moments of quiet over the amphitheater as the spectators realized that the incredible struggle was entering its final phase. The bull dug in its hooves and began to push, forcing Conan back toward the wall, heading for a spot just below where most of the chiefs sat. Conan's feet gouged a twin path in the turf as he resisted every inch of the animal's progress. The bull's breathing became labored and his tongue lolled from his mouth as he strove to drive the man against the wall and crush him like a fly. Two paces short of the wall, Conan stopped the bull.

They stood like a bronzen statue for long moments, Conan's arms spread wide toward the ends of the horns for leverage, muscles chiseled into rigid prominence, face empurpled with effort, sinews creaking audibly with the titanic strain. Sweat poured from him in pails as he put forth more strength than any mortal man could be expected to. Slowly, remorselessly, the bull's head began to turn. Conan's left arm raised one horn as the right forced the other down. Moving barely perceptible inches at a time, the great head came around as the neck twisted.

The wide horns were almost vertical now, and it seemed impossible that man or beast could stand an ounce more strain. The limit had been reached, and something had to give way. There was a faint crackling sound, and Conan released the horns, stepping back as the great beast collapsed, its neck broken. One great eye rolled in its socket for a moment, then it was darkened by death. The animal's last breath went from it in a long sigh, then it was inert upon the ground.

Conan stood trembling with exhaustion, not hearing the frantic cheers, his eyes upon the great bull he had slain. Then he looked up at the sound of an inarticulate scream. It was Atzel, pointing down at him and yammering curses so garbled that none could understand him.

Rage spread its red mantle across Conan's face. From some deep reservoir within him he found a last store of strength. With a tigerish leap he scrambled up the arena wall and onto the sloping turf of the spectator's area. His great hand shot out and grasped Atzel by the throat. The crazed old chief's eyes bulged with terror as he saw the death he had brought upon himself.

"Damn you to Hell for a torturer of women and children!" Conan bellowed. "Crom curse you for a *nithing*!" He grasped Atzel's belt and hoisted the big man, kicking and squalling, over his head. None sought to hinder him as he strode to the edge of the arena. "And demons gnaw your guts forever for making me kill this noble beast!" He accompanied the final malediction with a mighty heave, and Atzel sailed screaming through the air to land on the upthrust horn of the King Bull. With a sickening crunch the horn pierced his back and burst out through his breastbone. Atzel saw the foot of bloody horn that stood out from his chest and opened his mouth to scream, but produced only a great fountain of blood that soon stopped pulsing from his mouth.

Conan leaped back down into the arena, but this time his knees buckled and he fell heavily to the ground, his great strength drained at last. Shouting and cheering, others followed. They made a litter of shields and spears and rolled Conan onto it, then raised the litter to their shoulders. Aelfrith's men cut her bonds and lowered her gently to another litter while a chief wrapped her in a magnificent cloak.

"Bring them hither!" shouted the chief Conan had spoken to on the road. The two were brought to the edge of the arena wall and the chief looked down upon them in deep perplexity. "A thing has happened here today, and for the life of me I cannot decide whether it was a heroic feat out of the old legends or a terrible sacrilege. The King Bull is dead. A chief is dead. Blood has been shed in the sacred precincts. How shall we resolve this matter, my fellow chieftains?"

"What has Utric the Lawspeaker to say?" said the silver-helmed chief.

A gray-bearded elder rose and walked to the edge of the wall, where he looked down at the man and woman, the corpse of Atzel, the carcass of the great bull. He closed his eyes and stood in deep thought for several minutes while the assemblage maintained a respectful silence. At last his eyes opened.

"This is my judgment: Atzel was the evil behind these happenings. In his madness for vengeance he accused the innocent Aelfrith and went so far as to seize her person for purposes of revenge. To save himself from suspicion, he committed the hideous sacrilege of suborning the King Bull himself for his purposes. The gods have been angered at this, and decreed that because this King Bull was defiled he must die before his time. To that end they sent this mighty champion to slay him in the only lawful way: with his own strength, using no weapon. In this way he was the triple instrument of justice: He slew the defiled King Bull, he saved the unjustly persecuted Aelfrith, and he executed the vile Atzel. In recompense for his sacrilegious treatment and untimely death, the gods allowed the King Bull's own horn to be the ultimate instrument of Atzel's death.

"Let no man interfere with or offer violence to these just people. I have spoken."

Laughing and cheering wildly, Aelfrith's men bore their chieftainess and her champion out of the arena and back toward Cragsfell. Conan was only half-conscious, and those bearing his litter heard him mutter some words none of them could understand. He was speaking his native Cimmerian, and he was saying: "Damn you, Khitan, and your game-playing gods."

When Conan awoke upon his bed in Cragsfell he found himself unable to move. He felt, it seemed to him, very much like a man who has accidentally fallen into a mill and has now emerged after spending an hour or two between the great grinding stones. After an hour of wakefulness he was able to raise his head on neck muscles that screamed with agony. His body, as he had suspected, was near as black as a Kushite's, a single, solid bruise from chest to toes. He let his head fall back and thought of other great battles he had fought. None had been more desperate, more demanding of strength, intelligence, and courage than this conflict with the King Bull.

Later, a woman came in to feed him broth, and soon he was demanding stronger food. He asked after Aelfrith and the woman told him that the chieftainess was sleeping deeply, and might not wake that day.

"And the child?" Conan asked.

"Playing with her dolls as if nothing had happened," the woman said. "Praise Ymir, she is too young to understand what happened, and she slept through the butchery you and the lads accomplished in rescuing her. It has passed like a bad dream for her, to be forgotten in the morning. Besides, she has the blood of warriors in her veins."

The next day Conan was able to stand and walk about his bedroom, and then into the great hall to take his place at the tables. All were amazed to see him on his feet so soon. He paid a visit to Aelfrith's chamber, and found her barely able to sit up in bed and speak.

After four days of recuperation he was able to mount his horse and ride a mile or two, and he knew that very soon he would be hale. Increasingly, he cast his gaze northward. He had intended to be in Cimmeria by this time. By his calculation he was nearing the last day of departure upon which he might have some confidence of arriving at the slopes of Ben Morgh in time.

On the eve of the day he had chosen for his departure, Conan took to his bed early, after a meal at which he had eaten hugely and drunk uncharacteristically little. He was about to snuff the candle when he heard a scratching at the door of his chamber. Aelfrith entered, still moving a little stiffly. This night she wore a long gown of green silk, bought from some Zamoran trader. She crossed to the side of his bed and looked down upon him.

She did not waste words. "Do not go, Conan. Stay with me. I will make you a king. Be my husband and we will breed children such as the northlands have never seen, strong and beautiful. Since Rulf was slain, I have desired no man, but you I will serve all my days."

If he could not be kind, at least he could be brief. "No, Aelfrith. I must be away upon the rising of the sun. I have sworn my most solemn oath to complete my mission, and by now you know that I honor my given word. The days grow shorter already. I must be on my way on the morrow or violate my trust."

"Will you not return to me when your duty is done?" she asked despairingly.

"I cannot. From boyhood I have been a wanderer, and I must wander all my days until I fulfill my destiny. That destiny does not lie here; I can feel it in my bones. I shall know what my destiny is when I meet it. I am sorry, Aelfrith. I have never met a worthier woman than you, but our fates are not linked after this night."

She drew herself to her full height. "So be it. I am a chieftainess and you are a hero. I'll not beg and you'll not yield." She leaned forward and pinched out the flame of the candle. In the sudden darkness Conan heard the faint rustle of silk as the green robe whispered to the floor. Then she slid into the bed and their arms were around each other.

"I do not recover as swiftly as you, Conan," she breathed. "Be careful of my back." Then they spoke no more.

Six

The Land of Mist and Stone

Two men sat upon an outcropping of stone, keeping watch over a small herd of shaggy, longhorned cattle. One man was middle-aged, with grizzled beard and hair, the other young and beardless, but there was a strong family resemblance in their craggy, powerful features.

Their hair was black, hacked off crudely at shoulder length and square cut above their level brows. Their eyes were identical sapphire blue. Both men had rangy, muscular builds, and despite the biting wind they wore only brief tunics of rough homespun and short cloaks of wolfskin, with sheepskin wrappings on their feet, cross-gartered below the knee.

They held spears, and each had a dirk and a long, heavy sword sheathed at his belt. These were Cimmerians, and no Cimmerian went unarmed after earliest childhood. These weapons were severely plain, but finely made, for weapon-smithing was the only craft practiced with devotion in Cimmeria.

"There's a man coming up the mountain," said the younger man.

The older shaded his eyes and looked down the slope. He saw a tiny figure making its way slowly up the rugged slant of rocky land. "You've good eyes, lad. He'll be here before the sun's much lower."

"Enemy?" the young man asked. He drew his sword and tested its edge.

"What enemy comes alone onto Canach land? He's a Cimmerian, anyway. No lowlander walks with that stride in the mountains."

This meant nothing in itself. The mountain clans fought unceasingly among themselves. The new arrival was still so far away that eyes untrained by the vast distances of the mountains would never have seen him, much less been able to judge his stride.

"Who might it be?" the younger mused. "I know of no clansman who has been away in the lowlands. Not in that direction, at any rate."

"Not since you can remember, lad, but I think I know who that one is." Far below, the growing figure was leaping from one rocky outcrop to another rather than scrambling around them. "Yes, that's Conan, the blacksmith's son."

"Conan?" the boy said. He knew the name. The smith's unruly son had made a name for himself before seeking his fortune in the lowlands. "I'd thought him dead long ago."

"As did I," agreed the elder. "He was with us when we took Venarium. Only fifteen years old in those days, younger than you are now, but a proven warrior."

"Venarium," breathed the younger enviously.

The story of that great fight was sung around the fires throughout the mountains. The Aquilonians had pushed a settlement across the Bossonian Marches and on to land held by the mountain clans for a hundred generations. Settled by the Aquilonian's tame Gundermen and Bossonians, the frontier town of Venarium had reared its crude ramparts against the marauding raiders. But when the Cimmerians came, it was not as raiding clansmen, but as a whole race gone to war. Clan enmities were put aside for one screaming day and night of incredible ferocity, and the howling, black-haired horde had swept aside the disciplined courage of the lowlands like chaff before the arctic wind.

Prominent amid the struggling had been the young Conan. Envy grew bitter in the youth's heart. There had been no such notable battling in the few years since he had been old enough to go to war, and he could take little pleasure in the knowledge that Cimmerian cattle now grazed where the city of Venarium had stood. Besides, he had a deeper sorrow gnawing at his heart.

Conan saw the cattle on the mountainside above him, and soon he spotted the two men keeping watch over them—and over him as well, he knew. He had left his horse in the keeping of a homesteader three days before. This steep, rocky land was death to a plains-bred horse. Only mountain goat and stag and the tough little Cimmerian cattle could live on these slopes. And, of course, the Cimmerians themselves. Mist blew in wisps and skeins across the fells, for it was almost always misty and drizzly in the Cimmerian uplands. The abundance of rock, the thin soil, and the great amounts of rain fathered many springs; since setting foot in the mountains he had never been out of earshot of falling water. He had almost forgotten that.

Conan wondered who the men above might be. Kinsmen, most likely. He was on land held by his own clan, if his clan had not been utterly destroyed.

He had not yet found a village, but that was not unusual. The Cimmerians were semi-nomadic, wintering in a different mountain glen each year, returning to the same site perhaps only one year in ten. Many such deserted sites lay behind him, with roofless walls of piled dry stone. The villagers took their precious roof poles with them when they moved from place to place, for Cimmeria was a treeless land.

Conan drew his cloak closer about him. There was a

cutting wind blowing out of Hyperborea; and unless he was much mistaken, they were in for an early snow tonight. He had found kinsmen none too soon. Now, at least, he could see that these were indeed his kin. Even at a distance the craggy features of the Canach were unmistakable. In these inbred upland valleys, each clan had a distinctive physiognomy, and the square jaw of the Murrogh was as recognizable as the high forehead of the Tunog or the long nose of the Raeda.

"Greeting, Conan," the older man said when he was close enough.

"Greeting, Milach," Conan said. For all the excitement the two showed, they might have parted days before. "You've grown some silver in your hair since last we met. Who's the lad?"

"I'm Chulainn, your kinsman, and I'm a grown man." He said this not with the windy posturing of the city-bred adolescent, but as a simple statement of fact.

Conan acknowledged it with a curt nod. Henceforth, he would treat Chulainn as a warrior.

"My sister's son," Milach said. "And blooded in brushes with the Vanir and the Murrogh."

"That is good," Conan said. "A young man needs exercise for his weapons."

He did not ask how many kills Chulainn had, for such things were irrelevant. Cimmerians did not take heads or hands or any of the other ghastly trophies prized by other northern peoples. When a clansman was old enough to bear arms for the clan, it was assumed that he would do what had to be done, and if an exceptional feat of arms drew praise around the council fires, yet it was assumed that every blooded man was a competent warrior. Proven cowards were rare in the mountains, and they were not tolerated.

Now the faint drizzle was being replaced by huge flakes of

snow. Conan looked up at the lowering clouds. "First snow of the season. Is there shelter hereabout?"

"There's a good place a short way from here," Milach said. "Plenty of shelter from a storm. Chulainn, let's drive the kine down into the Broken Leg Glen."

Conan helped the men drive the twenty or so shaggy, surefooted little cattle the mile separating them from the small valley. When the beasts were driven into the skimpy pasture, the men retired to Milach's "shelter," which turned out to be a mere rock overhang, which shielded them slightly from the snow that was falling ever thicker. They made no attempt to build a fire, for fuel was too precious to waste on the mere comfort of herdsmen in winter pasture.

Conan drew his cloak more closely about him against the growing cold. The other two did no such thing, but they politely refrained from making any remark at this unwonted display of sensitivity.

"Does my father's brother, Cuipach, still live?" Conan asked.

"Dead in a Vanir ambush, these three years," Milach said.

"And my cousins Balyn and Turach?"

"Dead in the feud with the Nachta," Milach told him.

"The Nachta?" Conan said. "I thought we'd slain all their fighting men years agone."

"We did," Milach confirmed. "But the boys grew into more, and they're breeding another batch of them, last I heard."

Conan nodded. It was an old story in these mountains. In the fierce feuding many a clan had been pared down to a single male to carry the name. The Cimmerians married young and bred many children, though, and such a clan could be strong and numerous again in two or three generations.

"How did you find the southern lands?" Chulainn asked.

"I found them much to my taste," Conan said. "They

glitter with gold and the folk wear silk instead of sheepskin. The food is rich and spicy, and the wine is sweet. The women are soft and smell of perfume instead of peat smoke and cattle.''

"Men have no need of such things," snorted Milach. "Things like that soften a man."

"Best of all," Conan pressed on, "they fight all the time, and a man who's handy with his weapons can make something of himself."

"Fighting?" Milach said. "Is that what you call it? I'll wager they've taught you to fight from the back of a horse, as if a man's legs were not good enough, and to wear armor into a fight instead of your own good skin." His tone was one of unbounded contempt for such effete warmaking.

"That's the way of it in the South," Conan said. "What do you know of it? I've been on battlefields swept with the thunder of ten thousand horsemen, when the drums beat and the trumpets snarl and the banners blind you, so bright are they. These mountains see nothing of real war. I've been on a sea full of burning ships and smashing oars and hulls split in twain by bronzen rams. That is real fighting."

Milach snorted his contempt again. "Only fools and cowards need beasts to make themselves taller. And who would want to fight over a stretch of water? Once you've taken it, what do you have? Is not one bit of water much like another?"

"You've seen the sea?" Chulainn said. "I have always wanted to travel and see such marvels."

Conan was pleased to see Chulainn rouse from whatever melancholy held him, for he seemed to be gloomy even by Cimmerian standards.

"Aye, I've seen sea and desert and steaming jungle. I've been in cities so huge that all the clans of Cimmeria would not fill one of the smaller quarters. There are temples of marble reared so high you'd think they were built by gods instead of men." His eyes took on the faraway look of a man in a dream. "It is there that a man can test himself. There you are not bound by clan and custom. A wanderer without a coin in his purse but with a good sword and a strong arm and a brave heart can win for himself a kingdom."

"Do not listen to him, nephew," Milach said. "There's nothing for one of us down there. A man should stay by his kinsmen. Where is your kingdom, Conan? To my eye you have little more than when you left to go live with the Aesir years ago."

"I've won fortunes and lost them," Conan said. "And I'll win more. Perhaps one day I'll sit on a throne, if it suits me. Meantime, there's much of the world still left for me to see."

"Is the South not full of sorcery?" Chulainn asked. "I have heard there are magicians thick as a ram's fleece down there."

"Aye, there are a plagued lot of them," Conan admitted uncomfortably. "Never content to leave men to their own follies and always stirring up some mischief with gods and demons and such."

"You see?" Milach said.

"Still," Conan went on imperturbably, "I'll accept them as part of the price of a life that's worth living. I'd rather be dodging some wizard's spells than watching cattle and sheep, or breeding a pack of brats and huddling around peat fires for the rest of my life." Conan lay down on the stony ground and rolled into his cloak. After a moment he sat up and reached out a long arm to scoop up an armload of snow, which he packed into a large, hard ball. When its shape suited him he lay back, rested his head on the snowball, and was soon asleep.

Milach watched Conan gloomily. "You see?" he said to Chulainn in a voice of great sadness. "This is what living in foreign parts can do to a man. This was once a mighty warrior, but so soft has he grown that now he must have a pillow to sleep!"

*   *   *

The woman stepped from the doorway of her peat-roofed stone hut to see the three men coming down the hillside, driving the cattle before them. A layer of white coated the higher slopes, but the snow had not reached this lower glen. She was curious to know who the third man might be, for only two of her men had gone up days before to give the kine the last of their summer pasturing before being taken down to the winter's village.

"Wife," Milach said as they drew near, "we've brought a kinsman to visit."

"So I've seen," she said. "Good day, Conan. You've grown since I saw you last, but you still favor your father." She was a tall, gaunt woman, as gray and hard as the stone of her native mountains.

"Greeting, Dietra. Your gray hairs do you honor." This was a compliment in a land where the great bulk of the people died young.

"Come inside. There's food on the hearth." She pushed aside the hide curtain, and Conan followed her in.

The hut was full of peat smoke, and there was a pot steaming on the hearthstone. His mouth watered. So famished was he that his stomach was drawn into a tight knot. The eve before, he and his two kinsmen had shared a few lumps of hard cheese, and he had brought out the last shreds of dried meat from his pouch.

The clansmen found this no hardship. On the contrary, they found the dried meat a veritable feast. Conan, on the other hand, had become accustomed to gorging himself frequently. He had eyed the cattle hungrily, but slaughtering beeves before killing time was unthinkable, unless they be stolen from an enemy.

"Are you home for good now?" Dietra asked. "It's long past time you wed and increased the clan. Jacha Onehand has a pair of strong, unwed daughters not far from here."

"Nay, I only visit this time. I've much left to do, and I want no wife or child to slow me."

"Then I see the years have not improved you," she said.

She took some crockery bowls and began spooning food into them with a long-handled wooden ladle. She passed the steaming bowls to the men, who scooped the mush into their mouths with their fingers. Conan made a wry face. It was oat porridge, almost tasteless. He had forgotten about oat porridge.

Dietra caught the look. "Surely you did not expect wheaten bread? Wheat grows in the lowlands, oats in the mountains. In hard years we live on naught else."

"Do not be too hard on our kinsman," Milach said innocently. "He's grown accustomed to better things down in the soft lands."

Conan glowered at him. "You'd have gone there, too, years ago, had you the spirit."

Dietra cracked him across the back of the head with her ladle. "Have you forgotten the manners you were raised with, that you insult your kin beneath his own roof?"

Conan rubbed the back of his head and wiped off the spattered porridge. "Nay, I've not forgotten," he said ruefully, "but I am beginning to remember why I left."

"If you're not here to settle down," Dietra said, "then why did you come?"

"Is it not enough for a man to want to visit his home and his kin?" Conan demanded.

"No," she said. "Another man, perhaps, but not you. Something's drawn you back here, and I fear it's a thing that bodes no good for the clan."

Conan reflected that there was no gulling a Cimmerian woman of one's own blood. They could follow their men's thoughts with an accuracy a necromancer would envy.

"I have a mission," Conan said. "It need not involve the clan, but I'll want to talk to the headmen before I set out on the last stage of it."

"On the morrow," Milach said, "we take the roof poles and drive the kine down to the wintering place. Most of the clan should be there within a few days. What's the nature of this mission?"

"Time enough to tell when the chiefs meet," Conan said. "But it's on my own head, not that of any other."

Chulainn gave his clean-licked bowl to Dietra. "I'll go see to the kine," he said. He nodded to Conan and pushed through the hide curtain.

"What ails the lad?" Conan asked when Chulainn was outside and out of earshot. "Some sorrow gnaws at his heart, that's plain."

"There was a girl," Dietra began, "a girl of the Murrogh. They met at the midwinter fair down by the border when the clans were at truce. He wanted her to wife"—she shot a glare at Conan—"like any *good* clansman."

Conan affected to ignore this.

"He got a band of cousins together and they set out for Murrogh land to bring her back," she continued.

"A feud-wiving, eh?" Conan grinned. When two clans were at feud, it was an ancient and honorable tradition for young men to make forays into enemy land to get women. This way, a man gained both a wife and honor, and the clans were prevented from growing too inbred. "And what happened? Did her father and brothers thrash them and send them back home empty-handed?"

"That they did not," said Milach, taking up the tale. "They arrived at the girl's steading unseen, for Chulainn's been schooled well in the lowland forest; but when they reached the main house, they found it devastated. The walls were torn down, and the bodies of men lay all about, and some of the womenfolk as well, but the younger women and the children were gone."

"So," Conan grunted, "a Vanir raid. It's unfortunate, but doubtless he'll find another lass."

"Not Vanir!" Milach protested. "Nothing was taken but the girls and children. Good weapons were left where they fell. The Murrogh trade down on the border, so they have more silver than most. The lads saw silver coins and ornaments scattered about along with the other rubble. Vanir never would have left them."

"Worst of all were the bodies, though," muttered Dietra.

"What about them?" Conan asked.

"They were torn asunder," Milach said in a low voice, "as if by great beasts. The young men had seen bodies beast-rended before, by wolf and bear, but this was done by no clean creature. Its claws and teeth were not those of any animal we know . . ." His voice trailed off as if he were unwilling to say more.

"Tell him the worst," Dietra said grimly.

"Some of the bodies were partly eaten," Milach said.

"Eaten?" Conan said, still mystified. "Well, even so, if it were wild beasts, it is not unlikely that—"

"Not eaten as a wolf will eat a man," Milach insisted. "The flesh had been cooked over fires, and there were still half-gnawed limbs on wooden spits! What creature but man cooks his food?"

Involuntarily, Conan's hand went to the amulet that hung from his neck. "Cannibalism! Crom!" Such a thing was unheard of in these mountains. Not even the oldest legends spoke of such. "Was this the only such incident?"

"The only one we know of," Milach said. "By the time Chulainn got back it was mid-spring, and time to take the cattle to high pasture. We've been here since, and have seen nobody from below. Heard you nothing as you traveled hither?"

Conan shook his head. "Until I reached clan territory I avoided people, not knowing how the feuds were going. I saw men from time to time, but I did not seek them out. The man I left my horse with, down where our lands start, was a tight-lipped old fool. I doubt he'd have told me if the seat of my trews were aflame.''

"That must be old Chomma," Milach said. "He's addle-pated, all right, but trustworthy. Well, we'll hear more of this soon enough, when we get to the wintering place.''

Conan brooded upon what he had heard. Surely, this had nothing to do with his task here! Somehow he could gain little confidence in this thought. Much as he tried to avoid them, evil and sorcerous doings had a way of seeking him out. No wonder, he thought, the boy had a sad face.

Seven

In the Kingdom of the Great River

The barge plying the broad river bore a single tall mast, but its triangular sail hung slack from the long, slanting yard. As the wind had died, the barge was propelled by long sweeps driven by the brawny arms of slaves. So wide was the river at this point that its current was scarcely apparent, and it lay like a glittering silver shield beneath the relentless southern sun.

The banks of the river were lined with palms, and the fertile land along both sides was intensively farmed by peasants who toiled in the benevolent climate to bring in two or even three crops per year. The peaceful aspect of the scene, and the gleam of temples visible in the distance, belied the essentially primitive nature of this land, Stygia. The women who washed out laundry along the banks in the noonday sun would be well away from the riverside by dark, for then it became the haunt of the great crocodiles of the Styx, and huge hippopotami would come lurching ashore to ravage the crops the peasants had toiled so hard to plant and cultivate. The people had to accept this, even with the consequent loss of life, for these beasts were protected by the priest-kings of the land, as were the omnipresent vulture and cobra. In the

127

homeland of the serpent cult of Set, it was a capital offense for a peasant to kill any serpent, though it threatened his own child.

The woman who sat beneath the awning that protected the stern of the barge thought of none of these things, for they were so much a part of her life that anything else seemed barbarous and alien. In any case, her mind was on more important matters. The plans of years were coming to fruition, and she had much work to do before she could be assured of utter success. She knew well the unwisdom of impatience, though, and the only sign of restlessness she showed was a slight tapping of her fingertips against the arms of her chair.

The master of the barge walked astern and bowed before Hathor-Ka. He was a short, swarthy man dressed only in a brief white kilt and headcloth. "My lady, we shall reach your landing around the next bend of Father Styx."

She nodded and turned to the man who stood beside her. "Is all ready, Moulay?"

The desert man nodded to her. "All is packed below. Shall I raise your standard?"

"Yes. I want no delay when we reach the landing."

Moulay took a rolled cloth amidships and attached one end of it to a rope that hung from the mast. As he hoisted it up the mast, the cloth unrolled into a long black banner. Embroidered on the cloth with golden thread was Hathor-Ka's personal device: a scorpion whose tail was a serpent forming a circle around the desert arachnid. This would signal her servants ashore that their mistress was arriving on this barge.

Around the bend they caught sight of the great stone pier that thrust out into the river. As they approached, a small crowd gathered on the dock, awaiting the arrival of the barge. This was part of Hathor-Ka's huge estate, and all who gathered were her slaves, servants, the serfs who worked her land, and the priestly staff of her temple and shrines.

A long-armed black man cast a mooring line onto the dock. The rope was made fast to a bollard carved in the likeness of a crouching scarab beetle while the rowers skillfully worked the purple-sailed vessel alongside the gleaming marble pier. Slaves came aboard to transport Hathor-Ka's goods ashore just as a team of panting men arrived, bearing a pole-suspended litter. These men were not slaves but shaven-headed acolytes from the temple maintained by Hathor-Ka.

The priestess stepped ashore, mounted the litter, and seated herself on a throne of ivory and fragrant wood beneath its cloth-of-gold canopy. The lean but brawny acolytes hoisted the litter to their shoulders and set out for the temple palace, walking in a skillful, broken step that made for a smooth ride. Moulay stood behind the throne with his hand on his sword hilt, even though they were on Hathor-Ka's own land.

A man ran up and made his obeisance, then fell into step beside the litter. He wore the dress of a farm servant, but his plain white kilt was of the finest silk, and his headcloth was striped with gold thread. In his hand was the whip of an overseer.

"My lady," he reported, "since you left us we have brought in a fine harvest of wheat, along with the usual lentils and onions, and we have planted another crop. There were three thousand two hundred eighty-four slave deaths, and five thousand seventy-five live births, most of which will probably survive. Of other livestock, the cattle—"

"Excellent, Ptah-Menkaure," his mistress interrupted. "Submit a full accounting in writing this evening. I especially want to see the figures on the stone quarried for the new temples at Khemi. The priests there are eager to begin construction."

"It shall be done, mistress," the steward said, prostrating himself in the dust. Unlike many of her colleagues in the sorcerous hierarchy of Stygia, who were mainly virtual ascetics, Hathor-Ka was among the most powerful landowners of the nation. Her wealth was as vast as her wizardry was potent, and through one or the other she controlled much of the land of the great river.

The litter was carried along a slightly raised road paved with white limestone, which slanted from a far escarpment down to the river, cutting through fertile and well-cultivated fields where peasants were even now hard at work. At intervals the road was flanked by figures of greenish-black stone crouching on pedestals, figures that had characteristics both human and animal, and which bore a disturbing aspect. The workers here did not like to look at these sculptures directly, for if studied too closely, they often seemed to have moved when one gazed at them again.

In a land of soaring, if oppressive, temples, that of Hathor-Ka was of surprisingly modest dimensions. The god she served was not a deity who required grandeur. The temple palace itself was surrounded by smaller buildings, in which lived Hathor-Ka's servants, slaves, priests, and acolytes. She alone lived in the palace.

The acolytes bore the litter into the hypostyle hall of the temple portion, flanked by rows of columns with lotus-shaped capitals, dim in the overhead gloom. The thick walls had only narrow slots for windows, set high to prevent profane eyes from observing the rites performed therein. The purpose of these slot windows was mainly to disperse the smoke of the incense as well as the less agreeable smells that sometimes rose from the altar. Most illumination came from torches and lamps and from the great fire basket before the high altar.

The litter was lowered to the polished pave, and Hathor-Ka alit. She was greeted by a shaven-headed priest, distinguishable from the acolytes only by the cloak of leopard skin which cascaded from one shoulder, leaving the other bare. The priest knelt and touched his forehead to the floor, almost touching Hathor-Ka's sandals.

"O Lady-Who-Sits-by-the-Right-Hand-of-Father-Set," he intoned, "welcome to your home. We who are your servants wish you ten thousand years of life."

"Rise, SenMut," she said. "Even I do not hope for ten thousand years; but if our plans bear fruit, I may have nine hundred, and so shall my servants. Is all well?"

The priest arose. "Quite well, my lady." No longer speaking in ritual tones, the man had a soft and pleasant voice. "We have carried out the rituals you prescribed to the very letter, and we have kept close watch on your colleagues."

"There is only one who troubles me," she said. "What of Thoth-Amon?"

"Our spy in his household says that in recent weeks he has spent much time in the trance of the black lotus. It is clear that he is engaged in the preliminary stages of some mighty wizardry, but he shows no sign of knowledge of the missing Skelos fragment."

"Has he been in contact with Turan, or Vendhya, or Khitai?"

"He received a communication from the great Vendhyan mage, Jaganath, just days after you left," SenMut told her.

Hathor-Ka bristled at the name. "What was the nature of this communication?"

"Just an exchange of pleasantries," the priest assured her, "apparently in answer to some enquiry of Thoth-Amon's concerning the properties of a certain Vendhyan strain of the blue lotus. Jaganath promised to send samples at the plant's next blooming, along with seeds and a soil sample. The message appeared to have been months upon the road."

"I am much reassured," said the priestess. It was the kind of thing great sorcerors traded only when they were not discussing their greatest lore. "Reward our spy. And, SenMut—"

"Yes, mistress?"

She gave him a look that might have killed a cobra. "Better you had never been born than that I should find such a spy in my own household."

The priest folded his hands across his breast and bowed deeply. "You need have no fear, mistress. The security of your secrets is ever my dearest concern, as the safety of your blessed person is looked after by Moulay."

Hathor-Ka, trailed closely by Moulay, walked around the altar and through the square doorway into the living quarters beyond. A small group of slave girls greeted her and conducted their mistress to her bath. The hot water had been conveyed hither the instant Hathor-Ka's standard was seen from the landing, the event relayed to the palace by burnished bronze shields flashing in the Stygian sun, the same signal that had brought her litter to the shore.

Moulay followed even into the bathing room. The slave girls aided their mistress in undressing, and she stepped into the steaming water, fragrant with exotic oils.

Unlike many of Hathor-Ka's house servants, Moulay was not a eunuch. He watched the slave girls in their steam-dampened shifts with interest, but no lewd thoughts crossed his mind at the sight of his naked mistress, beautiful as she was. To Moulay she was an object of fear and adoration, in whose service and protection he would gladly lay down his life, but he could never look upon her as a man looking upon a woman. To any who might suggest to him that Hathor-Ka was a beautiful and desirable female, Moulay would have accorded an instant's incredulous wonder at such unprecedented insanity before slaughtering the man without mercy. To consider his mistress as an ordinary mortal was to Moulay little more than sacrilege.

"This business of Jaganath disturbs me, Moulay," Hathor-Ka said. "The communication with Thoth-Amon seems innocent enough, and I am satisfied that Thoth-Amon knows nothing of my plans. If such a one so nearby were planning anything, I should feel it. Jaganath, though, is subtle. It would be just like him to send prattling letters to his sorcerous colleagues to distract suspicion from his true activities. You are sure that there was a party of Vendhyans in Khorshemish while we were there?''

"Just two of them," Moulay said. "The fabric merchant I spoke to said he knew Vendhyans by sight, especially by the cloth they wore upon their bodies. There was a fat, middle-aged man, and a small, slender youth. There may be no connection. They might have been merchants."

"Trading what?" demanded Hathor-Ka. With a sponge and scented oil she was cleansing her body with the dispassionate deliberation of a man washing a chariot. "Did these men have goods to offer? Were they scenting out trade routes? Had they approached city officials with bribes to receive favorable treatment in the markets?"

"As you know, my lady," Moulay protested, "there was neither time nor opportunity to carry out an investigation of these itinerant Vendhyans."

"I know, Moulay," Hathor-Ka said. "And I may be exercising myself over nothing. However, with the stakes of this game so high, I cannot but be suspicious. Vendhyans are most rare so far west, and to find two of them in the same city where we are carrying out a crucial task smacks of more coincidence than I am prepared to swallow. I would not know Jaganath by appearance, as I have never seen him, although there are ways that those of us who practice the Art have of recognizing one another. It seems, though, that this Vendhyan 'merchant' was careful to keep out of sight, something unique among merchants, to my experience."

"But if it was your rival," Moulay said, "what was his purpose? He did nothing to interfere with our actions that I could detect."

"He might have been spying," Hathor-Ka posited. "He

might have been spying on me, tracking me to find out what I was doing. He might have been trying to hire the Cimmerian himself. If so, he was unsuccessful, for I would have known any such subversion from that unsubtle savage. I suppose it might have been coincidence. That is the most untrustworthy of propositions, but Khorshemish is one of the crossroads of the world, and two persons on similar missions may meet at such places. Whatever the reason, however, I do not like it. Of all my sorcerous rivals, after Thoth-Amon this man Jaganath is the most dangerous, and the one I would least like to see in possession of the Skelos fragment.''

"How could he have come across it?'' Moulay asked. These subtleties of the sorcerous arts repelled him, for he was a desert man of direct action, yet he would not criticize his lady's doings.

"These things do not go by the common rules of chance,'' Hathor-Ka said. She stepped from the bath, the steaming water cascading from her shapely body and her thick hair. As her maids began toweling her, she explained: "Many times, a document or artifact will seem to thrust itself under a mage's nose, as if by a will of its own. This means that there are higher powers involved, and that they seek to play us like pawns. If Jaganath has stumbled across the fragment, and Thoth-Amon has not, it is because those powers have wished it so.''

"But, my lady,'' Moulay said unhappily, "if these powers have taken a hand, how may you and your rivals and colleagues hope to prevail? Surely you will not wish to compete against the gods?''

"Fool!'' Hathor-Ka barked. Then, more gently: "No, you are just ignorant in these things. If I were content to acquiesce to the will of the gods, I would be a mere priestess. Instead, I have chosen to be a sorceress, to control events and even to compel the very gods to my will! If these gods or powers seek to play a deep game with me, then I shall seek to play better.''

Moulay was willing to obey his mistress no matter what happened, but the thought of crossing swords with the gods brought forth sweat on his usually undampened brow. ''And what of this northland god, this Crom, of which the barbarian spoke? Has Crom any power?''

''I have read somewhat of these northern deities,'' Hathor-Ka said as she donned the light robes held out by her chamber slaves. ''They are real gods, if minor ones, but nothing to compare with our Father Set.'' She made the Sign of the Serpent, which was echoed by the others in the room.

''Ymir of the Northlanders and Crom of the Cimmerians are little more than giants who have attained godhood through millennia of being the strongest beings in their cold northern wastelands. They have no sorcerous secrets, and they take little interest in the doings of men. They pay scant attention even to their worshippers. The true gods, the gods of the South, connive and plot ceaselessly to gain yet more power over the Earth. It is through manipulation of this power lust among the great gods that we sorcerers gain our power.''

Talk like this made Moulay uncomfortable. ''But,'' he said, ''if these northland gods are weak, why is this most important of events to take place upon Crom's mountain?''

Hathor-Ka was silent for a while. Then: ''I have wondered that myself. There are many more fitting locations here in the South. However, the gods no doubt have some reason for choosing this place. There must have been a good cause for that chapter of Skelos to be lost even from the few known volumes thought to be complete. It is as if the gods wish that only sorcerers of the first rank could find the writings, then make their way to the remote corner of the Earth, where they could try their skill at gaining ultimate power.''

"Then why not Thoth-Amon?" said Moulay, greatly daring. "He is held by all to be a wizard of the first rank."

To his relief, instead of growing wroth, Hathor-Ka merely wrinkled her brow in thought. "It may be that the powers have some other fate planned for Thoth-Amon."

Eight

The Gathering of the Clans

For the first time since he was a boy, Conan drove the cattle
down to the wintering place. Instead of a sword he bore a
wand in his hand to whip the recalcitrant kine down from the
high pastures, where the lowering clouds promised snow.
With his kin, Milach and Dietra and Chulainn, he carried his
portion of the roof poles on a brawny shoulder down to their
new quarters.

Strangely, these things he had chaffed under and hated as a
youth felt proper and even reassuring now, and he did not
even resent it when his elders from time to time treated him
like a child. This, too, was Cimmerian custom. If a fight
portended, then he and Milach and Chulainn would draw
their weapons and be fellow warriors together. Otherwise
Milach and Dietra might treat Conan and Chulainn like youths.
Conversely, Conan and Milach might behave like contempo-
raries while Chulainn became the inept child. And always,
within the household Dietra would treat all the menfolk as
infants, whereas on the battlefield she would be sent back to
the high glens while the men, from striplings to oldsters, plied
their weapons among the foemen.

They found themselves to be among the last clansmen who

137

had gathered to make up the winter village. This wintering's gather of the clan was as large as any Conan could remember, some three or four hundred clansmen all in one place. The Cimmerians were not a numerous folk as the southerners reckoned such things, but they made up in quality what they lacked in numbers. Every man was a fighting man, even the one-handed artisan who was quite willing to use that hand to wield a weapon. The women were tall and strong; their children were active and grew up young.

Despite the Nordheimer appelation of "blackhairs," not all Cimmerians had hair of that somber hue, though dark hair predominated. While most had eyes of gray or blue, brown eyes were not completely unknown. What distinguished the Cimmerians from their neighbor tribes was their strength, their sturdy physique, their language, and, above all, their relentless willingness to fight to the last drop of blood.

Conan and his kin drove their cattle into the common ground among the other livestock and closed the gate poles behind them. There they would graze all winter, if the snows were not too severe. In the spring they would be sorted out according to their brands. This had been Cimmerian custom from time out of mind.

When the cattle had been attended to, Conan and his kinsmen picked up the roof poles from where they had stacked them and found the hut shell Dietra had staked out. For the rest of the day they put up the poles, cut turf for the roof, and stacked peat and dried cow dung outside the door for fuel. Compared to the life Conan had grown accustomed to in the South, this was primitive beyond belief, but he could feel himself gaining strength from it. Milach was right; this was the proper life for a man, even if a steady diet of it would be too much for one with Conan's wanderlust.

As he set the last of the turves on the roof, Conan looked down and saw a group of men assembling before the door of the stone hut. Some of them he recognized. After unhurriedly packing the last turf into place, Conan slid to the ground. His weapons he had left piled with those of his kinsmen inside the hut, but for the first time in years, in the presence of fierce armed men, he did not feel threatened when unarmed. These were, after all, his kinsmen, even if they did not approve of him.

Conan brushed the dirt from his hands as he walked up to the tall, graying, bearded man who stood before the others. This man looked very much like Conan himself, except for his long, dark beard. His weapons were plain but of the very best quality. In dress he looked like an ordinary clansman, but something set this man apart.

"Greeting, Canach," Conan said. While he and all the others belonged to the Clan Canach, this man was *the* Canach, the *Canach of Canach,* chieftain of the clan.

"Greeting, Conan," said Canach. "It has been many winters since we have seen you. Your sept has almost died out. Have you returned to join us once more?"

"For a while, at any rate," Conan answered him. "I've a mission to accomplish here in these hills, and I must speak of it before the chiefs."

"That you shall," said Canach. "But you must wait your turn, for there is much to be spoken of when all are gathered. I rejoice to see you, Conan, though there have been hard words between us in the past. This winter we may need all of the clan's best fighting men."

"Is it to be a spear-wetting, then?" Conan asked. "It seems a strange season for it."

"Everything about this business is strange," Canach said. "You will hear about it at the gathering this evening." The chieftain and his sidemen turned and left.

Conan resumed his weapons and walked about the little village, renewing old acquaintances and inquiring after friends and kinsfolk. Without surprise he found that most of his old friends were dead. Mortality was always high in the mountains, and Conan's companions had been wild youths like himself, inviting an end to their careers ere they had fairly begun.

Fires were being built all about, for here in the lowland near the Pictish Wilderness, wood was relatively plentiful in this glen that had not been occupied for ten years. Not until late winter would they have to resort to peat for fuel. Around the fires, pots of beer brewed in the lowlands were passed around, and people sang the eerie, dirgelike songs born of this wild land.

As the sun set, its afterglow shone luridly upon the snow-capped crests of the higher elevations. Down in the valley, though, the usual autumn mist and drizzle prevailed, and it would be the passing of another moon before snow blanketed the lowlands. Hunting parties had brought in a few wild boar and stags from the nearby wood-clothed hills, and now the sharp odor of the roasting meat filled the air of the village. Among the men impromptu contests were in progress in leaping, foot-racing and stone-throwing. Unlike their Nord-heimer or Pictish neighbors, the Cimmerians did not contend among themselves in swordplay or even in stick-fighting, for fighting was a serious matter among them. Cimmerians drew their weapons against another man only with intent to kill.

Before the bonfire in the center of the village the chiefs and elders sat on the ground, gnawing on beef bones and passing beer jars among themselves. A place was made for Conan at this fire, and a joint of stag was thrust into his hand by a shock-headed girl of fifteen or so, whose fierce gray eyes took in his massive frame from scalp to toes with the unmistakable calculation of a woman sizing up a prospective husband. Word had gone out that Conan was back, and that he was yet unmarried. Cimmerian males in their prime were always in short supply.

Conan wrapped a chunk of smoking stag flesh in a flat oatcake and bit into it, chewing the tough but delicious meat and reliving a hundred other highland feastings, when he had fought with the other boys over the leavings of their elders. He washed the good food down with a long draught of Pictish barley beer.

A gray-haired elder sitting next to him said, "Greeting, kinsman. I knew your father and grandfather."

"And I remember you, Anga," Conan said.

The old man frowned slightly. "You've picked up an odd accent, living in foreign places."

"They say much the same of me in the South," said Conan with a shrug. "It seems I'm destined to speak no tongue to perfection!"

Unlike their Aesir and Vanir neighbors, who were boisterous to the point of insanity in their feastings, the Cimmerians remained solemn even on the most joyous occasions. The warriors did not stand up and boast, nor did they fight, no matter how freely the beer flowed.

As soon as his immediate appetite was satisfied, Conan found himself longing for a good brawl, but no blood flowed. "At an Aesir feasting," he told his neighbors, "there would be steel drawn by now, and the songs would shake the rafters, and the fighting men would be proclaiming the names of chiefs they had slain."

Unimpressed, Anga said, "It is good, then, that you have come back to a place where men know how to comport themselves."

"Yes," said a man with a long, sad face, who sat on Conan's other side, "who but a fool or a coward boasts of the men he has slain? What boots it that the dead foeman be a chief? Friend or foe, the measure of a fighter is in his arm and heart. I have engaged many a lowland swineherd who wounded me sorely, and I have seen chiefs fall to the sword of a youth on his first bloodletting." Others nodded and complimented the wisdom of these words.

"Still," Conan persisted, "in other lands they know the

value of merriment. There is song and the music of harp and flute. There are dancing girls and jugglers and beast trainers. Here, our songs sound as if we were mourning the dead."

The others looked at him as if he were speaking a foreign tongue.

"Never mind," he said disgustedly, "you would never understand."

Conan saw Chulainn walking about at the edge of the firelight, and he excused himself, taking a pot of beer from the circle. He walked to the young man and thrust the pot into his hand.

"Here, cousin," Conan said, "drink some of this. A man should not be long-faced on the first night in winter quarters."

Chulainn took a brief drink and handed the vessel back. "My thanks, cousin," he said shortly.

"Look, kinsman," Conan said, "I have heard somewhat about the lass. You are not the first to lose one. Gather your friends together, and we'll go get you another."

"I want only Bronwith," Chulainn said levelly. "We plighted our troth."

"Well," Conan grumbled uncomfortably, "from what I heard, your vow is canceled. Even Crom will not hold you to a pledge made to the dead."

"I do not know that she is dead," Chulainn insisted. "Her body was not among those at the steading."

"Are you certain?" Conan asked. "They say the bodies were in no condition—"

"She was not there!" Chulainn said vehemently. "I would have known!"

"Still, she is lost to you. You might as well give her up."

"Never," said the young man. "I swore to her by Crom that I would come for her, and neither her kinsmen nor the demons of the sky or the mountains can keep me from bringing her home."

Conan was about to comment on the unwisdom of lightly

making oaths in the name of Crom, but the memory of his own recent indiscretion stayed him. "How will you find her? Once they have been led to the coast in chains, captives never come back; you know that well."

"They were not led to the coast this time. This was no slave raid of the Vanir. It was some work of demons or madmen. The captives were herded northeast."

"Northeast?" Conan pondered, drinking deeply of the beer as he considered the geographical possibilities of his country. "Toward Asgard, then? Or Hyperborea?"

"No. There are many good low roads and passes to those lands, or to the Border Kingdom. We tracked them for days, and their way led always higher, into the loftiest crags, where only the white goats live."

"Up near Ben Morgh," Conan muttered, his scalp crawling.

"Yes. We were within sight of the peak of the sacred mount, just below the Field of the Dead, when a dense cloud descended. We could not see so much as a hand before our noses. It was no natural mountain mist, but a cloud black as a Van's heart, yet there was no smell of smoke. I would have gone on, by feel alone if need be, but my companions would have none of it. They bore me bodily back."

"Well," Conan said, "it may be that you and I shall soon have work to do together. Wait until I have spoken with the chiefs."

"Work?" said Chulainn. "What work?"

Before Conan could answer, an elder rose and, standing in the firelight, sounded a long, deep blast on an ancient horn. This was the great summoning horn, a cherished treasure of the Canach. It was carved in one piece from the long, curled horn of some great beast unknown to these mountains, and was wrought with curious figures and runes over its whole surface. Clan legend had it that the horn had belonged to the first Canach.

Conan and Chulainn moved closer to the fire, where the

clan chiefs sat. Canach was there, along with the heads of the largest septs and families, and the oldest and most prestigious warriors, although many of these were but simple householders whose fame and position in the clan were due to their skill and prowess rather than to clan position. Others were there as well, and these drew Conan's surprised attention. One, seated next to Canach, was a middle-aged man with hair braided in the long temple plaits of the Raeda. Another's face was painted battle-ready blue, as was the custom of the Tunog. Conan wondered what brought these chieftains to this gathering, for among the ever-feuding clans of Cimmeria, peaceful meeting ordinarily took place only at the midwinter fair or the fair held in early spring.

Canach rose to his feet and held both hands high. The great horn blasted twice and all fell silent.

"Clansmen of Canach!" the chieftain shouted. "All of us, not just Clan Canach, but all the clans of Cimmeria, face a grave new danger. Not since Venarium have we stood in such peril. We must stand together and fight together lest we perish one by one. It is decreed that all feuds must cease during this time of mutual danger. There must be no vengeance-slaying, no feud-wiving, and no cattle-raiding until the clan chieftains declare the peril past."

A babble of dismay swelled like a wind among the audience, for in the long, dull months of winter these were the principle diversions of the clansmen. The great horn blew once more for silence.

"You have all heard by now of the feud-wiving undertaken by young Chulainn and his cousins, my own son among them, and of what they found in Murrogh land. After my son told me of what they found, I traveled among the clans, bearing the white shield of peace, to learn whether there had been other such incidents." As he paused his listeners waited silent and enthralled. It had been many years since a chief had borne the white shield. "I learned of many

. . . at least a hundred steadings wiped out. These who sit beside me will tell you their stories." He turned to the man with the long temple plaits and spoke the accustomed formula: "Rorik of Clan Raeda, I bid you speak to my clansmen."

The man stood. "I am Rorik," he began, "brother of Raeda of Raeda, and I come bearing the white shield. In the ten moons past, six households of Clan Raeda were annihilated. Forty men and women were slain, and at least as many children borne away into the high mountains. Clan Raeda will not raise sword against other Cimmerians until this danger is gone from among us." With these simple words Rorik sat down.

"Twyl of Tunog," Canach said, "speak to my clansmen."

The blue-faced man stood and leaned upon the shaft of his spear. "I am Twyl, a senior war counselor of Tunog, and I come bearing the white shield. In this summer four homesteads of the Tunog were destroyed, with the loss of thirty slain or abducted. Across our border two households of the Lacheish were destroyed. We men of Tunog have painted our faces for war, and we will not wash it off until this danger is no more. Until that time we make peace with all the clans." The Tunog chief resumed his seat.

"From what Chulainn and my son and the others have said," Canach intoned, "this danger comes from the high mountains near Ben Morgh. It is not enough that these unclean creatures slay the living, but they also defile our dead, for only through the Field of the Dead can they enter or leave that area. It matters little what manner of creatures these are. They are our enemies. They walk on Cimmerian land, and they must die."

"Have any caught sight of these demons and lived?" asked a grizzle-bearded warrior.

"A boy of Raeda was herding sheep near one of the houses when it was struck," Rorik said. "He ran to see what the commotion was about. From a high cliff he saw the steading cloaked in a strange black mist, such as he had never before seen. He lay on his belly to watch until, in time, the black cloud moved away, to the northeast. He heard from within the cloud the wails of the young. Later he saw the ruined huts and corpses left behind. In that steading died Chamta, our greatest champion. His heart had been torn from his breast and devoured. On the sword of Chamta were found scales clotted thick with black blood. These were not metal scales, such as the Vanir wear for armor, but more like the scales of giant fish or serpents. As no one would touch such unclean things, they were burned where they lay.''

''Tomorrow,'' Canach went on, ''we shall send out the Bloody Spears to summon the fighting men of all the clans to the Standing Stone in the Field of the Chiefs.'' He pointed to the half-disk of the moon, perched on the shoulder of the mountain to the east. ''When the moon shines full once more, all the fighting men of the clans shall be assembled before the Standing Stone.''

''Not all!'' said Conan as he strode forward into the full light of the fire. ''I'll not be with you. I have other matters to attend to.''

There were expressions of dismay and disgust from the assembled men. Several of those nearest him drew back, as if avoiding defilement. Canach glared at him in mixed anger and disbelief. ''You were always a wild one, Conan, but you were never a coward ere now!''

''I am not afraid,'' Conan growled, ''but I have a previous commitment.'' In as few words as possible he described the mission he had undertaken for Hathor-Ka. ''So you see,'' he concluded, ''if I wait for a gathering of the clans and a march through the Field of the Dead, I will not reach the peak of Ben Morgh before the equinox. I go thither on the morrow.''

Canach spat. ''Would I had died before I saw the day when a kinsman of mine held loyalty to a foreign witch higher than the good of his clan.''

"My loyalty is to my word!" Conan bellowed. "I swore by Crom, and if any man seeks to make me false to my oath, he'll eat steel, though he were my own brother!" Conan clapped a hand to his hilt and a hundred men drew their weapons and the rasp of a hundred swords clearing their sheaths echoed through the glen.

"Hold!" Canach shouted. The clansmen froze where they stood. The chieftain continued to glare at Conan. "You are a mighty fool, Conan, and you always were; but a coward you are not. It takes a man of heart to challenge the whole armed strength of Clan Canach. Go on your cursed mission, which I doubt not is part and parcel of the woes that have befallen us. If you learn anything of use to us, make haste to join the clans on the march. And if you are captured"—he pointed a finger at Conan and spoke in a voice as grim as doom—"you shall die under torture without speaking of our gathering."

"I'll not talk," rumbled Conan. "When did this clan ever breed weaklings? And Canach, I charge you, when you send around the Bloody Spears, to send one to Wulfhere of the Aesir, if he still lives. Tell him to fetch his band to fight beside us. Say Conan summons him. It is a debt of long standing between us."

A warrior stood to speak. A great scar slanted from brow to chin, the knotted scar tissue almost closing one of his eyes. "When did we ever need help from the yellowhairs?" he demanded.

"Now," said Twyl of Tunog. "Now we need all the aid we can get, by Crom. With what we face, I would accept aid from the Vanir!"

A tall youth strode from the shadows into the firelight. "Conan does not go alone upon the morrow," Chulainn said. "I go with him."

"You had better have a good reason," Canach said. "If you seek the glory of being first to strike against our foe, you disgrace your house. Your place is with your kinsmen."

"I, too, swore an oath," said the youth with simple dignity. "I have waited too long to honor it. Conan's words have reminded me of my duty."

"Ah, well," Canach sighed, "go if you must. I cannot fault a man for standing by his word." His stern eyes pierced the gloom beyond the circle of firelight. "But these two only! All other men of fighting age shall go with me to the Standing Stone!"

Then, pointing to a young man far back from the fire, he ordered: "My son, take your younger brothers and a few cousins and seek the three families who have not yet arrived. See if these monsters have done away with them. The rest of you"—he stared fiercely about him—"prepare for a hard march and a harder fight!"

In the darkness of midnight Conan, Chulainn, and Milach walked silently to their hut at the far edge of the encampment. At the door they turned and looked back over the village, faintly illuminated by the dying fires before many of the dwellings. To them came a sound like the steady droning of a swarm of insects. It was a scraping, singing sound, and they knew that no insects made it. It was the grinding of whetstones upon the edges of sword and dagger, ax and spear. Fierce at their most peaceful, the Cimmerians prepared for war with a deliberation that was truly awesome.

"There will be blade-wetting in plenty for all," Milach said. He turned to Chulainn. "Are you sorry now that you missed Venarium, lad?"

"At least you fought a human enemy that time," Chulainn said. "I would sooner face ten thousand men than these nameless creatures on Ben Morgh."

"We know from Chamta's sword that they bleed when cut with steel," said Conan. "And if they cut and bleed, they'll die, by Crom! Now let's get some sleep. Before the sun is over the mountain, we'll be on our way to Ben Morgh."

Nine

In the Field of the Dead

Starkad slapped his arms for warmth, for even his great cloak of wolf and marten fur did not serve to keep out the highland chill. His breath streamed out upon the morning air as steam between the cheekplates of his polished iron helm, embossed with plates of silver. Cold it was on the mountain. When Starkad's freebooters had awakened that morning, every man's armor was gray with frost.

The chieftain stared up past his noseguard at the form seated on a bare rock high overhead. It was Jaganath, up to some devilment, Starkad did not doubt. Ordinarily, the Vendhyan was far more sensitive to the cold than any Nordheimer, but there he was, sitting cross-legged on ice in the teeth of the bitter wind, dressed only in a loincloth and turban. His obscenely fat body was exposed to weather as evil as any Starkad had ever known.

The younger Vendhyan, Gopal, wrapped in furs so thick he might have been a small bear, came sidling up to Starkad. "My uncle works powerful magic, northman," he said.

"He looks asleep," Starkad replied. "Why does he not chant and shout? He is making no sacrifices. I see no flames or smokes."

149

"Those things are for simple children," Gopal said. "The truly great feats of magic are performed here." He tapped a gloved forefinger against his fur-hatted temple. "Truly great mages, such as my uncle, can spend many months in a trance, communing with the gods and working mighty sorcery."

Starkad looked down at the little man and snorted, sending twin streams of vapor to either side of his noseguard. "At our great festivals we hang as many as a hundred prisoners in the sacred groves, and cut the thoats of others over the holy stones. That is what pleases Ymir, and brings us victory in war. That is the kind of magic I trust, none of this mumbling and meditating." The younger man just kept his superior smile.

Starkad's mind was not eased by his own words. How did the man stand the cold?

"This cold is unnatural," Starkad said, to change the subject. "Even this high in the mountains the air should not be so cold. It is not yet midautumn, and the cold is that of the depths of winter."

"There are great sorcerous matters afoot," said Gopal. "The gods are uneasy; the powers of heaven and Earth and the underworld struggle for supremacy. At such times the great wheel of eternity pauses in its turning, and accustomed things are no longer as they were."

Gopal waved his arm skyward. "Behold! In the heavens have appeared ten new stars this year. Comets have flared in the constellations of the Scorpion and the Dragon, only to disappear without warning. Strange creatures are seen in the sea, and winters of exceptional severity are followed by summers of great heat and dryness. Twice this year heavy rains have flooded Stygia, something not seen in generations. The very Earth has shaken with the battles of restless dragons in its depths."

Starkad shuddered. "Say no more. I regret that I ever

agreed to escort you and your mad uncle on this fool's mission.''

"Can it be," Gopal taunted, "that the mighty warriors of Vanaheim know fear after all?"

Starkad reached out to seize the little man, then thought better of it and let his heavy arms drop. "Every warrior fears black sorcery, you fool. There is no dishonor in that. To buy the favor of a god with sacrifice is one thing. This playing with powers beyond human ken is another. I like it not.''

"But you do like gold." Gopal smiled.

"Aye, I like gold very much. If you had not so much of it, I would not be here, but back in my hall like any sensible chief. It is a good thing for you that I fear your uncle's sorcery, else I should have long since slain the two of you and gained your treasure.''

Gopal laughed. "And well for you that you fear him so. Think you that such a mage has aught to fear from a petty pirate chieftain? The great Jaganath has sent great armies down to bloody ruin.''

"Then why does he need an escort?" asked Starkad triumphantly.

"Not because he has aught to fear from your savage Cimmerians," said Gopal haughtily. "But because he has great magic to perform when we reach our destination, and he does not wish to be distracted in the midst of his rites.''

Their discussion was interrupted by the arrival of a glowering group of Vanir, led by the huge warrior who had questioned this expedition in Starkad's hall. "Starkad, we must speak," he said.

Starkad turned his back on the apprentice sorcerer and leaned casually on his ax. "What must we speak of, Gurth?"

"The men and I have been talking together," Gurth rumbled. "This is no natural weather we have come upon. This is a false winter caused by demons. And it is bad luck to travel with sorcerers. So we have decided to kill these out-landers, take their gold, and go back to our hall.''

"So, *we* have decided, have we?" Starkad said with a murderous gleam in his eye. "And were these discussions so important that your chieftain could not be allowed to take part in them?" He glared at his men, but none save Gurth would meet his eye.

Without warning Gurth raised his ax, aimed to split Gopal's skull. As the Vendhyan stood in shock, mouth open and eyes wide, Starkad swung his own ax across and caught Gurth's descending weapon in the angle between the head and the haft of the chieftain's ax. In almost the same move the chieftain swung the butt of his weapon into the side of Gurth's helmet. Gurth sprawled on the ground in a rattle of scales, and Starkad raised his ax to split him on the ground, but the downed man rolled swiftly aside and the blade rang against the frozen earth.

Then Gurth was on his feet again and the two men circled, each with one hand near the butt of his weapon, the other near its head. The rest of the hirelings maintained a diplomatic silence, knowing that a cheer for the loser would be long remembered by the winner. They formed a wide circle around the struggling warriors, for ax fighters required much room.

With a howl of demented rage Gurth swung at Starkad as the chieftain was backed against a crag of rock; but Starkad leaped nimbly aside, and the ax head struck sparks from the stone. In that instant, while Gurth was off balance, Starkad's ax came around in a hard, vicious arc and bit into the scales that protected Gurth's spine. Gurth cast up his hands, his ax flying away. As Starkad wrenched his weapon free, Gurth toppled stiffly to lie facedown upon the cold ground. Starkad stepped forward and swung his ax a final time. Gurth's head rolled away from his body, the red beard severed just below the chin. Tufts of red whiskers were carried away on the chill breeze.

Starkad hefted his bloody weapon and spoke with deceptive casualness to the watchers. "If there are others who wish to dispute my leadership, I am warmed up now, and this is a good time to settle the matter." He looked around, but none of his men seemed inclined to challenge him. "Good. We shall resume our march into Cimmeria."

Jaganath, now dressed in his heavy furs, stepped around the corpse, fastidiously avoiding the widening pool of blood. "Have we been set upon by enemies while I meditated, Starkad?"

"Just a small dispute concerning our course of action," said the Vanir chief. "All is now settled. Are you ready to march?"

"I am," Jaganath assured him.

"Today we will cross into Cimmerian land," Starkad said. "From here on, the hand of every man we see will be turned against us. With luck we'll get close to Ben Morgh without being seen, for Cimmeria is thinly settled compared to Vanaheim. We may even reach our destination without trouble. But we shall not leave without a fight."

To his surprise, Jaganath laughed. It was a huge rumble that came from deep within his vast belly. "Just get us there, Starkad, and have no fears about our return." His nephew joined in his laughter, and the Vanir stood mystified, sure that both were mad.

Conan and Chulainn set out before first light. They took nothing with them save their weapons and heavy cloaks, flint and steel for making fire, and a bag of black bread, dried meat, and slabs of hard cheese. They did not bother with water bottles, since a traveler in the Cimmerian highlands was never more than a few paces from fresh water. They walked with the hillman's long stride that covered the miles more efficiently than a horse's uncertain hooves yet left them unfatigued at the end of a day's travel.

They had plotted the straightest possible line of march, and were able to use the best routes and all the daylight hours because of the truce with the other clans. Even so, it was a long and arduous journey, taking them ever higher into the fastness of the mountains.

Late in the afternoon of the fifth day they saw, silhouetted against the lowering sun along a mountain ridge, men marching in single file. Instinctively, Chulainn started to dive for cover. Then, remembering the truce, he sheepishly rejoined Conan.

"Old habits are hard to break." Conan grinned. "Those must be the Galla, by the look of their topknots."

"Perhaps we had better take cover anyway," Chulainn said. "They are a distant clan, and the Bloody Spear may not have reached them yet."

At that moment the men on the ridge caught sight of the travelers and waved their spears overhead as a sign of peaceful intentions. Had they meant harm, they would have howled a war cry and charged. "Let's go talk to them," Conan said. "They may have seen or heard something of use." The two men trotted to the ridge.

The Galla were considered wild and primitive even among Cimmerians. Their warriors were tattooed all over their bodies in intricate whorls and spirals, and the hair knotted high on their heads was ornamented with carved bone amulets and charms. They bore long, flat shields of wood, and, alone among the Cimmerian tribes, their favored weapon was a knotty-headed club, made from the stone-hard wood of a stunted tree native to their clan territory. A few bore iron-headed spears. Their only garments were brief kilts of wolfskin, and their tattooed feet were bare.

Without preamble the leader of the Galla said, "Why are you not going to the Standing Stone?"

"We have another mission," Conan said. "We go to Ben Morgh."

"What business have you on the sacred mountain?"

"Business of our own," Conan said gruffly. "How long have you been on the march?"

"A runner came to us with the Bloody Spear two nights gone. We have been on the path since first light yesterday."

"Most armies would take a week to cover the distance between here and Galla land," muttered Conan.

"Have these demon-things struck in Galla land?" Chulainn asked.

"Four families wiped out," answered the leader. "We are eager to see if they have brains to scatter." He shook his fearsome club, whipping the massive weapon about his head as easily as if it were a wand.

"We'll not keep you from the gathering of spears, then," Conan said.

Without a further word the Galla set off at a steady trot, which they could maintain all day. Late as it was, they would put many more miles behind them before darkness forced a halt.

"Those will be good men to have beside us when the battle comes," Conan said as he and his companion resumed their march.

"I am sorry to miss the gathering," Chulainn said wistfully. "Never have I seen a great army in one place. It would be something to tell my grandchildren."

"You'll see them, if we survive our mission," Conan assured him. "If not, then no sense worrying about armies and grandchildren."

That night they rested beneath a rock overhang while a light snow began to fall. Beneath the sheltering rock they found a few turves of peat left from some herdsman's store, and they quickly struck a fire with flint and steel. The cheering flames pressed against the dark. The two men stared brooding into the fire for a while, each occupied with his own dark thoughts.

"Conan," Chulainn asked at last, "what do you think we may be up against? What will we find on Ben Morgh?"

"How should I know? Monsters, demons, tribal spirits out of Kush, for all anybody has seen of them."

"But why do they take prisoners?" Chulainn persisted.

"For slaves, maybe," Conan said. "Or for food."

"Then why only women and children?"

"Perhaps they make better eating," Conan hazarded. "Grown Cimmerian men may be too tough for them."

Chulainn stared into the fire, a picture of despondency. He did not want to picture his Bronwith as a feast for some nameless horror from a madman's nightmare.

As they approached the Field of the Dead they could see a lurid glow in the sky above the hulking form of Ben Morgh. In the dimness they could just make out the stark outlines of cairns raised to Cimmerian chieftains and heroes in ages past. A light dusting of snow still lay on the ground, but the sides of the cairns were bare and dark.

"What is the cause of that glow?" Chulainn said. "Can it be fire? There is neither wood nor peat on Ben Morgh."

"You ask a great many questions," Conan said, "and you ask them of one with no more answers than you have yourself. Were I you, I would save my breath for more important things, such as fighting."

"And who might we be fighting?" Chulainn asked.

"To begin with, the lurking swine on the other side of this cairn." With this, Conan sprang up the mossy side of the pile of stones next to them. Chulainn, Cimmerian to the bone, spent not an instant in standing dumbfounded, but scrambled up the cairn behind his companion before Conan's sword was fully drawn. At the crest of the cairn they saw two crouching forms waiting with polearms ready to hew down unwary passersby. These scarce had time to look up as the two black-haired Cimmerians descended on them.

The shapes below seemed roughly human albeit misshapen; but the hiss loosed from the throat of the first came from no human larynx. Conan was swinging as he leaped down, and his sharp blade plowed through the skull of his chosen target before his feet touched earth.

Chulainn landed too far from his foe, and the creature lunged at him with a broad-bladed glaive on a short pole. Chulainn sidestepped the clumsy weapon and replied with a thrust of his spear, which barely penetrated the scaly hide over the monster's chest. With an enraged hiss the creature spun unexpectedly, and a long, thick tail lashed around, caught Chulainn in the side, and sent him tumbling against the cairn. The glaive came up for a deathblow, but Chulainn rolled aside and Conan's sword skewered the creature from back to front. With a vicious hiss the serpent-thing expired.

"Crom!" Conan said, wiping his blade. "It takes some real force to push a blade through these things. They grow their own armor."

Chulainn staggered painfully to his feet. "I am sorry, Conan," he wheezed. "I know we needed one for questioning. I thought I had that one, but my spear would not go in."

"We'd have had no answers from these beauties," Conan said. With his dirk he pricked forth the tongue of one. It was long, thick, and forked. "If these things have a language, it is one no man understands, I'll wager. Tongues like this could form no human words, save, perhaps, the secret speech of the serpent priests of Set."

"Set?" Chulainn said. "Is that a god?"

"Aye, and an evil one. Set may be behind these things, for all the sorcerers of Stygia are minions of that vile god." Chulainn could sense behind Conan's steady-spoken words a deeply ingrained horror of the supernatural.

"Surely this Set cannot challenge Father Crom on his own mountain," Chulainn said.

"Wager no coins on what gods and demons can or cannot do," Conan observed. "At least we know this lot die if you strike hard enough. Remember that trick with the tail, though. That kind of blow can take an honest fighting man by surprise. I'd like to get a better look at these things. But we dare not strike a light this close to Ben Morgh."

"I wonder if these were posted here," Chulainn said, "or if they were sent to intercept us."

"I would give a great deal to know that myself," Conan said. Did their enemy know that they were coming? The thought was unsettling.

Abruptly, Conan turned and began walking so fast in the direction of the mountain that Chulainn had trouble keeping up with him. "Now, about that light in the sky," he continued as if the incident with the two lizard-things had never transpired. "In the South I have seen a kind of black stone burned for fuel. It comes from the ground, where there is no wood or peat, but a thick and stinking smoke comes from it, and I see no smoke up there."

They had almost reached the upper end of the Field of the Dead when they saw a figure seated atop a small cairn, perhaps one of the oldest monuments in the ancient burial place. The trespasser sat motionless, a cold breeze fluttering what appeared to be tattered garments, but the travelers could see only its outline against the bloodred sky. Two swords hissed snakelike from sheaths as the Cimmerians strode to within ten paces of the cairn.

"Speak swiftly if you do not want your blood to feed some old chief of our race," Conan demanded.

The creature shifted on its seat and cackled. "Say, northerner, you like to buy another amulet? I sell, very cheap."

For several seconds Conan stood speechless, rooted in one spot. "Crom!" he said at last.

"No, just Cha the fortune-teller. Crom live higher up." The Khitan mountebank jerked a thumb over his shoulder in the direction of Ben Morgh.

"You know this oldster, Conan?" Chulainn asked. He had not been able to understand the exchange.

Cha turned his face to the younger Cimmerian. "Conan and I old friends," he said in mangled Cimmerian.

"Is it human?" Chulainn asked. "It talks worse than a Pict."

"He's human," Conan told him. "In his own way." He turned back to the Khitan. "Why did you pretend to be a mere seller of amulets and charms, Khitan?"

"What the matter?" demanded Cha in tones of hurt outrage. "You not like my amulet? Bet you not be here right now if not for my amulet!"

Conan thumbed the keen edge of his sword. "I do not like being played with, Khitan," he said in a low, dangerous voice. "That bitch Hathor-Ka played me for a fool, and now I find you have done the same."

"From the start I tell you you just playing-piece for the gods," Cha said. "You mad now because it true?"

"True or not," Conan growled, "I feel like killing somebody for it, and you're handy." He started to ascend the small cairn.

"Wait," the Khitan said hastily. "You need me, and I need you."

Conan paused. "Why do I need you?" he asked suspiciously.

"Because I very great magician, while you just fighter. Up there"—he pointed toward the glowing crest of Ben Morgh—"is great magic. Bad magic. You need more than swords to fight magic."

"From the look of this," Conan growled, "we'll need more than your piddling amulets."

"No fear," the Khitan said, smiling teeth showing in the dimness, "my magic plenty powerful. How you think I get here?"

"I was about to ask that." Conan looked puzzled. "Chulainn, I last saw this little beggar in Khorshemish, a city many weeks of travel to the south, yet here he is ahead of me. How did you do it, mountebank?"

"Easy," the Khitan said, descending from the cairn and adjusting his rags. "I flew on a dragon. Now, you want to go up the mountain?"

Mystified, the two Cimmerians trudged on uphill alongside the shabby Khitan sorcerer.

The Field of Chiefs lay silent and deserted in the first gray light of dawn. No clan farmed here, and none grazed its cattle and sheep amid the eerie, strangely carven stones of the field. So mossy were they grown that one could stand in their midst for a great while before noticing the geometric patterns wrought upon their surfaces, and even longer before realizing that the geometry thus represented was not the same as that taught by the wise men of Aquilonia. The Cimmerians knew nothing of geometry, canny or uncanny, and had never noticed that particular strangeness.

The stones lay scattered about the little plain—odd, humped forms, upon which the moss seemed to grow equally upon all sides, unlike ordinary moss. In the center of the field towered the Standing Stone. It was a stark shaft of black rock and no such stone was native to these mountains. Its surface was rough and pitted, but no moss grew upon its surface. According to immemorial legend, this stone had been a missile in a long-ago war between Crom and Ymir. Ymir, god of the Nordheimers, had challenged Crom for the suzerainty of the North. Ymir, who was lord of storms and king of the frost giants, had sent a terrible, freezing winter, and many thousands of Crom's subjects had died. When he thought that Crom was sufficiently weakened, Ymir and his giants had marched upon Cimmeria. Crom, unweakened, had torn the great stone from a mountaintop in Hyperborea, still glowing from the heat of the internal flames of that mountain. It had arced for many leagues through the air and landed in this spot, directly before the advancing army, so close that it singed Ymir's beard. The Nordheimer god, seeing that Crom was in no way weakened, had turned in his tracks and gone home. After that time Crom had made sure to imbue his people with the extraordinary endurance of extremes of cold and heat that so characterized the Cimmerians.

The boy thought of this legend as he climbed the Standing Stone, his fingers and toes finding easy purchase on the rough surface. Cimmerians are climbers from birth and this one swarmed up the side of the vertical stone as swiftly as a civilized youth would have climbed a stair, and he reached the top without the slightest trace of breathlessness. He was the first to arrive. He had awakened in the dark of night and had stolen from the camp in order to arrive here ahead of his kinsmen. Now he would be able to tell his grandchildren that he was first among the clansmen to reach the Standing Stone upon this hosting. If he survived the fighting.

The youth wore the blue face paint of Clan Tunog and little else. Despite the biting wind he did not trouble himself with a cloak and only a wolfskin loincloth eased the bite of a wide belt heavy with the weight of sword and dagger. He had left his spear leaning against the base of the stone. His long black hair streamed like a banner in the breeze as he stood in the alert half-crouch of the mountain-bred warrior. Had he known it, an artist of the civilized lands would have considered him to be the very picture of the savage, warlike north, but he neither knew nor cared about such things. He slitted his gaze against the wind and awaited the coming of the clans.

The boy's keen eyes caught the first movement just as the rising sun peered over the mountain crest to the east, flooding

the Field of Chiefs with a bloody light. From several directions he saw lone runners converging upon his point of
vantage. These were the best runners of each clan, bearing
their Bloody Spears ahead of the main body. Within minutes
the field was black with dark-haired warriors, for the
Cimmerians do not march stolidly to battle like civilized
armies, but instead run at the mile-eating trot of the high
valleys.

As they neared, each runner cast his spear at the great
stone in accordance with an ancient custom no longer understood but still practiced at such times. "Greeting, warriors!"
called the youth atop the stone.

A Raeda with plaited hair looked up and grinned. "I had
hoped to be first. You arose early this morning, I'll wager."

"You would win," the youth called. "Come on up and
see such a sight as few men ever behold in a lifetime!" The
young runners scaled the stone with the agility of monkeys
and soon crowded together on the treacherous footing as
casually as Aquilonian loungers in the great square of Tarantia.

"They come!" said one. "Raeda, Tunog, Canach, Lacheish,
Dal Claidh, all the clans in one place. Was there ever such a
sight?"

One pointed to the northeast, where a long file of men
were trotting through a narrow pass, their spearbearer at their
head. "Yonder come the wild Galla, by the look of their
topknots. I have never laid eyes upon a man of that clan.
They are said to be uncommonly fond of battle." This was
an awesome pronouncement coming from a Cimmerian.

"Ahh," exulted a youth whose temples were shaven in the
fashion of Clan Lacheish, "does not the light of morning
glitter most fairly upon the spearpoints of such a host?"

Now a grizzled chieftain reached the base of the stone and
he stood with fists on hips, staring up at the boys. "You've
gazed your fill, now come down from there. There's little

fighting to be found atop the Stone, and much work to be done down here.''

As the young men descended the stone several other chiefs joined the one who had hailed them. Among them was Canach. As the chief who had called for the hosting, he was leader of the clansmen, at least as far as any one man could lead the wild tribes of Cimmeria, even in time of peace. ''We gather quickly,'' he said with approval. ''We'll not have long to wait before we set forth. Even the Galla have arrived early on the first day.''

''The Galla travel faster than most,'' said Raeda. ''Others will be arriving throughout the day. Some of the lowland clans may not arrive until the morrow.''

''I hope that they do not take longer than the midday to arrive,'' Canach said. ''I feel that time is important now. We must set off before the sun is much past its zenith tomorrow, with or without all the clans.''

Throughout the day the men gathered. There was no making of speeches. All knew why they were there and they were ready to fight. No more need be said. They sat talking around small fires, some of them eating from their scant supply of marching rations. By nightfall the last of the clans had arrived. All the able fighting men of Cimmeria, save only Conan and Chulainn, were present for the hosting at the Standing Stone.

Canach was sitting at a fire with his fellow chiefs when a final group arrived, and these were not Cimmerians. ''Foreigners come,'' a man said quietly. Canach stared into the dimness outside the circle of firelight. He heard the faint click and jingle of arms, sounds that the Cimmerians did not make even when fully armed. Ordinarily, these sounds would have had him reaching for his weapons, but this time he was certain that those who approached were not foes.

Three men stepped within the firelight. ''I was told that I would find the chieftains here,'' said the tallest. Like the others, the speaker had long yellow hair and beard. Unlike the Cimmerians this man and his followers wore helmets adorned with horns short enough to be clear of a sword blow, and coats of iron or bronze scales. They also wore many ornaments of gold set with gems.

Canach and the others stood, but their hands did not stray near their weapons. "We are the chieftains of Cimmeria," said Tunog, oldest of the chiefs. His snowy hair and beard contrasted weirdly with his blue-painted face.

"You are the Aesir warband Conan spoke of?" asked Canach.

"We are," said the leader. "I am Wulfhere, son of Hjalmar, and a prince among the Garlingas when I am not an outlaw. Just now I am under outlawry for a manslaying. My men are outlaws as well. I left most of them at the edge of your camp."

"Sit," said Canach, gesturing graciously toward the bare ground. "We would offer you food and drink, but we came with but little by way of refreshment."

"We came better prepared," said Wulfhere. He reached back and one of his men handed him a bulging skin of wine. Wulfhere upended it and took a long pull, then offered it to the Cimmerians.

Canach shook his head, as did the other chiefs. "Thank you, but we'd not have our kinsmen see us drinking while they went dry."

They sat for a while in silence. Unlike their cousins the Vanir, the Aesir were not unceasingly hostile to the Cimmerians. Aesir and Cimmerian fought only most of the time. Indeed, there had been spans as lengthy as a year when the two peoples were at peace. Each looked upon the other with a certain disdain, but with a wary respect for the fighting prowess of the other. The Aesir were as tall as the Cimmerians on the average, but they often had a somewhat heavier build. Like all northern peoples they were strong and fierce, but unlike the Cimmerians they were fond of feasting, revelry, and drunkenness. They loved adorning themselves with bright ornaments, preferably stolen from someone else. The Cimmerians considered them to be shamelessly self-indulgent. There was an old Cimmerian proverb about these people: "The only good thing about the Aesir and the Vanir is that they kill so many of each other." Indeed, where enmity between Cimmerian and Vanir was ferocious, that between Aesir and Vanir was maniacal. This was in spite of the fact that the Aesir and Vanir worshipped the same gods, spoke the same tongue, and had almost identical customs. In fact, the only noticeable difference between the two was the color of their hair—Vanir red and Aesir yellow. But then, civilized men have fought over differences less significant.

"Have these demons plagued you as they have us?" asked the shaven-templed chief of Lacheish.

"They have," Wulfhere confirmed. "Three steadings that I know of wiped out, all of them in the border country up near your folk. At first some thought it was your raiding, but we soon saw that this was no work of Cimmerians. Until your runner came, though, we had no idea where to go to get our vengeance. Were you willing to wait, you could have the whole Aesir race here to aid you."

"We'd as soon not have the whole Aesir nation on our land," said Canach with a faint smile, "even in alliance."

"We'll have to make do, then," said Wulfhere. "Whatever our numbers, this threat must be eliminated and we must have vengeance."

All the others nodded. This was the language that all northerners understood.

Ten

On the Mountain of Crom

"Why do they take my people prisoner?" demanded Conan of the slight magician who walked through the snow beside him.

"He who do this preparing great sorcery, great spell, want maybe great sacrifice."

"Like the Vanir?" Chulainn asked. "They buy the favor of Ymir with sacrifices in their sacred groves."

"Maybe so," Cha said, "but I think much more. Not buy favor of god, but give evil spell much force. Earth, sky, stars, planets, all in strange order. Many spells, not used in thousand years, possible now."

"I understand nothing of this," Conan said, "but you say you, too, know nothing."

"Mortal man know nothing for sure," Cha agreed, "all is illusion. Duke Li say—"

"Enough of your eastern maunderings!" Conan barked. "From now on, if you have no plans to contribute, keep your thoughts to yourself. Warn us if some sorcerous danger lies ahead. We will take care of the rest without your aid."

"You not trust me?"

"I trust nobody who claims to fly on dragons," Conan said.

They continued to climb, forced to breathe deeply in the thinning air. As their path wound higher, Conan noticed that the snow disappeared from the ground, and the air seemed distinctly warmer. Soon he saw that his companions' breath no longer steamed from mouth and nostril.

"It's getting warmer," Conan said.

"Even a northern barbarian has powers of perception," Cha said, chuckling. "Am I not good teacher, to bring this out in you?"

"Will your amulets cure a split skull, Khitan?" Conan asked, grasping his hilt.

"You true barbarian, all right," Cha mumbled. "One answer for everything."

"One answer is all you need for most questions," Conan said.

"Do all Khitans talk as much as this one?" Chulainn asked.

"I think so," Conan replied. "People who live in cities have little to do but talk."

"At least we Khitans have somebody worth talking to," Cha said, "and things worth talking about. What you Cimmerians got to talk about? Cattle? Snow? We . . ."

Conan silenced him with a sharp wave and hiss. The three stood frozen and silent. There was nothing to see except the lurid glare in the sky, but faint sounds were drifting down from the mountain, hellish sounds of raucous chanting and screaming, underscored by a deep, rhythmic thunder of drums.

"It sounds like the lamentations of damned souls," Chulainn said.

"Maybe that what you are hearing," Cha told them.

"We'll never know unless we get closer," Conan said.

They advanced, but very cautiously now, keeping to the deepest shadow, and silent as shadows in their movement. Conan noted with approval that Cha moved with the same silent assurance as the Cimmerians and did not seem to be using magic to do it. The Khitan was perhaps as large as a twelve-year-old Cimmerian child, and he was in a foreign land and approaching an unknown, dreadful danger, but he did not seem to be afraid.

Chulainn came close to Conan and whispered, "I think that some civilized people are not as soft as I have heard." Conan just nodded.

Jaganath examined the corpse on the frozen ground. It was that of a very young man, features fixed in a snarl of rage and hate. He was beardless, with black hair and gray eyes that now stared at nothing. The right hand was still clenched around the grip of a long, straight sword, somewhat narrower than the weapon favored by the Vanir. In the other hand was a spear. Jaganath looked up to see the three wounded who stood talking to Starkad.

"This lone boy did so much damage?" the Vendhyan asked the chieftain.

"I told you they were doughty fighters," Starkad said. "And this one had a mission he thought was so important that he chose to fight his way through a hundred Vanir rather than run like any sensible man."

"What mission?" asked Jaganath.

In answer Starkad stooped and grasped the spear in the youth's left hand. He had to step on the wrist and twist strongly to wrench the weapon loose. He held it up for Jaganath's inspection. It was brown-black from the point to the socket of the spearhead.

"It is filthy," Jaganath said. "Do these Cimmerians not clean their weapons?"

"This is a Bloody Spear. It means a gathering of the clans. Runners go out to all the clans bearing these spears and those who receive them gather at a place called the Field of Chiefs."

"What kind of blood is it?" Jaganath asked with professional interest.

"If the cause of war is the killing of Cimmerians by foreigners, they use the blood of the victims. Otherwise, the clan that sends out the call assembles its warriors and they cut their arms to bloody the spears."

"Why are the clans being called together?" Jaganath said.

Starkad looked down at the corpse. "He does not seem inclined to tell us, but I doubt that our little incursion is sufficient cause. We are still far from the Field of the Dead, and they have no way of knowing that is our destination. For a sally by a hundred men, the blackhairs would send out the fighting men of one clan, no more. They must be facing some serious threat, perhaps another invasion from Aquilonia."

"If that is so," said a Van, steam coming from the midst of his red beard, "then they may be too busy to bother us." The others nodded eager assent.

"So I am hoping." Starkad smiled. "They are being called from a spot far from here."

"How do you know that?" Jaganath asked.

"The blood on that spear is three, perhaps four days old. You would not believe me if I told you how far one of these mountain goats can travel in three days."

"We have runners in the mountains of Vendhya too," Jaganath said. "So now this little escort duty does not look so onerous, eh?" The mage smiled tauntingly.

"We were never afraid," Starkad maintained. "But who wants a hard fight if none is needed?"

"I thought you Vanir enjoyed fighting," Gopal said.

"For honor, yes"—Starkad shrugged—"or for vengeance, or sport. But when it is for gold, we prefer the gold without the fight. Fame lives after a man is dead, and is worth bleeding and dying for. Gold is something passing. It may be worth risk, but only a fool dies for it."

"So, northern barbarians are philosophers," Jaganath said. "Truly the age of miracles is upon us."

*   *   *

Two Cimmerians and one Khitan lay upon a rocky outcrop, peering down into a vast pit from which came a hellish illumination. Only their heads as far as the eyes protruded over the lip of the stone. High on the east face of the mountain above them gaped the entrance to the huge cave called the House of Crom. Conan had seen the entrance once as a boy, when the clan had come to the Field of the Dead to bury the old Canach, slain at Venarium. The pit they now gazed into had not been there at that time.

The thunder of the drums was a constant cacophony now, and the screams and groans of those below formed a discordant harmony to the steady drumming. The pit was filled with mist and steam, from which sprang occasional tongues of unnatural, smokeless flame. Vague shapes could be made out within the fog, some human, others hunched and shambling and unfit to share the clean air of the mountains with true men.

"Whence come those flames?" Conan asked in a whisper.

"They are ignited vapors," the Khitan said, "which come from inside the earth, and are like the breath of dragons of Khitai. I know of a place where it comes to the surface by the sea, and the peasants use it to boil down sea water for salt."

"Nobody is making salt down there," Conan said.

"The sky lightens to the east," Chulainn said. "We had better find a place to hide before we are seen."

Conan looked up the face of Ben Morgh. The ice that crowned its summit reflected the earliest rays of the morning sun. He looked back down into the pit. "I want to get a better view of what goes on down there," he said.

"Your friend is right," Cha urged. "Best be away from here. Come back when dark again."

"A few more minutes," Conan said, his calm tone masking the inner horror he always felt in the presence of wizardry. "I want but a glimpse of it. How can we fight what we do not understand?"

Then they heard a new sound. It was a rumbling even deeper than the tone of the drums, and somehow they knew that its origin was in no artificial object, but was rather some huge, unthinkable creature in the mist below. For a moment, against a new flaring of the unnatural flames but still obscured by the mist, they could just discern the awesome shape of a moving creature so immense that the mind rejected it. Then, most horrible of all, the rumbling voice, so low-pitched as to hang on the threshold of human hearing, began to form alien but unmistakable words.

"Let us leave this place, Conan," urged Chulainn with a faint tremble in his voice.

"That sounds like a good—wait." Conan held up a hand to delay his two companions, who were about to beat a fast retreat. They paused, and their gazed followed his.

The monstrous form was sinking out of sight, and the flames were gradually lowering, as if the infernal fires were dying. The tormented screaming continued, but it seemed to recede, as if into a great distance. The shadowy forms no longer moved against the wall of mist. Last of all went the drumming, which became fainter for a while, then ended abruptly in mid-beat. For a while all below was silence. Then a thin breeze began to whip the lingering mist to tatters, revealing a huge open pit to the early morning light. There were no creatures in it, human or inhuman, living or dead. The craggy floor was carved into strange, uncanny shapes unpleasant to look upon, but there were no openings anywhere to indicate how or where the pit's late inhabitants had gone.

"Now let's get out of here," Conan said.

The three slid backward on their bellies until they were well away from the pit, in the bottom of a narrow, rocky gully identical to a thousand others radiating from Ben Morgh. They descended until they found a tiny, cramped cave just big enough for the three of them, and there they huddled as the first rays of the rising sun streamed into the mountain valleys.

They plucked some scrubby shrubs and brushed away tracks that might lead searchers to their hiding place. Then they piled the brush against the entrance.

"Tell us, great magician," Conan said, "what did we just see?"

Momentarily, the Khitan sat with eyes closed, mumbling to himself. At last he came out of his self-induced trance. "I think it is a thing from the most ancient legends. It is from before the Book of Skelos, before Python of Acheron." The ancient shook his head. "Nay, those things are recent compared to what we saw in the pit this night."

"Then you saw more than I did," Conan said dryly, "for I saw nothing but fog and flame, though I'll own I heard some hellish sounds I'd not care to hear again."

"You have not eyes of a magician. I see more than you, I hear more; I understand more." The Khitan had lost his half-intelligible chatter and spoke with clarity. "This thing is an evil so ancient that it existed before storied Atlantis rose from the sea only to be swallowed again. This Earth is ancient beyond the dreams of philosophers, yet the thing in the pit is more ancient still. Many times have the wizards of mankind driven it away to the gulfs outside the time and space that spawned it, yet always has it found a way to return, called back by the overweening ambition of foolish mages who dreamt of absolute power."

"Where did it go when the sun rose?" Conan asked.

"Below. The thing has bent the creatures of the underworld to its bidding, and they have hewn it tunnels to reach the surface, as they carved that pit. They can close these tunnels so cunningly that no ordinary man may find them."

"How long until the equinox?" Conan asked.

"Six days," the Khitan answered.

"How may I get into the tunnels?" Chulainn asked. "I must find Bronwith if she lives."

The Khitan looked from one man to the other, his slit eyes wide with amazement. "You mean you both will go through with your plans, knowing what you know now?" He eyed the two stony faces and broke into his maddening cackle. "If I know you barbarians so interesting, I come here long time ago!"

Eleven

In the House of the Sorcerer

For a day and a night Hathor-Ka had been performing the longest and most delicate ritual she had ever attempted. The Demon Star was in the eye of the constellation called the Serpent for the first time since the fall of Python more than one thousand years before. That last juxtaposition had coincided with the destruction of the terrible empire of Acheron by the barbaric Hybori. Hathor-Ka intended to use this opportunity to bring about an equally devastating change in the order of the world.

Only the closest of her acolytes assisted her in this rite. The less experienced would have been killed or driven insane by the sorcerous forces unleashed within the temple. Even the faithful Moulay had to stand guard outside the gate.

The walls and floor were covered with hieroglyphs, and the air was thick with incense as Hathor-Ka chanted shrilly in a tongue never intended to be spoken by human voice. Red streams dripped thickly from the altar onto the marble floor and Hathor-Ka's hands, bare arms, and heavy robe were likewise stained red. Behind her the acolytes chanted and played curious instruments that made rhythmic sounds that were not quite music.

175

Above the altar a wavering cloud formed a shimmering, shifting veil that for brief moments clarified to reveal sickening gulfs of space that the mind could not encompass while retaining sanity. Gradually, a hideous shape came into view. Against the void its size was impossible to calculate, but the inescapable impression was of overpowering immensity. Its colors were not such as the eye felt easy in gazing upon, and its unstable shape bespoke an origin far removed from the narrow band of time and space known to man.

As the thing neared the window to another world which Hathor-Ka had created, the sorceress chanted with renewed intensity. Her face was impassive, but sweat poured from beneath her diadem to stream down her face and soak her robe. The acolytes, now terrified, did not pause in their duties.

The being called forth by Hathor-Ka's spell extruded a limb like a tentacle and reached through the veil. Instantly, the temple was filled with a stench so vile that all the energy the acolytes possessed was required to keep them at their tasks.

At strange places along the tentacle were jointed claws and sucking mouths with circular rows of teeth. Though the limb was studded with jewellike eyes, they seemed blind in earthly light. It groped blindly, stopping as if at an invisible barrier when it encountered the rows of hieroglyphs that surrounded the altar. At last the tentacle touched one of the streams of blood that flowed from the altar and followed it to the stone. More of the limbs came into the room. Horrible, obscene sounds arose as the blood and fragments of the sacrificial victims were consumed.

Hathor-Ka's chant changed tone, and the tentacles withdrew, leaving no trace that there had ever been a sacrifice. Deep, rhythmic sounds came from beyond the veil, as if those in the temple were hearing a distant echo, swelling into an unearthly counterpoint to the chant of the sorceress and the acolytes. Slowly, the shape withdrew into the unthinkable gulfs that had spawned it. The window shrank and dispersed.

Hathor-Ka let her arms fall and she almost collapsed, but the strong arm of SenMut saved her from falling. "You must rest, mistress," he said. "Even the strongest of mages would be exhausted by the pace you have kept."

"I shall, SenMut," she said, wearied beyond all previous experience. "Purify the temple and store the tomes and devices securely. Double the guard. There is great danger of detection now."

"It shall be done, mistress."

Hathor-Ka retired to her chambers to bathe and rest.

She awoke from a deep and dreamless sleep to find Moulay standing by her bed, gently shaking her shoulder. "Awake, mistress. Your house has been broken into and despoiled."

"What?" She flung back the silk coverlet and arose. Her bed stood on a dais carved in the likeness of a coiled serpent, and she descended the tiers of its immense body to a small table. "Explain instantly." From the table she took a pitcher that contained a potion of herbs steeped in water. It was specially mixed to help her wake quickly.

"The crypt below your temple, where you keep your sorcerous screeds and instruments, has been entered. One of my men passed by the temple entrance on his rounds and smelled something amiss. It was blood. He ran to fetch me since he is forbidden to enter the temple. I went inside and saw corpses in the crypt. Even I dared not enter that room, so I came straightaway to wake you." His mistress was already striding from the chamber.

Hathor-Ka descended the steps to the crypt behind an acolyte who held high a lantern. Behind her came Moulay, with drawn sword. "Where is SenMut?" she asked.

"He was in the crypt, mistress," said the acolyte, whose hand made the lantern tremble slightly. "He and three others had the second watch this night. He seemed most eager to guard your possessions well.''

"How so?" she asked, frowning.

"He bore with him a sword, something he had never done before."

With trepidation the acolyte stepped within the crypt. The lantern luridly illumined the ghastly scene inside. From the top of the steps, they had been able to glimpse only inert arms and legs. Now they saw three corpses, their blood carpeting the floor. One pale hand still pointed at an obscene statue set in a niche in the wall.

Moulay turned two of the bodies over with a foot. "Stabbed in the throat," he reported. "Done quickly. They were taken completely unawares. He must have had the blade in the third one's throat before the first struck the floor." None of the bodies was SenMut. "But how did he get past my guards?"

Hathor-Ka stepped past the dead, pointing hand to the niche. She turned to the acolyte. "Leave the lantern and go. Say nothing to the others before I return." When the acolyte was gone she twisted certain of the perverted excrescences upon the statue in the niche. A section of the wall swung away to reveal a dark tunnel. "This is where he went," she said. "This crypt was the tomb of a high priest before my family built the temple and villa atop it. The tunnel was made by tomb robbers in ages past. It emerges in the fields not far from the river, beneath a small shrine. One of my ancestors hid both entrances as a convenient escape route in times of danger."

"How knew SenMut of this?"

"Never has the secret been outside my family," she said. "It must have been Thoth-Amon. Through his arts he has discovered this passage and suborned one of my acolytes." She was pale and shaking with fury. Moulay had never seen his mistress so overwrought. "How long? For how long has Thoth-Amon had free access to my house?"

"Why did he not come himself?" Moulay asked.

"I have set sentries which he and his creatures cannot pass. But none of them would prevent an acolyte of mine from leaving with stolen goods."

"What was taken?"

"Need you ask? The Skelos fragment, of course. He may have taken other things, but that is the important one. I must get it back."

"If Thoth-Amon has it in his possession, will it do any good to have it back?"

"Yes. The fragment is not like a schoolboy's lesson, to be memorized and used at will. The physical possession of such things adds great force to the sorcerer's spells. That is why the great books of magic are so valuable, while later copies with the same text are far less so." She made further adjustments to the statue, and the passage closed again. "On the morrow I shall have workmen fill the tunnel with stone. Now get some of your best men together, desert men adept at night raiding. We shall pay my colleague Thoth-Amon a visit tomorrow night."

For the rest of the night and through the next morning, Hathor-Ka rested. Then she began making preparations. With draughts and spells she fortified herself, gaining strength, speed, and endurance for the night's work. She would pay dearly for this in the days to come, but the stakes were such in this game that considerations of mere pain and exhaustion were trivial. She assembled arcane devices of crystal and bone, and studied occult spells, the mere reading of which chilled the air. As the sun lowered she entered her courtyard, where Moulay and his men were assembled.

Moulay had chosen a dozen warriors, all of his own tribe and fanatically loyal to Hathor-Ka. Each was muffled to the eyes in the cowl and veil of their tribe, and dressed in close-fitting trousers and tunic covered by a flowing robe. Their garments were dyed gray and tan to blend well with the desert. They bore swords, daggers, and short bows. Each man wore beneath his tunic a jerkin of fine mail sewn down to a silken vest so as to make no sound. Their black eyes gleamed with eagerness, for they were raiders by temperament and found their sentry duties here tedious.

"All is ready, my lady," Moulay said. Grooms led in their horses, bridled with rope and shod with rawhide for the sake of quiet. She signaled and they mounted.

"We climb the eastern escarpment to the high desert," Hathor-Ka announced. "By the time the moon stands high above the river we shall arrive at the sphinx of King Rahotep. We leave the horses there and proceed afoot. When we reach the house of Thoth-Amon you are to remember two things above all: No one is to offer violence to Thoth-Amon, and I want the traitor SenMut alive."

They sped from the gate and climbed the road toward the great escarpment that separated the fertile valley of the Styx from the high desert. Peasants trudged toward their hovels with tools shouldered, and they looked up curiously to see the horsemen pass. Horses were little used in Stygia, where most travel was by foot or by river. Only caravaneers rode camels, and few but the desert raiders rode horses.

The road that slanted up the escarpment has been carved from the solid rock in ages past as a means of moving troops quickly from the river landings to the border forts where they might be needed. Stygia had faced no enemies from that direction in many centuries, but it was still Hathor-Ka's duty, as owner of the adjacent land, to keep the road in good order against future need.

The desert atop the escarpment was all but uninhabited, yet it was dotted here and there with the ruins of ancient forts, temples erected to forgotten gods, the hovels of long-dead hermits and desert mystics, and the enigmatic statues and monuments that stand in every corner of Stygia. Despite the concentration of the vast bulk of the population in the narrow, fertile strip bordering the great river, the priest-kings felt it necessary to make their mark wherever they claimed sway over the land.

Moulay rode in the lead, unerringly finding their path through the desert night, while Hathor-Ka scanned the moon-lit sky for sign of flying minions of her sorcerous rival. Should she catch sight of a batwinged form, she had spells ready to render it invisible to the watcher, or to bring it crashing to the desert. The drugs she had brewed and con-sumed caused her vision to reach farther than mortal eyes should see, and everything she perceived was bathed in shimmering silver light.

The sphinx of King Rahotep reared its immense bulk against the starry sky, and they reined their horses in the shadow between its great paws. No man now could say for what purpose it had been erected, or, rather, carved, for it had been hewn from a single outcropping of sandstone. So ancient was it that little now was known of Rahotep except for his name and a reputation for abominable practices. Above the lion's body, with its dragon's wings, the face of the wizard-king glared into the desert as it had for uncounted centuries.

"I saw no watchers as we rode," Hathor-Ka said.

"There were none on the desert," Moulay told her. She removed her robe and stowed it in a saddlebag. Beneath it she wore garments similar to those of the men, save hers were made of fine black silk. She wore no mail and bore no weapons, but slung from her shoulder was a bag containing items of great potency.

Before setting out on the last leg of their journey, Moulay sent out two men to screen their flanks and another to travel a hundred paces ahead. Then they set off, not at a walk but at a loping run. As they ran, the men chewed on the petals and leaves of the blue lotus for strength and stamina. Mile after mile they covered, until they came to the crest of a ridge that overlooked a small oasis fringed with palms. Near the dark pond stood a featureless house surrounded by a high wall.

"Guards?" Hathor-Ka whispered.

"I see three atop the wall," Moulay said.

One of the desert men came to them and stretched forth an arm, pointing to a movement just north of the house. "Roving patrol," he reported. "They come this way."

"We can deal with them," Moulay told Hathor-Ka. "And we can gain the top of the wall undetected. Know you the way into the house?"

"I have had a spy there for many years," she said, "but now I do not know whether she has been sending me true information."

"Give us our orders, mistress, and we shall do your bidding," Moulay said.

"First, remove that patrol. Then, get me atop that wall. A glance should tell me whether my intelligence is correct. I shall have further orders for you at that time."

Creeping along the ground, keeping to the shadows painted on the desert by moonlight, rock, and bush, Moulay and several of his men reached unseen a spot beside the track that Thoth-Amon's guards were treading. There was a faint clicking of harness as the guards drew nearer, and Moulay's men readied themselves, some drawing daggers, others holding bowstrings between their hands.

The approaching footsteps slowed and then stopped. The lead guardsman, wearing a helm never meant to encase a human head, turned this way and that, as if sensing something. It emitted a loud hiss but no more as a bowstring whipped around its neck and was drawn taut. At the same instant the other guards were suffering the same fate as a desert man garrotted each from behind while another man in front gutted it with a curved dagger. Sounds of struggle were brief and faint.

Hathor-Ka came close to examine the corpses as her men

cleaned their weapons. "Lizardmen from the isles east of ancient Lemuria," she said. "Thoth-Amon cast his net of conjury wide to find these."

With the same uncanny silence and swiftness, the raiding party approached the wall guarding the house. The guards atop the wall were oblivious of the recent slaughter and spoke to one another in the unmistakable voices of men. At the base of the wall one of the desert dwellers knelt on all fours and another stood atop him, back to the wall and cupped hands held before. A third sprang lightly up and his foot was caught by the second man, who boosted him to the top of the wall. In this fashion six men gained the walk inside the wall unseen and unheard. Within the space of a few heartbeats one of the men was waving to those below and the rest ascended the wall. The sentries lay dead at their posts.

Hathor-Ka surveyed the courtyard with slitted eyes. There were no more guards in evidence, but that did not mean that the house was without protection. With her enhanced vision she could see a circle of strange runes investing the house in a narrow band on the ground.

"All of you follow me closely," she ordered.

They descended to the ground and followed Hathor-Ka until they stood in a small group next to the magical barrier.

"We must not interrupt the magical circle," Hathor-Ka said.

Moulay nodded, although he could see nothing on the ground to which his mistress pointed.

She arranged the men in a tight huddle and took a short wand from her pouch. Starting at a point to one side of the band of men, she began to draw a loop of similar runes encircling them, rejoining the great circle on the other side. As she drew she saw the runes glow with a weird greenish light, though the others saw nothing. When the second circle was complete she erased the runes before them and led her men across the barrier. Behind them, the circle, now with a peculiar loop, continued to glow in a fashion only Hathor-Ka could see.

The great door stood open. Thoth-Amon apparently believed his human, unhuman, and sorcerous defenses to be more than adequate. The band entered the house, which was silent except for the sound of a small fountain that tinkled in the vestibule. No candle or lamp relieved the darkness, and Hathor-Ka muttered a spell. She could see, but her men needed light if they were to be of any use. A point of light appeared by her head and grew into a softly glowing sphere that drifted to the ceiling, revealing bizarre frescos of strange worlds and beings.

A single door opened from the vestibule, revealing only a rectangle of blackness. Hathor-Ka walked past the fountain and entered the room. The ball of sorcerous light followed, as did the men. She signaled for the others to halt. At the far end of the chamber, seated on a throne atop a low dais, was Thoth-Amon. The great mage wore an enveloping black robe, and all that was visible of him was his ascetic, shaven head and his hands.

"Is this what you seek, Hathor-Ka?" he asked, holding up a large ragged-edged piece of parchment.

"You know that well. Give it back to me, and all shall be as though naught has passed between us."

"Let us not bandy foolish words, Hathor-Ka. Would I have subverted your acolyte and revealed my knowledge of your hidden tunnel if I had intended to return what I took from you?"

"No. And you would not now be speaking if you had not some offer to make. Name your price."

"It is true," the wizard said, "that you entered so easily because I willed it so. What I have for you is not a price, but an offer of alliance."

"Alliance?" she said suspiciously. "Why should I wish to ally myself with you?"

"Because you have no chance of making yourself supreme mage otherwise." He held up the parchment once more. "This is useless to you without the full text of the Great Summoning of Powers."

"I command that spell!" Hathor-Ka insisted.

"You do not. Only two mages in all the world have the full knowledge of the greatest of all spells. I am one. The other is the Vendhyan, Jaganath. Nine others have the incomplete version which you learned from Khepteh-Sebek, whom you seduced and then murdered."

Hathor-Ka bristled and glared, but she did not try to deny the accusation.

"Your efforts were wasted," Thoth-Amon continued. "Six lines of verse are missing from this version, along with five important gestures. To attempt this spell at the great conjunction would result only in a death unsurpassingly hideous. By Father Set I swear this."

"What is your proposal?"

"I shall instruct you in the proper ritual of the Great Summoning. When you travel by the Double-Goer spell to Ben Morgh upon the equinox, you shall take with you my own spirit-double. When the ceremony is complete we shall be equally powerful and shall rule jointly."

"Trust him not, mistress," hissed Moulay. "If he has this spell, as well as the fragment, why does he not take all and become sole ruler?"

"Because he has no way of traveling to Ben Morgh by the equinox," she answered. "Had he found the Skelos fragment first, he would not be bargaining with me now."

"Do you accept?" Thoth-Amon demanded.

She considered the possibilities. Without the true Summoning she faced a horrible death. What if Thoth-Amon were to teach her a false spell? He had nothing to gain from that, as it would mean only that Jaganath would become supreme mage instead of her. Besides, there would be plenty of time to betray Thoth-Amon later. "I accept. But I want the traitor SenMut."

"Agreed. I have no use for him. He would betray me as easily as he did you." Thoth-Amon gestured, and two of his human servants entered with SenMut bound between them.

Hathor-Ka stared at the traitor with reptilian eyes, and he shrank beneath her gaze. "There is yet one ceremony to perform," she said. "It requires a sacrifice. You will do nicely, SenMut." His eyes widened as he realized what she meant, and the servants dragged him away screaming.

Twelve

In the Caverns of the Demon

"There must be an opening somewhere," Chulainn said. The sun had been up for an hour or more, and they were combing the bizarre pit in search of an entryway to the subterranean lair of the evil beings they had seen.

Conan rapped at the stone futilely, using the pommel of his dirk. Everything sounded and felt solid. Cha was examining the strange and grotesque formations scattered about the pit. Some of them were carved from the natural rock, others seemed to have been molded from melted stone. Still others were of no stone from this area and seemed in some odd way to have grown there.

"Khitan!" Conan called out. "Come help us find a way in. You can see the sights later."

"You too impatient," Cha said. "Much of interest here. Maybe never get opportunity to study such things again." He kicked one of the organic-looking stone objects lightly. "This thing not from this world. It is from the empty spaces beyond our planets. Never see its like before."

Conan, who was not sure what a planet was, refused to be impressed. "No time for that. We must go in there and find

187

our people and be out before the sun sets and they are on the mountain again.''

The Khitan made a circuit of the walls and studied the floor of the pit. ''No way in here,'' he reported at last. ''I think I know how they doing it, but we cannot use their way. We go higher up, into Crom's cave, maybe find a way there.''

Chulainn shook his head. ''We go in there only for the most important ceremonies. Few but chiefs ever enter that cave. We do not want to earn the disfavor of Crom.''

Conan noted paths worn in the loose stone and soil, as if there had been a good deal of traffic between the cave and the pit.

''With the houseguests he been getting lately,'' Cha assured them, ''two unwashed barbarians, one Khitan wizard, he probably never notice.'' He led the way up the mountainside toward the gaping mouth of Crom's cave. Inside, the cave was foul-smelling, its floor littered with wreckage and refuse, like a site where an ill-disciplined army has camped. The Cimmerians bristled at this further desecration of their god's sanctuary, but they said nothing. Conan nudged a pile of burned wood aside with his foot and uncovered several well-gnawed human bones.

They passed farther inside, where the weak sunlight scarcely reached. Ahead was an immense rock formation and the cavern expanded, its ceiling rising to disappear into the gloom overhead. Then they could see that the rock formation was actually the carved likeness of a pair of colossal feet. As their eyes adjusted to the dimness they saw that the sculpture towered out of sight overhead. It was in the form of a giant seated upon a throne, but they could see no higher than its chest. The head was lost in the obscurity.

''This is Crom,'' Conan said. ''Nowhere will you see another likeness of him. Who carved his image I know not, for my people do not have that art.''

"Once they did," Cha said quietly. "Your people are far more ancient than you can imagine, Conan. They were not always savages living in stony mountains."

Chulainn stared up in reverent awe, overcome by the gloomy majesty of his god. Then he lowered his gaze and saw a great rent in the stone just before the huge feet of the statue. He pointed, calling out: "What is this? The chiefs never said anything of a cave at Crom's feet."

"There was none," Conan said, striding over to look. "Mitra! They've carved stairs down to their lair!"

Cha examined the stairs slanting down into the darkness. "No, they did not carve them down. These stairs carved *up* from below. Look at tool marks." The Cimmerians had no knowledge of stonecarving, but they were willing to take Cha's word for it.

"Gather some of this wood and brush," Conan told Chulainn. "We will need torches." They found enough of the refuse to make several crude torches when bound together with withies. "They must have made the prisoners carry this up from below," Conan said, taking a flint from his pouch.

"I light," Cha said.

The others expected him to recite a spell to make fire. Instead, he reached into his rags and drew forth an odd mechanical contrivance of steel and stone, with a small bowl of oil-soaked tinder. Cocking a spring, he snapped it a few times, shedding sparks until the tinder burst into flame.

"Must be careful about using magic now," he explained. "These things maybe feel our presence if I disturb the ether with spells."

Conan stepped onto the stair and a warm breeze from below ruffled the flame of his torch. The breeze carried the taint of ancient evil and they could hear a faint sussuration, like the breathing of some vast animal. Each Cimmerian kept his free hand on his sword hilt as they descended, with Cha tiptoeing behind the two barbarians. The steps were not only wide but high, as if they were made for beings other than men.

Against all expectation the cavern grew perceptibly warmer as they descended. At the bottom of the steep stair they entered a long, smooth-floored tunnel that still continued to descend, but far more gently. Cha called for the others to stop for a moment while he took a close look at the walls. Instead of the bare stone of the higher tunnel, these were covered with a thin, hairlike growth of moss. He shook his head. "This place very, very old. Not like stair above. Either these creatures make way to surface from ancient cavern, or else they been digging for a very long time."

They continued the descent. Now they began to encounter smaller side tunnels meeting with the main one. "Keep to the big tunnel," Conan said. "That way we'll not get lost."

"What if our people are down one of these?" Chulainn pointed to one of the side tunnels.

"We can do only our best," Conan said. "We'll do nobody any good by getting lost."

The cavern began to widen, and the floor became less smooth and more like that of a natural cave. The warmth of unknown origin continued to grow. In the lower spots water had collected. The fine growth of moss on the walls became rank, and larger forms of sunless growth began to appear: huge toadstools, great ledges of thick, leprous fungus, hanging growths curled like a ram's horns, many other things far less describable. In the distance, out of the light from their torches, they could see that some of the growths glowed with a sickly luminescence.

"What kind of foul place is this?" asked Chulainn. The others had no answer for him. Now they could hear distinct sounds ahead of them. There was light coming from ahead too. They extinguished the burning torches and left the others beneath an especially hideous mushroom, where they could be sure of finding them again.

Ahead was a wide-arching entrance opening onto what appeared to be a very large chamber. Stealthily, they approached it. Lurid glares flickered across the ceiling of the tunnel, as if great fires were burning somewhere below the level of the entrance.

"Will there be sentries out?" Chulainn whispered.

"What they be guarding against?" Cha said. Nevertheless, the Cimmerians drew their dirks. They walked swiftly, in a half-crouch, wary as hunted animals. Despite the considerable amount of metal exposed about their persons, they made not the slightest clink or rattle. This skulking about beneath the surface of the ground repelled them, but they were prepared to endure anything, even death in the dark instead of in the pure mountain air beneath the sun. All that mattered was the rescue of their kin.

There was a great deal of noise coming from the chamber beyond, rumblings and croakings and screams of pain. Their tunnel ended in a ledge above a great sunken cavern, one larger perhaps than the throne room of Crom. The men lowered themselves to their bellies and crawled forward, silent as snakes. At the edge they peered over carefully onto a scene from a wizard's nightmare.

This time there was no obscuring smoke or fog to cover the hideous activities of the creatures below. The beings were of many types, all of them engaged in frantic if incomprehensible activity: herding human prisoners at the point of cruel-looking polearms, performing strange rites before ugly shrines, committing acts of seemingly pointless torture or violence, not only on their prisoners but upon each other.

Many of the things were of the reptilian sort that Conan and Chulainn had encountered in the Field of the Dead, but there were other types as well. There were vaguely humanoid things with jointed bodies like insects, and crawling giant slugs trailing slime. Huge, hairy spiders clung to the walls. Crouching ape-things pounded mindlessly on peculiar drums and creatures with batwings flitted silently through the cavern, apparently blind. Those were the creatures to which they could assign some degree of recognition. Others were so bizarre, with shapes so unstable and alien, that the sane and stable mind automatically rejected them. They were plainly of no world acceptable to humans.

The human prisoners, most of them children or young women, were herded and abused in a condition of abject degradation. Many behaved with mute apathy, some were clearly mad from horror, a few were belligerent and rebellious. The rebellious ones showed the marks of scourge and worse. The bulk of the prisoners seemed to be Cimmerian, although other peoples were represented: Aesir and Vanir and Hyperborean among them, along with races unknown to Conan, who had traveled more than most.

In an obscure corner of the immense chamber, walled off in a pen of piled stones, sat a steely-eyed group of captive youngsters, most of them Cimmerians. At sight of them Chulainn started to rise, but Conan's hand on his shoulder kept the young warrior in place.

"Bronwith?" whispered Conan.

"It is she. In the corner, with the blue mantle."

Conan saw her immediately—a handsome, strong-looking girl of marriageable age, with black hair and large brown eyes. The blue mantle thrown over one shoulder was the only article of clothing she retained.

The others were in no better state. What clothing they had was so whip-shredded as to be no more than bloody rags. The girl's face was fearless, but her eyes darted about continually, not in panic but in ceaseless search for an escape. For an instant her gaze rested on the ledge where the eyes of three men peered over the rock rim, then she resumed her frantic search.

Conan touched the other two and they crawled back into the cave among the mushrooms. "You made a good choice, lad,'' Conan said. "That girl is pure Cimmerian. She saw us and gave no sign. The others with her are not as panicked as the rest of the prisoners. I'll wager she's been keeping them in hand."

"Aye," Chulainn said, pride fighting with fear in his voice. "And we must free her. The others in the pen are younger than Bronwith, and it will not be easy to get them all out of here."

"You speak the truth," Conan agreed. "And she'll not leave them behind. From the look of them they're mostly Murrogh, probably her kin, taken in the same raid she was."

"How you know the clan of naked children?" muttered Cha. The Khitan was strangely subdued.

"No other clan has so many brown-eyed bairns among them," Conan said.

Cha shrugged. "All look alike to me."

"How can we get them free?" Chulainn persisted. "There is no night here. Those things down there may never sleep, and there are far too many of them."

Conan turned to Cha. "Earn your keep, wizard. If you are such a great enchanter, use your skill and make us a way to rescue our folk. We will take care of the sword work ourselves."

For the first time the Khitan seemed agitated, even angry.

"You want me give myself away so you can free a few of your kin?" He swept out a skinny arm and pointed toward the hellish chamber. "You see that place? You think that is evil? That is one place, under this mountain. I fail here, then whole world be like that!"

"One problem at a time, wizard," Conan said imperturbably. "First, we get our people out of here and to a place of safety. Then, we see about your task. And I must finish my mission. I'll not be forsworn."

"Barbarians!" Cha grumbled. "Get hold of one idea, no room for anything more."

Chulainn looked puzzled. "We value our kin and our word. What else is there?"

Cha hissed in disgust. "So be it. I give you a chance, but you must be quick."

"All we need is a chance," Conan said. "And we are always quick."

"I no use sorcerer's weapons. Must save those for later. I make illusion. Distract demons down there. You have only moments to get your people free, up to this cave. Then you must run faster than the demons. I not able to help you then."

"Do it," Conan said. "Just tell us when you are ready."

Bronwith sat on the hard stone with her arms around her knees, waiting. She did not dare inform the others of what she had seen, for fear that some of the younger might give way to hope and accidentally reveal to their captors that something had changed. She drew the scant cloak closer about her shoulders, although the cavern was warm.

She had seen the eyes of three men looking over the stone lip. Two heads bore tousled black hair, the third was mostly shiny scalp. Was one of them Chulainn? If so, who was the other Cimmerian? And who might the third man be? Of course, it might be her own kinsmen. That seemed to be more likely. Chulainn might come for her alone, braving any terror to rescue her and honor his given word, but what clansman of his would risk his neck for the sake of a Murrogh woman?

Time enough to answer these questions later. Now she would hold herself in readiness to take whatever opportunity came to win freedom for herself and her young kinsmen. She was the eldest, and she felt responsible for them.

Bronwith was a tall young woman, sturdy and little wasted from her long captivity, despite the scant fare they had been given. The others were surprisingly healthy as well. Cimmerian children were accustomed to deprivation. They were not used to captivity, however, and did not make model prisoners. All of them were heavily striped with the marks of the barbed whips carried by the reptilian guards. Bronwith bore more stripes than many of the others. She had tried as well as she could to protect her younger kin, and she had paid for it.

As she waited she sang one of the sad songs of her race. Above the blue mantle her face was broad-boned, handsome, and intelligent. Best of all, her face was sane. Sanity had not been easy to hold on to in the last weeks. Or had it been months? It was difficult to keep track of days here in the caverns. They were taken to the surface sometimes to work in the pit for some incomprehensible purpose, but there was no way of knowing whether the nights when they worked were successive or widely separated. Her strong example had helped the others to stay sane as well, and keep them from despair.

That had not been easy either. They had been taken from their steadings by demons from hell. Some had seen older kinsmen slain and eaten by the monsters. Knowing the dietary preferences of their captors, they had refused to eat the few scraps of meat given to them in captivity.

Worst of all was not knowing. Why had they been brought here? What was in store for them? Until now Bronwith had thought that slavery was the worst fate that could befall her. Mere death was common and nothing to fear greatly. Like all Cimmerians old enough to make decisions, she had long since resolved to die before allowing herself to be carried off to some foreign land to be enslaved by an alien people. Awful as this was, at least captivity near home held the prospect of escape. She wondered when they would come.

Bronwith was almost dozing when she was jerked awake by a sudden lessening of the noise in the cavern. The stilling of the pandemonium was as shocking as the noise itself had once been. Those of the creatures that had necks were craning them to stare upward, where something untoward was happening.

Above them some new creature was materializing. As it took on form, it appeared to be roughly human, although gigantic. Its face was majestic and serene, and its body and legs were finely proportioned. It seemed to have dozens of arms, all of them in motion as it trod the measures of some intricate dance to unheard music. The whole apparition was bright blue.

A jabber of excitement broke out as the demons expressed their disconcertion in a cacophony of croaks, hisses, and screeches. Bronwith did not connect this with the men she had seen, but she was ready to make use of it to help effect their escape. "Be ready," she said to the others in a low voice, "this may be our chance." Quietly, the others shifted, stretching cramped limbs surreptitiously lest they hinder a quick dash for freedom.

Bronwith heard a low, warbling whistle and turned to see two men crouched to one side of the stone pen. One was Chulainn, and her heart leaped like a mountain stag in spite of her stony discipline. The other she did not know, save that he was a kinsman of Chulainn's from the look of his craggy Canach features. Chulainn beckoned and she signaled the others. Silently, all rose and moved in a limber crouch to the two men, who helped them over the wall. The sentries near the pen continued to stare stupidly at the dancing figure overhead. Luckily, it seemed that none of their adversaries were overburdened with brains.

Skirting the side of the immense chamber, the two men led the escapees to a narrow ledge that made a tortuous way up the wall to the cave mouth where Bronwith had first seen them. Even the youngest of the children were as surefooted as mountain goats and trod the treacherous ledge with ease. When the last was on the ledge, the two men followed. Miraculously, it seemed as if they had not yet been noticed. Overhead, the hypnotic dance continued.

They gained the cave entrance without being seen. "Chulainn," Bronwith said, but the older man interrupted.

"No time," he growled. "Run! You'll find a lighted torch up ahead, and a stack of unlit ones. Take them and stay to this cave. You'll find yourself in Crom's cave. Get out and head downhill, through the Field of the Dead. If you run fast enough, you'll find friends before these demons catch you."

"This is my cousin, Conan," Chulainn said.

"Conan," Bronwith said. She had heard the name before.

A tousle-headed boy of perhaps twelve spoke up. "Why should Murrogh trust a dog of the Canach?"

Conan grinned, spun the boy around, and kicked his backside in the direction of escape. "The Bloody Spear has been sent about, boy. We can fight at some more peaceful time."

"Forgive him," Bronwith said, "he is my brother and headstrong like all the men of my clan. What will you two be doing?"

"We'll stay a little behind to cover your retreat," Conan told her. "That dancing Vendhyan idol is just a conjurer's trick, and the demons will catch on soon, so go."

Bronwith gave Chulainn a quick, fierce kiss and then ran. The others went with her, except for the boy who had wanted to defy Conan. "Should a Murrogh flee and let the Canach protect him? I'll stay with the warriors." The boy thrust out his thin chest and picked up a jagged rock.

Conan spoke solemnly, all mockery gone. "We are the rear guard, Murrogh warrior. Who knows what lies ahead of them in these tunnels? Do not leave them without an advance guard."

The boy thought a moment. "Aye, you have the right of it. Good fortune, men of Canach." Clutching his rock, the boy ran toward the flickering light of the torch.

Conan grinned again. "You're marrying into good stock, kinsman. Those two would do credit to any clan."

Chulainn smiled, a man at peace. "I've come for her, as I swore. Now I can die and face Crom without shame." There was a change in the noise from the cavern behind them. "That's liable to happen soon, now. The foreigner's trick has been found out."

"Come," Conan said.

They trotted toward the escaping prisoners, careful in the dimness. It was not long before they heard the sounds of pursuit. There was a single reassurance to be had from this: their pursuers had not seen the escape and had no way of knowing which of the multitude of caves they had taken from the great chamber. They must split up and search all of them. Conan and Chulainn would not have to face the whole force of the demons.

They were not able to make the best time in the dimness and the unfamiliar environs of the caverns, and the sounds of pursuit grew closer behind them. Without breaking stride the Cimmerians drew their swords. When the first challenge came, it was not from behind but from in front. From one of the small side tunnels a pair of insectoid creatures sprang out to confront them. The beings were at least seven feet tall, angular, and shiny. In their multiple pairs of limbs each bore odd-looking weapons, with which they attacked.

Conan ducked a saw-toothed sword aimed to split his skull and hacked at the attacking creature's thorax, chipping away a chunk of horny chitin. The thing hissed and made a grab for him with its free claw. The pincer closed agonizingly around Conan's left arm. Its strength was terrible, and he knew he must slay it quickly. Desperately, he wedged the tip of his blade against the spot where he had chipped away the natural armor and thrust with all his might. Abruptly, the thorax gave way and the blue brand crunched through. With a hideous screech the insect man released him and sought to pull away. With both hands on his hilt Conan wrenched the sword free, releasing a yellow acid-smelling fluid. The creature fell to the floor and its shell rattled on the stone as it writhed in its death convulsions.

Swinging his fine blade in a great circle to clear it of the foul fluid, Conan turned to see that Chulainn had his enemy backed against a wall of the cave, vainly seeking to defend itself with a bizarre polearm. Chulainn bore in like an avenging fury, first shearing away an arm at its elbow joint, then hewing through a knee, and finally hacking off the misshapen head as the creature toppled. Conan watched with interest as the head sailed for many yards toward the great cavern. It made a faint thunk when it landed, far out of sight.

"Those were no easier than the lizards," Chulainn commented.

"They know these caves as well," Conan said. "Pray we meet no more of them."

They reached the long stair and began their climb. They could hear pursuit close behind, and with it the loud hissing of the tough lizard-things. They put on a little more speed. The high steps were awkward but they were mountain bred and were only slightly winded as they reached the top.

Crom's cave was filled with sunlight as they entered it, and the sound of ascending demons ceased behind them, with much frustrated hissing. The Cimmerians paused to catch their breath.

"Will the sunlight stay them?" Chulainn asked.

"For a while," Conan said. "But they were in daylight sometimes when they raided the steadings. We'd best be away from here before they gather another of their clouds and come after us."

They walked toward the entrance and Chulainn pointed to the still-burning remnants of the torches dropped by the prisoners as they fled. "Bronwith and the others made it safely this far. They must be halfway down the mountain by now.''

They stepped through the entrance. "Let's catch up with them. I'll not feel—" Then he saw what was waiting for them. "Crom's bones!" he swore as he jerked out his sword once more.

"Two more for our net," Starkad said. "But I'll wager we'll not take these two alive."

Thirteen

Wolves of Vanaheim

Conan took in the scene even as he drew his sword. The mouth of the cave was faced by a great half-circle of armed Vanir. There looked to be nearly a hundred of them. To one side stood a man in rich armor, probably a chief. Near him were two odd-looking foreigners. One Van lay dead, with his head crushed by a jagged, bloody rock. Stretched by him was Bronwith's brother, blood matting his tousled black locks. Bronwith and the others were herded between the Vanir and the cave. All this Conan's mind registered before his sword cleared his sheath.

"Vanir on Ben Morgh!" Chulainn shouted, his look growing crazed. To Cimmerians, the presence of Vanir on their sacred mountain was as intolerable as that of demons.

"Do as I do," Conan muttered.

He had been in this type of situation before. The Vanir were stretched into a wide semi-circle before the cave. At no point was the line of men more than two deep. It would be useless to take on all the Vanir, but it was just possible to carve a hole in their line and escape. The line was thinnest near the chieftain, but Conan selected a spot near the recaptured prisoners.

201

"Kill these two dogs," Starkad ordered.

The men began to close in, grinning. They had not yet advanced more than one step when, howling a wild Cimmerian war cry, Conan charged. A Van stepped from the line, ax raised high and shield held before his body. Conan came in low and chopped at the lower edge of the shield. The blue blade was not even slowed, but bit into the man's side, showering those standing nearby with bloody iron scales.

Conan put a foot against the man's chest and shoved the body away, tearing his sword free with a sucking sound. Spinning on one foot, he turned that movement into a blow at a Van closing in from his right. Striking backhanded and off balance, the blow was still powerful enough to split the Van's horned helm from temple to nasal, hewing through the haft of his ax in the process.

Two Vanir tried to close in on Chulainn, but he dived forward at them, going into a tumble that bewildered the attackers. As he rolled between them, Chulainn cut beneath the shield of the righthand Van, chopping his left thigh to the bone. The Van fell howling as Chulainn sprang to his feet behind them and struck at the lefthand man's neck below the helm. The head toppled to the stone and Chulainn was turning to engage more of his enemies before the body fell.

They had opened a gap in the Vanir line several yards wide. Conan turned to the prisoners. "Run!" he barked.

Bronwith stooped and hauled her brother to her shoulders as if the boy weighed no more than a sack of meal, and leading the others, she made for the gap. A Van made to grab at her, but Chulainn turned from the man he was fighting and sheared the Van's arm away before he could touch Bronwith. The moment's distraction cost Chulainn a shallow cut across the chest from the tip of the other man's sword, but he returned the blow with one of his own which bit through nasal and skull.

As the prisoners were escaping, Conan pressed against the

Vanir line, driving it back a little farther. The Vanir were brave but a bit disconcerted by this whirlwind of ferocity in their midst. He splintered a shield, chopped a decorative wing from a helmet, then whirled and ran.

"Flee!" he shouted at Chulainn.

The younger man broke off from his fight as abruptly as Conan and followed. It took the Vanir a moment to realize what was happening, then they began to pursue. It was hopeless. The Cimmerians were unencumbered except for their weapons, and were fleet and surefooted as mountain goats. The armored Vanir, unaccustomed to mountain terrain and thin air, could only lumber ineffectually after.

Starkad snorted with disgust as he saw his men panting to a halt a short way down the slope and turn back. The blackhairs were almost out of sight already. "This is the last time I set foot in Cimmeria with a pack of untried young fools. From now on I risk action against the blackhairs only with seasoned warriors."

Jaganath smiled slightly at the expression "the last time." Starkad did not see this. "If these two are typical of the Cimmerians," the Vendhyan said, "I do not wonder that you prefer to surround isolated farmsteads at night with over-whelming superiority of numbers."

"We were not expecting them," Starkad growled, "and my men were fools. It is easy enough for a man to get around behind a busy foe while two others engage him from in front. Then he can be hewn down with no risk to anyone. These men were idiots to charge in for single combat as if some skald were standing by to make a poem." He walked over to the group of dead and dying men. "What a slaughter to be wrought by a pair of blackhairs without helm nor byrnie between them."

Starkad stooped by the corpse of the first man Conan had slain. The split shield was still on the outflung arm. A huge rent in the scale shirt revealed a body split to the spine and the entrails steamed slightly in the chill air.

The Van chieftain straightened. "That taller blackhair, the older one, he must be some great champion of theirs. I would not have believed that any man living could strike such a blow. The younger one fought shrewdly, striking unarmored limbs when he could. The older man, though"—Starkad shook his head in disbelief—"he struck as if shield and armor were no more than smoke." He turned and glared at Jaganath. "Is this more wizardry? I have never seen a sword like the one he bore. Was it an enchanted blade?"

Jaganath shook his head. "I know little of swords, but I felt no aura from the one he used. Do not try to excuse your men's inadequacy by giving your enemy a supernatural helper. More than one ruler has made that mistake."

Starkad was stung by the rebuke, but felt too humiliated to answer.

"Let us go inside," Jaganath said. He and Gopal walked through the towering archway, and Starkad followed.

They stopped at the feet of the colossus and Starkad gazed upward, a little awed by the immense statue. "So this is old Crom of the Mountain," he said. "I shall have my men build a great fire so we can see his face."

For the first time Jaganath spoke with a tinge of uneasiness in his voice. "I do not think you would want to look upon his face." He was looking up into the obscurity as if he could see that face perfectly well.

Starkad looked down at the ragged pit in the floor, with its enigmatic steps leading downward. There were faint, shuffling sounds coming from down there. "Now, wizard, I think it is time you gave me some information. Why were those Cimmerians here? Except for the warriors they were all children and a few young women. They were fleeing from this cave and had the look of prisoners long-held. There is something down in that cave that I don't like the sound of. What errand have you in this place?''

Jaganath answered with his customary haughtiness. ''You have no need to know of my business here. Have no fear of what is below. My powers will protect you. As for the Cimmerians, these are matters of interest only to the most powerful of sorcerers, and you would not understand them. Rest assured that all is according to my plans.'' With a flick of his hand he dismissed these things as trivial. ''Tomorrow we shall rest, and I shall make my preparations. The morrow after that is the equinox, when I shall perform my rites. By the end of the first hour after sunrise my business here shall be concluded.''

Starkad had a strong suspicion that this wizard was not half as knowledgeable as he pretended, that he was as mystified as any about the presence of the Cimmerians. ''Until the morning of the morrow after next, then,'' Starkad agreed. ''An hour after sunrise we leave for home. We dare stay no longer. When those blackhairs we just saw reach their villages, every armed Cimmerian within three days march will be heading for this mountain.''

Jaganath nodded, smiling thinly. ''That will be satisfactory. I shall have no further need of you, then.'' Starkad went out to rejoin his men.

Gopal spoke to his uncle as soon as the Van was out of earshot. ''Is this truly as you had expected, uncle?''

Jaganath frowned. ''There have been other mages at work here, nephew. Powerful ones, of the first rank. Some foolish one has prepared a way for the demons beneath the earth and those of other dimensions to enter here. Those creatures should be left alone, until one has the full power. But who is doing this? Thoth-Amon? Hathor-Ka? Ming Tzu? I can think of none so powerful but so foolish.'' He looked about. ''But I am the one who is here on the spot, and all their machinations must come to naught if they be not present on the equinox. But yet I smell some strange sorcery here, and I know not whose it is, save that it is not part of these workings." He pointed down into the pit. Then he looked up once again at the towering figure on the carven throne. "And this Crom. He is not what I had expected."

Gopal was deeply disturbed. Never had he heard his uncle speak except with perfect self-confidence. The fact that some rival could shake that confidence caused the very earth to shift beneath Gopal's feet. "But you shall prevail, uncle," Gopal said shakily. "Surely you shall prevail!"

Jaganath shook off his foreboding and smiled once again. "Have no fear, Gopal. Upon the equinox I shall be the most powerful mage who has ever lived."

When they reached the bottom of the valley called the Field of the Dead, Conan, Chulainn, and the former prisoners paused for rest. Many of the younger children were not in the best of condition after their long captivity. Chulainn ran to the top of the cairn and looked back the way they had come. "No pursuit," he reported.

"I thought as much," Conan said. He sat on a rock and began cleaning his blade carefully. "What Van was ever worth anything in the mountains?" Satisfied that his blade was clean and free of nicks, Conan sheathed it and stood. Bronwith was bending over the inert form of her brother. She had carried the boy the whole way.

As Conan approached Bronwith rearranged what was left of her cloak somewhat more modestly. "He is alive," she said.

Conan bent and ruffled the boy's dark hair, which was clotted with blood. There was a ragged gash in the lad's scalp, but Conan felt no movement of bone beneath his hand. "He'll be all right. The Murrogh were ever a hardheaded clan."

Chulainn joined them. "What became of your foreign friend?"

Conan shrugged. "I know not. He has some business in the mountain, and I doubt not that he is about it now. He's able to take care of himself."

"What should we do now?" Bronwith asked. "Some of the children are not fit to travel yet."

"The demons may be out when dark comes," Chulainn said. "We met two here not long past."

"We stay," Conan said. "I'll not leave our people here to the demons or the Vanir. Not one more Cimmerian child will they have while I draw breath. We wait. The great host should be here soon."

"And if our enemies should fall upon us before then?" Bronwith asked.

Conan looked about him, surveying the surrounding cairns. "If so, then there are far worse places to die than among the great chiefs of our people."

They scoured the valley for enough fuel to last them the night. Conan took first watch at the upper end of the valley. As the sky darkened he saw Bronwith's brother climbing toward him. The boy's head was still bloodied, but his eyes were clear and his walk was steady.

"Greeting, warrior," Conan called.

"Greeting," the boy said. He sat by Conan. "My name is Bodhrann. I am sorry I did not get to see you slay the Vanir today. My sister says you fought well, for a Canach man."

"High praise from the Murrogh," Conan acknowledged.

"What were the Vanir doing on Ben Morgh?"

"I would give much to know the answer to that. I saw two foreigners with them, though. I doubt not they're the ones who brought the redbeards here. Wizards are getting thick as a ram's fleece on this mountain. They were easterners of some sort, and up to some sorcery, no doubt."

The boy shrugged. "No matter, they are foreigners, and

we shall kill them for profaning our dead. Is it true what my sister says, that there has been a great hosting?''

''Aye. The clans were called to the Standing Stone and they'll be here soon. By tomorrow, I hope. They'll waste no time. Then there will be a fight such as none of us has ever seen.''

Chulainn came up to them from the camp. ''They are all bedded down, as well as can be managed. Cold, hungry, injured, and tired, but happy.''

''Would you not be?'' Conan asked.

''I have a matter to discuss with you,'' Bodhrann said to Chulainn.

''Speak on,'' Chulainn said.

''You wish to wed my sister?''

''And I shall,'' Chulainn assured him.

''I'll not permit it! Our clans are at feud. You may have her only by taking her from her menfolk by force!'' The boy thrust out his jaw belligerently.

''The Bloody Spears have been sent around,'' Chulainn said. ''Feuds are at rest and there may be no feud-wivings.''

''Oh.'' Bodhrann looked perplexed. ''But who ever heard of man and woman of feuding clans being wed under a White Shield?''

''It may never have been done before, but it is what we intend to do as soon as we have enough witnesses assembled.''

''It is not proper!'' Bodhrann insisted. His outrage at being cheated out of a good fight was plain.

''I am happy that it is turning out this way,'' Chulainn said. ''I might have had to kill you in carrying her off.''

The boy snorted. ''You might have tried!'' He walked away, his thin back rigid with dignity. Conan watched him and smiled, but he did not laugh.

''What is our course if the host does not arrive by tomorrow?'' Chulainn asked.

''You've fulfilled your vow. Before dark tomorrow you

may take the others down the mountain. I doubt not you'll
encounter the host before long. I must stay here to fulfill my
mission upon the next morning."

"I'll stay with you," Chulainn said calmly. "No Canach
goes to his enemies alone while a kinsman is close by."

Conan gave him no argument, knowing that it would be
useless.

The demons kept to themselves that night, and the first
rays of the rising sun glinted from the tips of hundreds of
spears, advancing up the valley below. The children cheered
and waved as the army of wolfish men approached, devoid of
flag, banner, or standard. Although offensive weapons were
there in plenty, no man wore helm or armor, nor any other
protective gear save the light shield borne by some. Such
effete things did not suit the headlong style of attack favored
by the Cimmerians. Some men had casting javelins, but there
were no archers. The art of the bow was unknown in Cimmeria,
where no suitable wood grew to make the weapons.

"Was ever there so fine a sight?" Chulainn said. "Have
you ever seen so many fighting men all in one place?" The
young man's face glowed with enthusiasm.

"I've seen more," Conan grunted. "But none better."

Indeed, the whole armed might of Cimmeria would not
have amounted to a good-sized regiment in some armies
Conan had seen. Few clans could muster more than a hundred fighting males of adequate years, and the clans of
Cimmeria were not numerous. But Conan would not have
rated highly the chances of any civilized army, however great
its number, against this host. The legendary ferocity of the
Cimmerians more than made up for their lack of numbers.

They wore the paints and tattoos, the braids and topknots
of all the clans. They were of all ages, from boys little older
than Bodhrann to gray-bearded elders with gaunt limbs still
ready to wield sword. Their weapons ranged from the fine
swords of the chiefs to the crude clubs of the wild Galla.

Uniting them was a fierce pride and independence, the spirit that had kept the Cimmerians a free people for all of their long history.

The chieftains were in the van, and they came forth to meet Conan and Chulainn. "So," began Canach, "you still live. And I see you have found our people."

"Some of them," Conan said. He jerked a thumb over his shoulder. "There are many more up there."

Canach addressed Bronwith, who stood by Chulainn. "There will be food and blankets for the children. You must take them below to safety as soon as they are fed."

Bodhrann stepped forward. "I stay with the host!"

The chieftains frowned at him for this unseemly interruption, but Conan said: "He killed a Van up there. With a stone."

Wild-bearded old Murrogh looked at Bodhrann with approval. "Go join the warriors of our clan, then."

"Here," Conan said. He took the sheathed dirk from his belt and tossed it to the boy. "There may be no spare weapons for you. This should do until you can find a dead man's sword after the fighting starts."

"He should receive his first man's weapon from the hand of a kinsman," objected Murrogh, glaring.

Conan grinned at the old chief. "We're almost kin already. My cousin here is about to wed his sister." The old man clucked over such improprieties.

"Vanir on Ben Morgh," said Canach. "That is something strange."

"It is far from the strangest of what I have to report. But we have work to do. The Vanir have damaged many of our cairns. As soon as you have set up camp we should repair them, before night falls."

"They shall pay," said the war leader of the Galla, who had no hereditary chieftain. "I think our ancestors will find the taste of Vanir blood pleasing."

That afternoon they struggled to restore the toppled stones of their cairns, storing up yet another chapter of hatred for the Vanir. That night, as the peat fires burned low, they heard the strange tales told by Bronwith, Conan, and Chulainn.

In conclusion Conan told them of what he had learned of the demons' way of fighting and their weaknesses. "Remember, they look terrifying, but they die as dead as men. The scaly ones have tough skins, like Vanir armor, and you must hit hard to pierce them. They have wicked tails and use them in fighting. The things like big insects are easier to kill. Just crack them open. Killing Vanir I need tell you nothing of. There are others we did not fight, but doubtless they are as mortal as the rest. We saw something in the pit, something big as a dragon, but so strange I cannot describe it. I doubt we could do it much damage. Best to leave it to the Khitan sorcerer."

"Saw you any gold down there?" asked Wulfhere, the yellow-bearded leader of the little contingent of Aesir, come at Conan's summons in payment of a debt neither man would discuss with the others.

"I saw none." Conan shrugged. "In truth, I was not looking. I think only a fool would go down in those caves to look for gold. Let the demons come out and fight us in the open." He looked about and gave his last instructions. "Tomorrow is the equinox, when I must carry out my mission. I think that all these sorcerous doings come to a head then. The demons do not like daylight, so if they want to deal with us, they may attack tonight. You have brought plenty of wood and peat. Keep it close by the fires and be ready to build them up at sound of attack. Let each man get what rest he can now, and sleep with your weapons in your hand."

Fourteen

In the Realm of the Gods

Hathor-Ka felt like an acolyte again. It was not pleasant for one of the world's most powerful mages to occupy again a subordinate position after so many decades. Her youthful appearance was due to her arts, for she was more than a century old. Yet, only now did she realize how ignorant and faltering she had been.

In recent days Thoth-Amon had taken her into his house to put the final polish on her sorcerous education, and she was staggered by the breadth and depth of his knowledge. Until now she had considered herself and several other mages to be very nearly Thoth-Amon's equals in the sorcerer's arts. Now she knew how laughable her presumption had been.

The strange beings from other dimensions that she had established halting contact with after long experimentation were Thoth-Amon's communicants. He was more ancient than she had dreamed, and he controlled forces she had been unaware even existed. In the few days since her abortive raid, Hathor-Ka had learned more of the wizard's arts from him than she had known in all her previous years.

Thoth-Amon had guarded well the secret of his full power. Over his centuries he had changed his name and appearance

213

many times in order never to give a hint of the true extent of his power. Thus he had an unparalleled advantage over any potential rival. Many a foe had fallen to Thoth-Amon's wiles by mistakenly assuming himself to be the great sorcerer's equal.

"Are there others as powerful, as knowledgeable, as you?" Hathor-Ka had asked him.

"None," Thoth-Amon assured her. "Jaganath thinks he is, but his skill is no greater than was yours before you came to me. In far Khitai the Order of the Silver Peacock may rival me in knowledge, but they are a brotherhood, and no single one of them rivals me in puissance."

"I know them only by a few writings," she said. "Is there any possibility that they might band together as one to wrest power from us?"

"None. They are as much philosophers as wizards, and while their scholarship is vast, they foolishly will not indulge in certain of the more powerful forms of magic and demon-summoning. They deem these things evil or too dangerous to mankind. They sit and contemplate and dream, but they have no wish to dominate the world through their arts." He waved a hand in one of his rare dismissive gestures. "All other wizards are as nothing now. We shall be masters of them all when this rite is accomplished."

Hathor-Ka remembered this conversation as she went to Thoth-Amon's meditating room for her final instruction before embarking upon the Great Summoning of the equinox. The frame of the door was covered with hieroglyphs of great power. Without the proper counterspell, to cross the threshold would have meant her doom. She muttered the spell Thoth-Amon had given her and the door swung open silently.

Inside, the great sorcerer sat upon the floor. The room was perfectly plain and unfurnished; its walls, ceiling, and floor were unrelieved black. Before Thoth-Amon was a plain basin of carved obsidian which contained only pure Styx water.

Not for the first time Hathor-Ka wondered at the simplicity of Thoth-Amon's thaumaturgy in contrast to the elaborate props and rituals of her own practice. So refined and perfect had his technique become that he needed little more than his own mind to carry out his spells. The basin of water was merely a focusing device of his powers.

He did not look up. "Come, Hathor-Ka. Sit across from me and look into the water of Father Styx. This night we go on a journey so far that distance is not even a concept. We go past the limits of our very universe. You have had some success in attracting a few minor denizens of that universe to the site of your temple by tempting them with sacrifices. You have done this by establishing an interface between that universe and ours above your altar. These things have been made possible by the millennial juxtaposition of the heavenly signs foretold by Skelos. Now we shall go into that universe ourselves and you shall see some of the real powers of that world, and have some idea of the forces you have unwittingly been playing with. Come, gaze into the waters."

She sat and stared at the nearly invisible water. It was a simple thing; one of the first exercises given to a new acolyte. The meditation upon water was as ancient as Stygian sorcery. But just as a master musician practices every day the simple exercises he first learned as a student, so a sorcerer must return to the basic mind-concentrating rituals. His centuries of practice had taught Thoth-Amon that this was the most profound technique in all the art of sorcery.

As she stared into the bowl, gradually both water and bowl disappeared. Hathor-Ka found herself sitting amid the firmament. All around her was naught but black emptiness aglow with the tiny lights of myriad stars. She had been here before innumerable times, but only by herself. This time Thoth-Amon was with her, although he was no more visible than was she herself.

"We are now at a place far from our world, but nearby as

one reckons the vastnesses of space," he said. "The stars you see are familiar. Now we shall go far, toward the very edge of the universe." The stars before her seemed to lengthen, then to shift and glow fiery red. Soon she was aware of them only as streaks of red. This went on for a limitless time, for time here had no meaning. Eventually, the red streaks became thinner and fewer. At last the remaining ones shortened and became once again points of blue-white light. There were very few of them, and all were in a direction she knew was behind them.

"Each point of light you see," Thoth-Amon said, "is not a star, but a cluster containing *billions* of stars. Gaze now upon infinity."

She looked and saw only blackness of a perfection she had never dreamed.

"Here, at the edge of reality," he went on, "we cross over into another reality."

There was a shifting about them. The blackness remained the same, but she knew that it was different. Thoth-Amon turned them, and now she was looking upon distant lights. They were not the star clusters of the world she knew, but weird shapes that glowed with unnatural colors. The two began to move toward the lights, and this time there was no color-changing, although Hathor-Ka felt that the distances and speeds were comparable.

Up to and past the glowing things they went. Only her sorcerer's training and experience kept Hathor-Ka's mind from snapping beneath the strain of what she saw. Some of them were living creatures of unthinkable immensity, existing in tortured geometries that an ordinary mind would have rejected at once. On worlds distorted inside out she perceived flocks of creatures doing things that shocked even her hardened senses.

Once, briefly, Thoth-Amon took them down to the surface of what might have been a planet. It was almost normal

compared to some others she had seen, save that its shape
was a disk of changing thickness and its size was easily a
thousand times that of her own world. All on it was perfectly
visible despite the absence of any light source. In a city of
purple crystal, atop a tower many miles high, Thoth-Amon
conferred at some length with a wizard of this universe, a
thing made up of crystal shards of many colors and a solid
manifestation of musical tones together with a stench that had
physical presence. It was performing a ritual intended to
destroy its world and all in it, apparently as a combination
poem and practical joke.

Onward they went toward the center of this universe.
Eventually, the lights and manifestations became fewer and
she was aware of a form before them that was so vast that she
had not noticed it. It was a concentration of all the blackness
in this universe, and yet she could perceive its form in bits
and increments.

She was at first reminded of the tentacled, formless horror
she had managed to call to her temple through her grisly
sacrificial rites. This thing bore some relation to it, but its
scale was unthinkably more vast. It was infinitely more evil,
more horrible. Slowly, she gained more awareness of the
thing's form, its aspect and nature. Then it was as if she had
become blind. The horror of this thing was too much even for
her, and her mind shut it out.

"You must encompass even a thing like this if you are to
become a mage of the first rank, Hathor-Ka." Thoth-Amon's
soundless voice was relentless. "This is a god of this universe, and it is one of the least of them. I confer frequently
with the greatest of them. And this is one of the least alien of
the universes. There are many far more terrible than this."

When Hathor-Ka emerged from this journey it was as if
she awakened from a dream. This dream, though, had none
of the soft edges of real dreams, and it remained firm in the
memory without fading like a real dream. Had it been a true

experience? Was Thoth-Amon as all-powerful as he seemed? Or had this all been a form of mummery, implanted in her mind by the wizard's powerful hypnotic suggestion?

She thought long and hard on this. The experience had been dreamlike in its unreality, in the lack of a true sense of scale, in the ability to see in the absence of light. Yet, that could be explained if the mage was truly able to travel to other universes.

It was important to solve this riddle, because she had no intention of sharing power with Thoth-Amon. But if he were truly so mighty, did she dare betray him? The Skelos fragment said nothing about a joint rule by two mages. If she performed the ritual alone, she would become ultimate ruler, and all other wizards would be subordinate to her. Thus, be he ever so powerful, Thoth-Amon would be her servant. She determined to stake all on this belief. She realized the chance she was taking, but one who would not take great risks had no business seeking high power.

Starkad was worrying, something he seldom did. Encamped before the mouth of the cave, which none of his men would consent to enter, he sat regretting that he had ever undertaken this escort. He loved gold, but these foreigners did not have gold sufficient to balance the risk they were running. He had foreseen a brief incursion into Cimmerian territory, perhaps a few brisk encounters with the blackhairs, with the Vanir holding great numerical superiority, of course. A little blooding was good for the younger men, and gold was always welcome.

Now the whole foray was turning into a disaster. Already they had lost several men, and with nothing to show for it. The fine batch of prisoners they had bagged was gone, and they had not slain a single blackhair to salve their pride. Now, behind them, was a cave full of unholy wizardry and frightful demons the Vanir had only glimpsed. Far below them he could see the fires of the Cimmerian encampment, surely the largest Cimmerian army assembled since the sack of Vanarium. It would be strange indeed if even a handful of his band survived to return to the halls of Vanaheim again. He intended to be one of those, but many a chieftain had been deposed in the aftermath of undertakings less ill-starred than this one. A leader of the Vanir held position by the might of his own arm, but also by the example of his skill and luck. Men would not follow a man who had proven himself unlucky.

All around him his men were thinking the same thoughts. Some glared at him as they idly gnawed the rims of their shields. Starkad was roused from his gloomy thoughts at the approach of two men he had sent on a scout. One was Alfgar, one of his oldest and most trusted companions. The other was Hilditon, a youth noted for his skill in climbing, learned in his native cliff village, where all men scaled the rocky faces in search of eiderdown. The two squatted by him and spoke in whispers.

"It is no good, Starkad," Alfgar said, shaking his grizzled head. "We have been all over this mountaintop, and it is all sheer cliffs to both sides of us. The only way down is through that valley before us, the way we came."

Starkad turned on Hilditon. "There is no chance?"

"I might be able to make it," the young man said, "in daylight, with good ropes. But not the rest. It takes much skill and experience."

Starkad gestured behind him. "And if we climbed up over the crest? Might we find a better slope on the other side?"

"It is too rugged and too icy," Hilditon said. "And we would not know what we faced until we reached the other side of the mountain. The risk would be great, we would lose many men on the slopes, and it might all be for naught."

"Starkad," Alfgar said, "the time has come to speak of what we must do before the sun rises. The whole blackhair nation is down there in arms, and upon the morrow they will move against this mountaintop. It were best we were not here when that happens. The fat foreigner has some business tomorrow, upon the equinox. I know little of sorcerous things, but I would wager all my gold, all my land and cattle and wives and slaves that he means us no good. Let's be away from here, and quickly.''

"You speak wisely, old friend. If it were any enemy but the blackhairs down there, I would say let us go down and bargain with them. Even the Aesir will behave as reasonable men when there is nothing to be gained by battle. But the hatred of Cimmerians is as black as their hair and their hearts. They care nothing for gold and little for their lives. Besides, we have desecrated their holy place, and they will be more than a little annoyed. I warned the men about that.''

Alfgar shrugged. "We did not know there was a whole blackhair army after us then. Besides, what warrior can resist defiling the ancestors of his enemies?''

"It is done," Starkad said. "Not that the Cimmerians need much encouragement to thirst for Vanir blood.''

"Those two blackhairs cut their way through us," Hilditon said. "Might we not do the same? If we can carve a way through them, the bulk of us may escape. The blackhairs did not come all this way just to deal with us. We slew the messenger with the Bloody Spear almost as soon as we crossed into Cimmeria. They were gathering for this hosting even then. If we run for home, they may not pursue, being intent upon their business here on the mountain.''

Starkad nodded. "You speak wisely for a young man. This has been much my own thought as well. If we can get through, we might pick up many slaves on our way back, since the fighting men will not be guarding the steadings and villages. Thus we need not return empty-handed.''

"Whatever we do," Alfgar said, "we must do it before first light.''

"Very well," Starkad said, relieved to have his mind made up. "Get the men ready, and be sure they're quiet about it. We fight, and we run."

The two men, old and young, went around the camp and spoke in low voices to the little clumps of men. At their report the men ceased their discontented muttering and their lowering scowls changed to grins of anticipation. Whatever the odds, Northlanders would always rather fight than wait.

They arose and quietly prepared for a night march and battle. Many tied cloaks or blankets about their bodies to muffle somewhat the rattle of the metal scales and to prevent the clink of weapons and shields against armor.

Starkad thought of having them blacken their metal with soot from the fires, but decided against it. They might be willing to muffle their gear for the sake of stealth, but no Van going into what might well prove his last fight would want to make less than his finest display.

In all, Starkad was well content. If he had little chance, at least it was better than none. It was always good to be leading men into a battle. His only real grief was that they might all die and the story of this fight never be sung in the halls of Vanaheim. Songs and poems were the immortality of a hero. He whistled idly as he thumbed his ax, making sure that the edge was keen. His thoughts were interrupted by Jaganath, who had appeared soundlessly behind him.

"Are you going somewhere, Starkad?" he asked.

"Yes. We have decided to take a little stroll down the hill and have some exercise with the blackhairs. Then we will go home. You may keep your gold. I have a feeling I would have precious little use for it were I to wait for it."

"It grieves me to part company with you, but if this is your wish, of course I shall not stand in your way. However, I have something for you all which may be of help."

Starkad narrowed his eyes. "What might that be?" This foreigner was accepting his defection with strange equanimity.

"I have made up protective amulets for you all. They contain a sacred power that will protect you from the detection and the weapons of your enemies. Gopal, help me distribute these."

"This is generous of you," Starkad said as the wizard hung around his neck a tiny bag on a silken string. The younger Vendhyan was passing the amulets out among the other men.

"It is the least I can do." Jaganath smiled.

When all was ready the Vanir began their slow, quiet trudge downhill.

When they were gone, Gopal turned to Jaganath. "Uncle, are these Northmen truly as stupid as they seem?"

Jaganath smiled and nodded, setting his many chins aquiver. "Is their simplicity not sublime, nephew? They are so unsubtle that it is possible to outwit oneself in dealing with them by feinting and dodging an obvious counterploy that never even occurs to them. Now they are properly consecrated and ready for sacrifice. There is no sacrifice more pleasing than a willing one, and no sheep ever went to the altar more willingly than these fools.

"Now, come. These men shall not slow down that mob below, and among them is the Cimmerian hired by Hathor-Ka, if my pursuers and even my cursed gold failed their task. We must not chance it with the stakes so high. I am not yet sure who brought the demons here, nor for what purpose save stirring up the countryside, but I have a plan. There is a spell known to me that shall send the demons against those men camped in the valley. Thus will the Cimmerians be eliminated as a threat while at the same time the caverns will be vacated so that I may perform these important rites in privacy and uninterrupted."

"You always plan with such elegance, uncle," said Gopal with fawning admiration.

Far below them, in the bowels of the mountain, a skinny, ragged figure sat cross-legged in a dark side tunnel. From time to time it murmured some ancient chant. Then, in the dimness, it smiled.

Fifteen

The Battle Among the Cairns

The Cimmerian camp spread across the Field of the Dead to the flanking slopes that defined its limits. The mossy stones of the cairns had been restored to their proper order, and the worst of the defilement cleared away. A true purification was not yet possible. That could be done only with the blood of the defilers.

Conan walked through the camp, smelling the smoke of the peat fires and hearing the low talk of the warriors. In other armies the young and untried men would be chattering nervously of what was to come. Those with a little experience would be boasting of their past feats. True veterans would be holding their own counsel, seeing to their fighting gear and trying to get some rest. In this, as in most things, Cimmerians were different. In the snatches of conversation as he was passing the fires, Conan heard them talking of the everyday things of their lives: of their wives and children, of cattle and feuds and farming. It was as if they were gathered for a trading fair instead of a battle. Once again Conan knew he was an alien in his own land.

Only in the camp of the Aesir did he find the kind of congenial fellowship that he liked among fighting men. Here the yellow-haired warriors laughed and sang and passed around a huge skin of wine from the South while a few young Cimmerians stood around and gazed upon them as upon some strange animals. Conan strode into the circle of men and intercepted the wineskin as it was being passed. He upended it and poured a long stream of the yellow juice into his mouth.

"Hey, Conan, leave some for the rest of us!" Wulfhere had hair and beard so pale that it was almost white. He was a little older than Conan, but was already a famous chief among the Aesir.

He and his men were a startling contrast to the somber Cimmerians. Like their cousins the Vanir, the Aesir delighted in gaudy display. Their armor was of polished iron or bronze, and their helmets were crested with horns or wings or fantastic animal figures, often overlaid with silver or gold. Their arms glittered with bracelets and armlets of fancifully wrought gold, and many a swordhilt blazed with jewels. With mirrors of polished silver, many of these warriors were taking advantage of the firelight to comb and braid their beards or shape their long moustaches into dashing curves. Several songs were going at once. Like the Vanir, the Aesir were merry in hall or camp, wild in battle, and sad at home among their families.

Conan took a final swallow and passed the skin on to the next man. "Why did you not bring ale if this stuff is so precious?"

"Ale takes up too much space," Wulfhere said. "We wore out three slaves carrying this wine as it was. This had better be a good fight, Conan. We abandoned a promising raiding party against the Hyperboreans to come here."

"You'll enjoy it," Conan promised. "There shall be Vanir to kill, along with the demons."

"That will be good," Wulfhere approved. "And these creatures have raided into Asgard as well, this last year, but we had no idea where they had disappeared to until your messenger came. Whatever befalls, there will be many songs sung in the halls of Asgard about this fight.''

A one-eyed man with gapped teeth handed the wineskin back up to Conan. ''Come raiding with us when this is done,'' he said. ''It has been long years since you took the wolf's path with us. I should like to see what tricks you have learned in your wanderings.''

''That I may well do, Ulf. I make no promise, though. Tomorrow I may be dead, or you may be dead. Best to make no plans until the shield-cleaving is done.''

''Now you speak like a Cimmerian,'' grumbled Wulfhere.

Conan grinned. ''I've been with my relatives too much.''

He left the camp of the Aesir and walked up the valley to the upper watchpost. Here no fire burned, lest the guard's night vision be ruined. Chulainn stood here with another young man, who wore the Galla topknot.

''All quiet, cousin,'' Chulainn reported.

''It will not be for long,'' Conan predicted. ''We've no more than an hour until first light. I am sure they will strike us before that.'' They stood for a while in silence, their ears, eyes, and noses trained uphill, where danger lay.

It was the Galla warrior who raised his head first, his nostrils flared. ''They come,'' he said. Then the other two heard the sounds of men descending, still far up the slope.

''Fools,'' Chulainn said. ''To think they could sneak past Cimmerians in our own mountains.''

''Are demons among them?'' asked the Galla, lifting his long shield and swinging his terrible club.

Conan shook his head. ''The Vanir. Trying to escape is my guess. They'll serve to warm us up for the real fight.''

''You two have already killed some of them,'' the Galla said. ''You go rouse the others. I will stay here.'' His eyes blazed with eagerness to kill his enemies.

"No," Conan said, "we'll all walk back into the firelight. No sense fighting in the dark." Grumbling, the Galla obeyed.

As they stepped into the light of the first fire, Conan said simply, "Vanir coming."

Quietly, without fuss, the men picked up sword and spear and waited. The quieting of their conversation was the only sign that they were ready for combat.

When the Vanir were fifty paces away they cast off their muffling cloaks, raised their battle cry, and rushed into the Cimmerian camp. Their only chance was to plow through the camp in a solid mass, so they came in a wedge, with Starkad at its point. The Cimmerians rushed to meet them joyfully, all their solemnity gone in the frenzy of mortal combat.

The momentum of the wedge pushed the Vanir well into the camp, but as each succeeding wave of black-haired avengers broke against it, the wedge slowed and at last stopped. Then it was a desperate battle that broke up into a multitude of single combats. The Vanir sought desperately to hold a shield wall, while the Cimmerians, innocent of all strategic thought, rushed upon them screaming like madmen.

At the first rush of the wedge Conan was pushed back like the rest, able to strike only intermittently. Only his great strength and his superb sense of balance kept him on his feet while others fell and were pulped beneath the weight of the Vanir swine's-head array. Conan found a low rock behind him and he leaped nimbly atop it. The wedge split to pass the rock and he managed to split a skull as they passed. Then men within the wedge were stabbing at him with spears and Conan gathered his legs beneath him. With a spring that would have awed a Zamoran tumbler, he cleared two ranks of Vanir and landed outside the wedge once again. The Aesir who were fighting there saw and cheered the feat.

Conan ran to the top of the cairn and scanned the battlefield. The Vanir were desperately holding their tight formation, but their forward impetus had been lost. They had not as yet taken many losses, and they would not as long as they held together. The Cimmerians were far more numerous, but they could not make the weight of their numbers felt against the tight knot of men behind their shield wall. Once the Vanir lost their cohesiveness, it would be over swiftly. He looked uphill, but there was no sign of reinforcements yet.

The fires had been built up, and they provided a lurid light for the ferocious goings-on among the cairns. Men cursed and sang and struck, Cimmerian swords rang on Vanir scale, Vanir ax split heads and unarmored bodies. Over all rose the unmistakable stench of blood. Conan could almost hear the satisfied mutter of Cimmerian chiefs as the blood of their enemies trickled down to them.

Conan ran down the side of the cairn and launched himself at the knot of Vanir below. Splitting a shield and the arm behind it, he finished the redbeard with his second blow. A Vanir tried to take the place of the fallen man, only to have his head crushed by a Galla club. Conan shouldered his way into the gap thus made and hewed to both sides, each blow sending a Van howling to the ground. Grimly refusing to let the Vanir advance men to close the gap, Conan worked his way farther in, widening it. Others forced their way in behind him, and the Vanir wedge began to break up. The clamor of striking weapons and screaming men was deafening, and the ground was growing slippery. As the fighting grew more and more desperate, men became truly insane with fury. Conan saw an As throw away his shield, tear off his mailshirt, and dive headfirst into the midst of the Vanir. He was hewn to pieces within moments, but he died with his teeth buried in the throat of a Van. The Vanir howled and foamed, biting the rims of their shields and stamping, each impact of their feet raising a spray of blood from the soaked ground.

The Vanir broke into small knots, then into pairs standing back to back, finally into single warriors with no thought except to take as many enemies with them as they could.

Conan saw the chief he had seen upon leaving Crom's cave and rushed to fight him. There was no thought in any mind of sparing the remaining Vanir. Centuries of hate and vengeance forbade it, and the Vanir would have considered the offer an insult in any case. Once battle was joined, it was always fought to the bitter last in the North.

The Van chieftain grinned mirthlessly as he saw Conan. His armor was still whole, and his elaborate helm bore only a few shallow nicks. He had been busy, though, for his ax was bloody from head to butt, and his hands and arms were bloodied to the shoulders. "Come play with me, blackhair!" he called to Conan. He shook his ax. "Come kiss the maid who has spurned so many of your kin. Perhaps she will like you better!" If Starkad was exhausted from the fight, he showed no sign of it.

"More Vanir blood for our fathers!" Conan shouted, rushing to the fight.

Starkad dodged his first blow and sent back another that Conan avoided only by a desperate dive to the ground. The follow-up ax blow rang against the ground an inch from Conan's back as he rolled. Then Conan was on his feet and his blade rang against Starkad's helm. As the chieftain staggered back Conan hewed a leg from under him. Before Starkad could fall, Conan's third blow split him from shoulder to belt. Standing over the fallen man, Conan spun his sword overhead in a great circle, shedding blood and scales in a wide arc.

Around him the fighting was over, and men stood panting from the terrible exertion. Canach approached Conan. "That was well done, kinsman," the chief said. "It is good for the young men to see a real warrior at his work."

"The battle was ill done, though," Conan said, glaring at the heaps of dead. "We lost too many just to kill so few Vanir, not even a hundred of them. They must have taken at least as many of us. There are ways to handle such a situation without such losses."

Canach shrugged. "That is not our way of fighting, and the Vanir are doughty fighters, not like your soft southerners. Besides"—the chief managed a faint smile—"I did not notice you holding back and pondering stratagems."

Conan grinned ruefully. "You have the right of it. In the end I am as Cimmerian as the rest. Do not let the men relax. I think there will be more fighting before the sun rises."

"Good," said Canach. "Many had no chance to wet their blades. I would not like to take them home discontent."

The sky to the east was beginning to turn gray when old Milach came to him, accompanied by Chulainn. Neither man was badly wounded, but their notched weapons proclaimed they had been in the thick of the fighting.

"I am sorry I thought you had become soft, Conan," said Milach. "I have been watching you in the fighting. You are not too far off your best speed and power even now."

"It must be the oat porridge," Conan said. "It makes a man lose the fear of death."

A glimmer up the slope caught Conan's eye. The sun was still below the horizon, but its earliest rays were shining at the very crest of Ben Morgh. Inexorably, the light would descend the slopes of the mountain, eventually reaching Crom's cave. He had to be in the cave when that happened. Conan went to a cairn and found the bundle of belongings he had cached there. Within a cloak was the flask given to him by Hathor-Ka. In one of the little encampments he found a fire pot, a small jar pierced with holes for bearing glowing coals in a bed of ashes. He did not want to waste time striking flint against steel when he reached the cave.

As Conan climbed the slope from the Field of the Dead, he found that others were falling in behind him. The sky was paling, and they no longer needed the light of the fires to fight by. All wanted to drive the demons from Crom's mountain home, and they would enter the caverns to do so should it prove necessary. Conan had expected the demons to strike ere now. Soon it would be light. Then he remembered the unnatural cloud they sometimes took with them.

There was a rising mutter when the warriors saw the gaping pit that had not been there before. This was a desecration as great as the Vanir defilement of the cairns. They were almost at the lip of the pit when all the horrors of Hell came boiling out of it. One instant, the field before the pit was empty. The next, Conan was fighting desperately for his life against something that looked like a cross between a moth and an ape.

The thing had long reddish hair and withered wings and gigantic compound eyes. Conan was more concerned with the wide-bladed glaive with which it was trying to kill him. It fought with no art he could interpret, but sliced at him with a clear intent to slay. It took him a few moments to determine its timing, then he stepped in and pulped its skull with his sword. The thing continued to flail away blindly until Conan hewed away its head, then it fell, still struggling futilely.

All around Conan was a demented battle being carried on by screaming men and things from a nightmare. The insect-creatures were dying easily, but the lizard-things were exacting a toll. Conan felt a fierce pride swelling in him. Any civilized army he had seen would have fled in terror from this unearthly force, and all their polish and discipline would have availed them naught. But this little horde of Cimmerians with their Aesir allies rushed to do battle as if they had no other purpose on Earth.

A howling horror of tentacles and batwings bore down on Conan, and he hacked it in twain, burying his blade half its length in the soil in the process. He wrenched the sword free and sunlight glimmered on its bluish length. Conan looked up the slope and saw that the light of the morning sun was almost to the level of the cave.

He had no worry over the progress of this fight. The things died, and if they could die, the Cimmerians would kill them all. He began to climb. Twice he was attacked by unclean creatures. Twice he shook their blood from his sword. Then he stood in the mouth of the cave.

The whole cave shook to strange vibrations. Far to the rear, near the feet of Crom, he could see two tiny figures capering about some sort of altar. He walked toward the rear, collecting firewood as he went. As he had suspected, he now saw that the two were the foreigners he had first spied with the Vanir. One of them, the smaller, saw Conan, and his eyes widened. Drawing a long dagger from his sash, the younger foreigner came at Conan.

Conan dropped his bundle of wood and smashed the fire pot down upon it. The dry wood caught quickly.

"Filthy barbarian!" squealed the young man, whom Conan now recognized as a Vendhyan. "How dare you interfere!"

The man darted in expertly, like a trained assassin. The dagger was a blur as it lanced toward the Cimmerian's belly. With an almost casual flick of his sword Conan sent the Vendhyan staggering back, hands clasped to his bloodied head, screaming.

The fire was going well now, and the first rays of sunlight were beginning to stream into the cave. Conan pried the stopper from the flask he had borne so far and poured a fine dust, like ashes, upon the flame.

"Hathor-Ka! Hathor-Ka! Hathor-Ka!" Conan's voice boomed through the cave like thunder, and his scalp prickled at the sorcerous forces being unleashed here.

His mission had been carried out. His vow was fulfilled and he could leave if he wished. Something kept him from making his escape, much as he wished to be away from these doings. A thick cloud of smoke formed over the flames of the fire he had built. Gradually, as if from far away, he began to hear a voice singing in a language never meant for human tongue. The smoke took shape and solidified, and the voice grew nearer, and he saw the beautiful, evil Stygian sorceress before him in the cave. Her feet amid the flames were not burned, and her garments stirred to a wind that Conan could not feel. She ignored Conan, and he watched awestruck as she walked toward the back of the cave. Drawn by a force he could not have named, Conan followed.

She stopped by the edge of the pit before the feet of Crom. Jaganath stood a few paces from her, sweat pouring down his fat face as he shrieked his spells. The two mages carried on each as if the other were not there. A deep rumbling came from the pit at their feet and the light within the cavern altered subtly. Conan stood in silence. His sword was clenched in his white-knuckled fist, but what use was a sword against the sorcerous forces being unleashed here?

Then yet another figure appeared. From behind the statue of Crom, a stately form emerged from shadowy obscurity into the light. It wore long, elaborate robes into the sleeves of which its hands were tucked. A towering headdress crowned the apparition. Although Conan did not know it, the latest wizard to appear wore the regalia of a Khitan Wizard of the First Rank, with the special attributes of the Order of the Silver Peacock.

"You have changed, Cha," Conan said.

"You look much the same. What you see before us is the spectacle of two foolish, presumptuous mages who think they can become gods."

"Can they?"

"It is possible." Cha removed a hand from a sleeve and stroked the long, snowy beard and dangling moustaches that spread over his breast. "But all shall take place as the gods wish."

Now the rumbling was all-pervasive. The chanting of the two wizards had become so high-pitched that it almost left the realm of human hearing. An unthinkable shape began to

ooze from the pit leading to the caverns below. Conan remembered it from the other pit. It was a writhing horror of
tentacles and jointed legs and sucker pads and fanged
mouths. It had eyes like jewels and in all was so unnatural
that Conan could bear to look upon it for only a moment.
Most horribly, it bore an unmistakable air of terrible
intelligence.

"This is the thing they have called from another universe," Cha said as calmly as if he were commenting upon
the evolutions of a country dance. "It is a sort of god which
they think will strengthen their spell. They are wrong. These
things give no help to this world. From that same world
Hathor-Ka brought the beings you thought of as demons. She
wanted them to round up prisoners and have them here, ready
for sacrifice. You and your Cimmerians foiled that. The
Vendhyan brought his own men for sacrifice, but they cheated
him and died cleanly. No advantage to either now."

Suddenly, Hathor-Ka's voice faltered while Jaganath's continued steadily. Her eyes widened with some awful knowledge. Lovingly, the monstrous thing reached out a tentacle
and wrapped it about her waist. It raised her slowly while she
chanted madly. Her chant broke into a shriek as it drew her
into one of its clusters of mouthlike orifices.

Jaganath's voice swelled to a triumphant climax and then
stopped abruptly. All was silent in the cavern. Then Jaganath
began to grow. He swelled and gained bulk and majesty until
he towered above the two little figures on the cavern floor.

"I fulfill the prophecy of Skelos!" he shouted ecstatically.
"I am master of all the sorcerers of Earth, until the next fall
of the Arrows of Indra!"

"No foreign wizard reigns in Crom's House!" Conan
bellowed. Striding to the huge figure, Conan took his sword
in both hands and, with all his weight and bulk behind it,
thrust the blue steel into the belly before him. To his own

astonishment, it went in easily and stayed there. He released the hilt and backed away.

Jaganath looked down in puzzlement, then smiled. "Think you that any weapon made by mortal hands can harm me?" He enveloped the hilt in his huge hand and tugged, but it would not pull free. Now Cha raised his arm and pointed at the sword protruding from Jaganath's vast belly.

"Behold the sword of the Kings of Valusia, forged more than four thousand years ago from a fragment of a meteor— one of the Arrows of Indra!"

Jaganath's face became transformed with rage. Frantically, he wrenched at the sword, widening the great rent in his belly. Blood, smoke, and flame poured from the wound, and Jaganath's demented howling reverberated through the cave, causing stones to fall from the ceiling. Slowly, the wizard-demigod began to shrink.

"This cannot be!" Jaganath shrieked, his voice dwindling as did his body. "I am a god! I am the king of sorcerers!"

Conan stepped forward and gripped the sword. With a powerful heave he pulled the blade loose from the obese body with a hideous wet sound. Jaganath collapsed to the floor, a mere fat man once again. Soon he was a fat corpse.

An unearthly sound came from the back of the cave. Conan looked to see the pit-thing coming toward them. Cha took Conan by the shoulder. "Time to go now!"

Cha's massive dignity disappeared as he gathered his long robes up around his skinny knees and dashed for the cave entrance. Conan wasted no time in following. Behind them a great rumbling began, and the whole mountaintop trembled.

They had gained the entrance when Conan stopped and looked back. The evil thing was still there, but something was different about the scene. Then he saw it. The throne of

Crom was vacant. His mind just had time to register this fact, then he saw a gigantic stone foot descend upon the squirming horror and the body of Jaganath, grinding them relentlessly into the stone floor.

Sixteen

Farewell to Cimmeria

Conan sat upon a rock outcropping with his cloak drawn close about him. Snow had been falling since he and Cha had come out of the cave. Winter had come to Ben Morgh, but any Northlander preferred the clean privations of winter to the unnatural warmth they had found on Ben Morgh. All day and all night the clans had scoured the caves beneath Ben Morgh, bringing out what captives they could find alive. Many were Cimmerians or other northern people, but some were of nations nobody could identify, not even Conan or Cha. The tunnel entrances of the lower pit gaped wide now, but nobody had been able to work up the nerve to look into the House of Crom.

Cha came up to Conan. Once again he was a ragged mountebank. "All out now. Lower caverns caving in. Soon this pit collapse as well. Your Crom not want them."

"Why did Hathor-Ka fail?" Conan asked.

"She ally herself with Thoth-Amon. He very great wizard, evil but very wise. He know better than to fool with these powers. He pretend to give her whole spell of Great Summoning, but he leave out crucial verse. He could have put an

239

end to this thing long ago, but he think it good way to get rid of rivals.''

"I hope I never encounter him," Conan grumbled.

Cha held out a hand, palm up. "Now, you give me back amulet? One of my best. I may need it."

Conan took the thing in his hand. "I paid for this. What will you give me for it?''

Cha grinned. "Tell you good fortune?''

"It had better be a good one, not like last time.''

"Very well. How you like this? Someday you be king of Aquilonia. Good, not so?''

"Well, I suppose that's worth an amulet." Conan took it off, not believing a word. He tossed the thing to Cha, who caught it, chuckling. "Good-bye now. Got to go catch my dragon." The old man disappeared among the rocks, and Conan shook his head, sorry to see the last of him.

At the bottom of the Field of the Dead he found the host assembled. A new cairn marked the burial place of the men who had fallen in the battle. The Cimmerians had completed their simple funeral rites and were ready to depart. Conan found Canach with the other chiefs. "What shall we do with these?" he said, gesturing toward the group of freed prisoners who shivered in the cold.

"Give them provisions and send them on their way, I suppose," said Canach. "Some of the women might make good wives. A little new blood now and then does not come amiss.''

"After the caves," said Wulfhere, grinning, "even Cimmeria might seem tolerable.''

They descended the slopes of Ben Morgh, and into the hills beyond. From time to time the fighting men of a clan would split off from the main group to return to their lands. All would be at peace until the last clan had returned home, then the feuds would begin once more. Once they all halted and looked up. Overhead, above the clouds, they could hear a sound, as of the beating of great wings.

By the time they reached Canach land all had gone except Conan's closest kin and the little band of Aesir. Near the winter village they halted for a last time. Conan and Chulainn stood together. Chulainn with his arm about Bronwith. "Will you stay the winter with us, Conan?" Chulainn asked.

"No, my place is not here. It was good to come back and see my kin, but it will be good to be away again. I go with Wulfhere's band, to winter in the halls of Asgard."

"Then good fortune to you, kinsman," Bronwith said.

Conan turned to go but something stopped him. The great sword at his waist did not feel right somehow. It had been his sword. Now it was not. He took it from his waist and handed it, sheathed, to Chulainn. "For your son," he said. With the Aesir, he mounted one of the little mountain ponies.

"Don't ride naked, Conan," said Wulfhere. The As tossed him a Vanir blade taken in the battle and Conan belted it on.

"Conan!" called Chulainn. Conan wheeled his pony to face his kinsman. "To which son shall we give this? We intend to have many. To the first? That one we shall name for you."

Conan thought for a moment, then said: "To the strongest." He turned again and, with the Aesir, he rode from the land of his people.

Look for the Next
Original Conan—Conan the Fearless—
Coming From Tor in January

The sun had made but a small part of its journey across the morning sky when Conan entered the city of Mornstadinos. From a distance the Cimmerian had been unable to perceive the convolutions of the narrow streets. He now traversed myriad alleys, cul-de-sacs, and cobbled roads, which appeared to have been laid out by someone besotted, blind, or mad. If a pattern existed to the maze, Conan was unable to discern it. Here sat a stable, full of horses and stinking of dung; next to the stable stood a temple, replete with cowled oblates; beyond that edifice, an open air market dealt in fruit and baked goods.

The barbarian's stomach rumbled, insistent in its hunger. He strode to the market, attracting more than a few stares at his muscular form. From a woven basket Conan extracted a loaf of hard black bread. He poked the loaf with one finger, then waved the bread at an old woman. "How much?" he said.

The woman named a figure: "Four coppers."

Conan shook his head. "Nay, old one. I do not wish to buy your house and grandchildren, only this loaf of stale bread."

The old woman cackled. "Since it is obvious you are a stranger, I shall make you a bargain. Three coppers."

"Again, I have no desire for the entire basket of these rocks you would sell as bread, only the one." Conan waved the loaf and scowled.

"Ah, you would cheat an old woman of her hard labor? Very well then, I will accept two coppers and the loss, so that you may think us hospitable in the Jewel of Corinthia."

"Where is your dagger, old woman? Surely a cutpurse who would steal my money must need a blade. Though I will allow that your tongue and wit are sharp enough."

The woman cackled again. "Ah, you're a handsome boy; you remind me of my son. I could not see you starve for want of a copper. One will buy you the best bread on the street."

"Done, grandmother."

Conan reached into his pouch and retrieved one of his few coins. He handed it to the old woman, who nodded, smiling.

"One other favor," Conan said. "You are right in calling me a stranger. Where might a man find an inn and some wine with which to wash down the best bread on the street?"

"A man of means might find a number of places. But a man who would haggle over a few coppers with an old woman has fewer choices, meseems. Down this road, two turnings to the right and one to the left such a man could find the Milk of Wolves Inn. And, if this man was some outlander who might not be able to read civilized writings, he might look for a picture of a wolf *salient* above the door."

"A wolf what?"

"Standing on her hind legs about to leap," the old woman said, cackling again.

"Well-met, then, mistress Baker. And farewell."

Conan located the Milk of Wolves Inn with no difficulty, and bearing his loaf of black bread, strode inside. The youthful hour seemed no barrier to the fair-sized crowd standing or seated at long wooden tables around the room. Most of the men appeared to be locals, judging from looks and clothing; several women were serving steaming bowls, and others offered hints of pleasures other than food or drink. He had been in many such places, passable, for the most part, and cheap.

The Cimmerian found a vacant place at one end of a table and seated himself. He looked around the room, scrutinizing the patrons. Most of the men were probably poor but engaged in some honest trade: coopers, smiths, tradesmen, and the like. To his left Conan saw a group of four men who looked more unsavory, probably cutpurses or strong-arm thieves. The largest of the four was of medium height, but very broad and heavily muscled, with dark eyes and blue-black hair; further, he had an enormous hook nose, which resembled a bird's beak. Conan had seen men with similar countenances before, men bearing a mix of Shemite and Stygian blood. This beak-faced one looked dangerous, not a man to turn one's back on.

Seated near the four were an odd pair: an old man with white hair and the weight of a good sixty or seventy winters riding his stooped shoulders and, a girl, a child of twelve or thirteen. The old man was dressed in a long robe with full sleeves. The girl, auburn-haired, wore blue hose and boots and a short jerkin of supple leather; additionally, she carried a short sword under a broad belt, in the Turanian style.

"Your pleasure, sir?"

Conan looked up at the speaker, a fat wench draped in a shapeless dress much stained by food and drink. He fetched out one of his last three coppers and held it up. "Would this buy me a cup of decent wine?"

"It will buy you a cup of wine. How decent such a beverage is I leave to your judgment."

"That bad, eh? Well, I am in no positon to be choosy. I shall risk the vintage."

The girl left, taking Conan's coin. The latter half-turned, to study the old man and the girl.

Conan quickly became aware that he was not the only person regarding the pair. The four he had marked as strong-arm thieves were also taking an uncommon interest. Such did not bode well for them, the Cimmerian figured. Well, it was not his business. He turned his gaze back toward the serving girl, who approached bearing an earthen mug brimming with dark red liquid. Some of the wine sloshed over the lip of the cup as she set it onto the table. Without saying anything, the girl moved off to see to other patrons.

Conan tasted the wine. In truth, it was not bad; certainly, he had drunk both better and worse. It would wash the bread down and help fill his belly, for now. Later, he could worry about his next meal. He broke a chunk of the black bread and tore off a mouthful of it with his strong teeth. The bread, too, was passable. He chewed slowly, savoring the taste.

Nearby, beak-nose gestured at the old man and girl with a quick movement of his head. Two of his companions rose from the table and began to sidle toward the pair. One of the men toyed with the handle of his dagger; the other man merely scratched at his scraggly beard.

Beneath drawn brows Conan watched, interested. He took another bite of the bread.

When the two men were a few steps away from the old man, several people seated or standing near the inn's door-way gasped. Conan glanced toward the door and saw men scrambling to get out of the way of something. He could not see what caused the commotion, but it was as if a wind cut a path through a field of tall grain. As the crowd rippled aside, the cause became apparent.

Scuttling across the sawdust-covered floor was a spider. This creature was like none the Cimmerian had ever gazed upon before. It was the size of Conan's fist, covered with fine hair, and glowed like a lantern inlaid with rubies: indeed, the thing *pulsed,* as might a throbbing heart.

Without hesitation the spider ran to the table at which the old man sat; in an eye blink it scuttled up a table leg; another second saw the glowing arachnid leap in a graceful arc to land squarely in the mug of wine the old man held in one gnarled fist. The wine emitted a loud sizzle, a pop, and a small cloud of red vapor suddenly floated above the mug.

With every eye locked into a stare upon him, the old man calmly smiled, raised the cup to his lips, and drank.

Beak-nose's two minions suddenly decided they had business elsewhere, that they were late for such business, and that further delay would be disastrous. At least it seemed that way to Conan as he watched the two men scramble over each other in order to be first to reach the door.

Behind the Cimmerian someone uttered an oath and muttered, "Magic!"

At that moment the girl seated next to the old man leaped up. She tossed a moldy sunfruit into the air. Conan saw her set and guessed what would happen. A heartbeat later the girl pulled the short sword from its sheath smoothly and slashed it back and forth at the falling fruit. At first it might have appeared she had missed with her strokes, but Conan's sharp eyes beheld the truth and he grinned even as the fruit continued its fall—now in four pieces instead of one.

The Cimmerian chewed another bite of bread. Here was a message for all who chose this particular morning to breakfast at the Milk of Wolves Inn: this old man and girl were not so helpless as they might appear; best to tread elsewhere for easy pickings.

Beak-nose was not amused. He glowered at the old man, his own cup of wine clutched so tightly that the knuckles of his dark hand were chalk-white.

Someone at the door gasped again. A second spider appeared, this time heading for the foot of the beak-nosed man's table. Without preamble the hairy arachnid scrambled up onto the rough wood and leaped into beak-nose's wine.

Conan laughed. A challenge! Would beak-nose dare to drink?

Uttering a cry of wordless rage, beak-nose leaped up and tossed the mug away with a backhanded flinging motion. The mug and its contents flew straight at Conan's face.

There was no danger, the Cimmerian knew. He raised one muscled arm to bat the mug away; unfortunately, the hand he chose contained the loaf of bread, the better part of which was as yet uneaten. The wine drenched the bread as the mug struck it, knocking Conan's breakfast onto the filth of the much-trodden sawdust floor. He stared at the bread as it rolled over three times, covering itself with a layer of grime.

In better times such an occurrence might be amusing, especially were it to happen to someone else; but at the moment Conan failed to see the humor. First his horse and all his gold had been lost; now, his food. The young giant took a deep breath, and the air fed his quick rage as wind feeds a hot fire.

Beak-nose had drawn his own blade and was advancing upon his intended victim. The child bravely pulled her own small sword and moved to cover the white-haired man, who tried to pull her back to safety.

Conan's broadsword hissed as the leather sheath stroked it in its passage. He raised his blade and clenched the handle with both hands. "You—you *scum*!" he roared.

Beak-nose turned in surprise. What he saw must have surely alarmed him, for he spun and tried to position his sword for a block or parry. At the same time the dark man tried to backstep away. He managed neither. Conan's sword caught him in the middle of the breastbone and a hand's span of sharp steel sliced its way downward, opening the man as might a vivisectionist, from sternum to crotch. The man's face contorted in shock as his entrails spilled through the massive rent in his body. He fell backward, his spirit already on its way to join his ancestors.

Conan's rage was only partially spent. He looked around for the fourth member of the band. This one, however, was not in evidence. The Cimmerian glared at the inn's patrons, who all shrank away from the big youth with the bloody sword. All save one.

The young girl approached Conan, smiling. She had sheathed her sword and when she drew near he saw that the girl barely reached his chest in height. With great reluctance he lowered his broadsword. He stared at the child. "Well?"

"Thank you, sir, for saving us." Her voice was warm. Indeed, the very air seemed to grow warmer as she stood there staring up at the Cimmerian.

"Do not thank me," Conan said, his voice still rough and angry. "The scum destroyed my breakfast. Would that he had put up a better fight, so that I might have made him suffer for it."

The girl's mouth opened into an *O* as Conan spoke, her face filled with shock and puzzlement.

The murmur of voices began to rise, to fill the inn.

"—you see that strike? Such power—!"

"—split him like a chicken—"

"—foreigner from some backwoods—"

A thin man with a jagged scar that lifted both his lip and left nostril came closer, warily watching the Cimmerian's unsheathed blade. He wore a splattered apron that might have once been white but now displayed the remains of too many spilled wine cups and meals to be more than a splotched gray. Likely the owner of the inn, Conan judged.

The innkeep glanced down at the dead man. His perpetual sneer seemed to increase a bit. "So, Arsheva of Khemi has finally picked the wrong victim." The man looked up at Conan. "Few men deserve such an exit from this life so much as he; he shall not be missed, and no mistake about that." He pulled a rag from the pocket of his apron and tendered it to Conan. "Here, wipe your blade, sir, lest Arsheva's gore chew with teeth of rust upon the steel."

Conan took the greasy rag and methodically cleaned his sword.

"Still," the man said, "the Senate's Deputation will no doubt eventually arrive for an investigation of Arsheva's passing. I trust you had sufficient reason to dispatch him to the next world?"

Conan slid his sword into his leathern home. "Aye," he began, "my reasons were just. This offal—"

"—intended to attack myself and my assistant," the old white-haired man said. "This man is our bodyguard; he was merely performing his job in protecting us."

Conan stared at him. What was he about? He started to speak, but the old man interrupted again.

"We shall finish our breakfast whilst awaiting the deputies. If you would bring my friend here a tray to replace the meal he lost, along with a bottle of your better wine, I should be most grateful." Here the old man raised a wrinkled and age-twisted hand bearing a small coin of silver. "And the balance of this for your trouble in this matter."

Scar-face took the coin, and nodded. "Aye. Obviously, a gentleman of means such as yourself will have no difficulties convincing the Senate's Deputation of your position in this matter." He drew back a chair for Conan at the old man's table. "I'll tend to your meal, sir."

Seated with the old man and girl, Conan waited for answers to his unasked questions. Earlier, he had held his tongue, reasoning that the old man had some purpose in coming to his aid. Perhaps it was merely to thank him for splitting the blackguard who would have attacked the girl. While unintentional, Conan had served them, certainly. But the barbarian now suspected there was more to be said than words of thanks.

The old man waited until the inn's patrons focused their attention elsewhere before he spoke. "I am Vitarius and this"—he waved his arm in its voluminous sleeve toward the girl—"this is Eldia, my assistant. I am a conjurer of small talent, an entertainer of sorts. We wish to thank you for taking our part in this matter."

Conan nodded, waiting.

"I sensed you were about to speak of your true reason for slaying our would-be assassin—he who slew your loaf of bread—which is why I injected my remarks."

Conan nodded again. The old man was not without sharpness of sight and wit.

"The deputies who will come to speak with us are corrupt for the most part. A few pieces of silver will expedite the resolution in our favor without a doubt; still, carving a man for knocking a loaf of bread to the floor is hardly considered just punishment in the minds of the Mornstadinosian Senate. Protecting a patron from attack by a cutthroat thief is sufficient reason to draw steel, however."

The young giant nodded. "I am Conan of Cimmeria. I have done you a favor and you have thus returned it; let us then consider the scales balanced."

"So be it," Vitarius said. "After breakfast, at least."

"Aye, that I will allow."

A serving girl arrived with a tray of hard rolls, fruit, and a greasy cut of pork, along with another cup of wine of a vintage better than the first drink Conan had partaken of. He ate with gusto, and washed the food down with gulps of the red liquid.

Vitarius watched Conan intently. When the barbarian was done with his meal, the conjurer spoke. "We are quits on debts; still, I have a proposition in which you might find some merit. Eldia and I demonstrate our simple illusions at street fairs and market gatherings and we could use a man such as yourself.''

Conan shook his head. "I truckle not with magic."

"Magic? Surely you do not think my illusions are magic? Nay, I work with the simplest of the arts, no more. Would I be in such a place as this were I a *real* magician?"

Conan considered that. The old man had a point.

"Still, of what use could I be to a conjurer?"

Vitarius glanced at Eldia, then looked back at Conan. "That blade of yours, for one. Your strength, for another. Eldia and I are hardly capable of protecting ourselves from such as the one you slew. She is adept with her own sword, for demonstrating speed and skill, but hardly a match for a fully grown man in a duel. My illusions might scare the superstitious, but in the end can hardly sway a determined assassin, as you have just seen."

Conan chewed on his lower lip. "I am bound for Nemedia."

"Surely such a considerable journey would be easier were you mounted and well-appointed with supplies?"

"What makes you think I lack such things?"

Vitarius peered around the inn, then back at Conan. "Would a man of property be spending his time in such a place?"

That reasoning was sound, but Conan followed the line a step further. "Then, good conjure artist, why are *you* in such a place?"

Vitarius laughed, and slapped his thigh. "Ah, forgive me for underestimating you, Conan of Cimmeria. That a man is a barbarian does not mean he lacks wits. As it happens, we are conserving our money for supplies; we, too, intend to leave this fair city, to travel westward. Our path will veer southward, toward Argos. We wish to—ah—travel in some style, in an armed caravan, and thus avoid possible encounters with the bandits along the Ophir Road."

"Ah." Conan studied Vitarius and Eldia. He had been a thief, to be sure, but he had nothing against honest work for a brief enough time. Besides, he was in no great hurry to reach Nemedia. In any event, the journey would be a great deal easier astride a good horse than on foot.

"A silver coin a day," Vitarius said. "We shall be ready to leave within the month, I should think, and surely such a short diversion would not inconvenience you greatly?"

Conan considered the sorry state of his money pouch. A good horse and supplies could be had for twenty or thirty pieces of silver, certainly. And such work, guarding a conjurer and his assistant from sneak thieves for a moon or two, could not be too taxing.

Conan smiled at Vitarius. "Master of glowing spiders, you have engaged a bodyguard."

Conan
the
Indestructible
by L. Sprague de Camp

The greatest hero of the magic-rife Hyborian Age was a northern barbarian, Conan the Cimmerian, about whose deeds a cycle of legend revolves. While these legends are largely based on the attested facts of Conan's life, some tales are inconsistent with others. So we must reconcile the contradictions in the saga as best we can.

In Conan's veins flowed the blood of the people of Atlantis, the brilliant city-state swallowed by the sea 8,000 years before his time. He was born into a clan that claimed a homeland in the northwest corner of Cimmeria, along the shadowy borders of Vanaheim and the Pictish wilderness. His grandfather had fled his own people because of a blood feud and sought refuge with the people of the North. Conan himself first saw daylight on a battlefield during a raid by the Vanir.

Before he had weathered fifteen snows, the young Cimmerian's fighting skills were acclaimed around the council fires. In that year the Cimmerians, usually at one another's throats, joined forces to repel the warlike Gundermen who, intent on colonizing southern Cimmeria, had pushed across the Aquilonian border and established the frontier post of

255

Venarium. Conan joined the howling, blood-mad horde that swept out of the northern hills, stormed over the stockade walls, and drove the Aquilonians back across their frontier.

At the sack of Venarium, Conan, still short of his full growth, stood six feet tall and weighed 180 pounds. He had the vigilance and stealth of the born woodsman, the iron-hardness of the mountain man, and the Herculean physique of his blacksmith father. After the plunder of the Aquilonian outpost, Conan returned for a time to his tribe.

Restless under the conflicting passions of his adolescence, Conan spent several months with a band of Æsir as they raided the Vanir and the Hyperboreans. He soon learned that some Hyperborean citadels were ruled by a caste of widely-feared magicians, called Witchmen. Undaunted, he took part in a foray against Haloga Castle, when he found that Hyperborean slavers had captured Rann, the daughter of Njal, chief of the Æsir band.

Conan gained entrance to the castle and spirited out Rann Njalsdatter; but on the flight out of Hyperborea, Njal's band was overtaken by an army of living dead. Conan and the other Æsir survivors were led away to slavery ("Legions of the Dead").

Conan did not long remain a captive. Working at night, he ground away at one link of his chain until it was weak enough to break. Then one stormy night, whirling a four-foot length of heavy chain, he fought his way out of the slave pen and vanished into the downpour.

Another account of Conan's early years tells a different tale. This narrative, on a badly broken clay prism from Nippur, states that Conan was enslaved as a boy of ten or twelve by Vanir raiders and set to work turning a grist mill. When he reached his full growth, he was bought by a Hyrkanian pitmaster who traveled with a band of professional fighters staging contests for the amusement of the Vanir and Æsir. At this time Conan received his training with weapons. Later he escaped and made his way south to Zamora (*Conan the Barbarian*).

Of the two versions, the records of Conan's enslavement by the Hyrkanians at sixteen, found in a papyrus in the British Museum, appear much more legible and self-consistent. But this question may never be settled.

Although free, the youth found himself half a hostile kingdom away from home. Instinctively he fled into the mountains at the southern extremity of Hyperborea. Pursued by a pack of wolves, he took refuge in a cave. Here he discovered the seated mummy of a gigantic chieftain of ancient times, with a heavy bronze sword across its knees. When Conan seized the sword, the corpse arose and attacked him ("The Thing in the Crypt").

Continuing southward into Zamora, Conan came to Arenjun, the notorious "City of Thieves." Green to civilization and, save for some rudimentary barbaric ideas of honor and chivalry, wholly lawless by nature, he carved a niche for himself as a professional thief.

Being young and more daring than adroit, Conan's progress in his new profession was slow until he joined forces with Taurus of Nemedia in a quest for the fabulous jewel called the "Heart of the Elephant." The gem lay in the almost impregnable tower of the infamous mage Yara, captor of the extraterrestrial being Yag-Kosha ("The Tower of the Elephant").

Seeking greater opportunities to ply his trade, Conan wandered westward to the capital of Zamora, Shadizar the Wicked. For a time his thievery prospered, although the whores of Shadizar soon relieved him of his gains. During one larceny, he was captured by the men of Queen Taramis of Shadizar, who sent him on a mission to recover a magical horn wherewith to resurrect an ancient, evil god. Taramis's plot led to her own destruction (*Conan the Destroyer*).

The barbarian's next exploit involved a fellow thief, a girl named Tamira. The Lady Jondra, an arrogant aristocrat of Shadizar, owned a pair of priceless rubies. Baskaran Imalla, a religious fanatic raising a cult among the Kezankian hillmen, coveted the jewels to gain control over a fire-breathing dragon he had raised from an egg. Conan and Tamira both yearned for the rubies; Tamira took a post as lady's maid to Jondra for a chance to steal them.

An ardent huntress, Jondra set forth with her maid and her men-at-arms to slay Baskaran's dragon. Baskaran captured the two women and was about to offer them to his pet as a snack when Conan intervened (*Conan the Magnificent*).

Soon Conan was embroiled in another adventure. A stranger hired the youth to steal a casket of gems sent by the King of Zamora to the King of Turan. The stranger, a priest of the serpent-god Set, wanted the jewels for magic against his enemy, the renegade priest Amanar.

Amanar's emissaries, who were hominoid reptiles, had stolen the gems. Although wary of magic, Conan set out to recover the loot. He became involved with a bandette, Karela, called the Red Hawk, who proved the ultimate bitch; when Conan saved her from rape, she tried to kill him. Amanar's party had also carried off to the renegade's stronghold a dancing girl whom Conan had promised to help (*Conan the Invincible*).

Soon rumors of treasure sent Conan to the nearby ruins of ancient Larsha, just ahead of the soldiers dispatched to arrest him. After all but their leader, Captain Nestor, had perished in an accident arranged by Conan, Nestor and Conan joined forces to plunder the treasure; but ill luck deprived them of their gains ("The Hall of the Dead").

Conan's recent adventures had left him with an aversion to warlocks and Eastern sorceries. He fled northwestward through Corinthia into Nemedia, the second most powerful Hyborian kingdom. In Nemedia he resumed his profession successfully enough to bring his larcenies to the notice of Aztrias Pentanius, ne'er-do-well nephew of the governor. Oppressed by gambling debts, this young gentleman hired the outlander to purloin a Zamorian goblet, carved from a single diamond, that stood in the temple-museum of a wealthy collector.

Conan's appearance in the temple-museum coincided with its master's sudden demise and brought the young thief to the unwelcome attention of Demetrio, of the city's Inquisitorial Council. This caper also gave Conan his second experience with the dark magic of the serpent-brood of Set, conjured up by the Stygian sorcerer Thoth-Amon ("The God in the Bowl").

Having made Nemedia too hot to hold him, Conan drifted south into Corinthia, where he continued to occupy himself with the acquisition of other person's property. By diligent application, the Cimmerian earned the repute of one of the boldest thieves in Corinthia. Poor judgment of women, however, cast him into chains until a turn in local politics brought freedom and a new career. An ambitious nobleman, Murilo, turned him loose to slit the throat of the Red Priest, Nabonidus, the scheming power behind the local throne. This venture gathered a prize collection of rogues in Nabonidus's mansion and ended in a mire of blood and treachery ("Rogues in the House").

Conan wandered back to Arenjun and began to earn a semi-honest living by stealing back for their owners valuable objects that others had filched from them. He undertook to recover a magical gem, the Eye of Erlik, from the wizard Hissar Zul and return it to its owner, the Kahn of Zamboula.

There is some question about the chronology of Conan's life at this point. A recently-translated tablet from Asshurbanipal's library states that Conan was about seventeen at the time. This would place the episode right after that of "The Tower of the Elephant," which indeed is mentioned in the cuneiform. But from internal evidence, this event seems to have taken place several years later. For one thing, Conan appears too clever, mature and sophisticated; for another, the fragmentary medieval Arabic manuscript *Kitab al-Qunn* implies that Conan was well into his twenties by then.

The first translator of the Asshurbanipal tablet, Prof. Dr. Andreas von Fuss of the Münchner Staatsmuseum, read Conan's age as "17." In Babylonian cuneiform, "17" is expressed by two circles followed by three vertical wedges, with a horizontal wedge above the three for "minus"—hence "twenty minus three." But Academician Leonid Skram of the Moscow Archaeological Institute asserts that the depression over the vertical wedges is merely a dent made by the pick of a careless escavator, and the numeral properly reads "23."

Anyhow, Conan learned of the Eye of Erlik when he heard a discussion between an adventuress, Isparana, and her confederate. He invaded the wizard's mansion, but the wizard caught Conan and deprived him of his soul. Conan's soul was imprisoned in a mirror, there to remain until a crowned ruler broke the glass. Hissar Zul thus compelled Conan to follow Isparana and recover the talisman; but when the Cimmerian returned the Eye to Hissar Zul, the ungrateful mage tried to slay him (*Conan and the Sorcerer*).

Conan, his soul still englassed, accepted legitimate employment as bodyguard to a Khaurani noblewoman, Khashtris. This lady set out for Khauran with Conan, another guard, Shubal, and several retainers. When the other servants plotted to rob and murder their employer, Conan and Shubal saved her and escorted her to Khauran. There Conan found the widowed Queen Ialamis being courted by a young nobleman who was not at all what he seemed (*Conan the Mercenary*).

With his soul restored, Conan learned from an Iranistani, Khassek, that the Khan of Zamboula still wanted the Eye of Erlik. In Zamboula, the Turanian governor, Akter Khan, had hired the wizard Zafra, who ensorcelled swords, so that they would slay on command. En route, Conan encountered Isparana, with whom he developed a lust-hate relationship. Unaware of the magical swords, Conan continued to Zamboula and delivered the amulet. But the nefarious Zafra convinced the Khan that Conan was dangerous and should be killed on general principles (*Conan: the Sword of Skelos*).

Conan had enjoyed his taste of Hyborian-Age intrigue. It became clear that there was no basic difference between the opportunities in the palace and those in the Rats' Den, whereas the pickings were far better in high places. Besides, he wearied of the furtive, squalid life of a thief.

He was not, however, yet committed to a strictly law-abiding life. When unemployed, he took time out for a venture in smuggling. An attempt to poison him sent him to Vendhya, a land of wealth and squalor, philosophy and fanatacism, idealism and treachery (*Conan the Victorious*).

Soon after, Conan turned up in the Turanian seaport of Aghrapur. A new cult had established headquarters there under the warlock Jhandar, who needed victims to be drained of blood and reanimated as servants. Conan refused the offer of a former fellow thief, Emilio, to take part in a raid on Jhandar's stronghold to steal a fabulous ruby necklace. A Turanian sergeant, Akeba, did however persuade Conan to go with him to rescue Akeba's daughter, who had vanished into the cult (*Conan the Unconquered*).

After Jhandar's fall, Akeba urged Conan to take service in the Turanian army. The Cimmerian did not at first find military life congenial, being too self-willed and hot-tempered to easily submit to discipline. Moreover, as he was at this time an indifferent horseman and archer, Conan was relegated to a low-paid irregular unit.

Still, a chance soon arose to show his mettle. King Yildiz launched an expedition against a rebellious satrap. By sorcery, the satrap wiped out the force sent against him. Young

Conan alone survived to enter the magic-maddened satrap's city of Yaralet ("The Hand of Nergal").

Returning in triumph to the glittering capital of Aghrapur, Conan gained a place in King Yildiz's guard of honor. At first he endured the gibes of fellow troopers at his clumsy horsemanship and inaccurate archery. But the gibes died away as the other guardsmen discovered Conan's sledge-hammer fists and as his skills improved.

Conan was chosen, along with a Kushite mercenary named Juma, to escort King Yildiz's daughter Zosara to her wedding with Khan Kujula, chief of the Kuigar nomads. In the foot-hills of the Talakma Mountains, the party was attacked by a strange force of squat, brown, lacquer-armored horsemen. Only Conan, Juma, and the princess survived. They were taken to the subtropical valley of Meru and to the capital, Shamballah, where Conan and Juma were chained to an oar of the Meruvian state galley, about to set forth on a cruise.

On the galley's return to Shamballah, Conan and Juma escaped and made their way into the city. They reached the temple of Yama as the deformed little god-king of Meru was celebrating his marriage to Zosara ("The City of Skulls").

Back at Aghrapur, Conan was promoted to captain. His growing repute as a good man in a tight spot, however, led King Yildiz's generals to pick the barbarian for especially hazardous missions. Once they sent Conan to escort an emis-sary to the predatory tribesmen of the Khozgari Hills, hoping to dissuade them by bribes and threats from plundering the Turanians of the lowlands. The Khozgarians, respecting only immediate, overwhelming force, attacked the detachment, killing the emissary and all but two of the soldiers, Conan and Jamal.

To assure their safe passage back to civilization, Conan and Jamal captured Shanya, the daughter of the Khozgari chief. Their route led them to a misty highland. Jamal and the horses were slain, and Conan had to battle a horde of hairless apes and invade the stronghold of an ancient, dying race ("The People of the Summit").

Another time, Conan was dispatched thousands of miles eastward, to fabled Khitai, to convey to King Shu of Kusan a letter from King Yildiz proposing a treaty of friendship and trade. The wise old Khitan king sent his visitors back with a letter of acceptance. As a guide, however, the king appointed a foppish little nobleman, Duke Feng, who had entirely different objectives ("The Curse of the Monolith," first published as "Conan and the Cenotaph").

Conan continued in his service in Turan for about two years, traveling widely and learning the elements of organized, civilized warfare. As usual, trouble was his bedfellow. After one of his more unruly adventures, involving the mistress of his superior officer, Conan deserted and headed for Zamora. In Shadizar he heard that the Temple of Zath, the spider god, in the Zamorian city of Yezud, was recruiting soldiers. Hastening to Yezud, Conan found that a Brythunian free company had taken all the available mercenary posts. He became the town's blacksmith because as a boy he had been apprenticed in this trade.

Conan learned from an emissary of King Yildiz, Lord Parvez, that High Priest Feridun was holding Yildiz's favorite wife, Jamilah, in captivity. Parvez hired Conan to abduct Jamilah. Meanwhile Conan had set his heart on the eight huge gems that formed the eyes of an enormous statue of the spider god. As he was loosening the jewels, the approach of priests forced him to flee to a crypt below the naos. The temple dancing girl Rudabeh, with whom Conan was truly in love for the first time in his life, descended into the crypt to warn him of the doom awaiting him there (*Conan and the Spider God*).

Conan next rode off to Shadizar to track down a rumor of treasure. He obtained a map showing the location of a ruby-studded golden idol in the Kezankian Mountains; but thieves stole his map. Conan, pursuing them, had a brush with Kezankian hillmen and had to join forces with the very rogues he was tracking. He found the treasure, only to lose it under strange circumstances ("The Bloodstained God").

Fed up with magic, Conan headed for the Cimmerian hills. After a time in the simple, routine life of his native village, however, he grew restless enough to join his old friends, the Æsir, in a raid into Vanaheim. In a bitter struggle on the snow-covered plain, both forces were wiped out—all but Conan, who wandered off to a strange encounter with the legendary Atali, daughter of the frost giant Ymir ("The Frost Giant's Daughter").

Haunted by Atali's icy beauty, Conan headed back toward the South, where, despite his often-voiced scorn of civilization, the golden spires of teeming cities beckoned. In the Eiglophian Mountains, Conan rescued a young woman from cannibals, but through overconfidence lost her to the dreaded monster that haunted glaciers ("The Lair of the Ice Worm").

Conan then returned to the Hyborian lands, which include Aquilonia, Argos, Brythunia, Corinthia, Koth, Nemedia, Ophir, and Zingara. These countries were named for the Hyborian peoples who, as barbarians, had 3,000 years earlier conquered the empire of Acheron and built civilized realms on its ruins.

In Belverus, the capital of Nemedia, the ambitious Lord Albanus dabbled in sorcery to usurp the throne of King Garian. To Belverus came Conan, seeking a patron with money to enable him to hire his own free company. Albanus gave a magical sword to a confederate, Lord Melius, who went mad and attacked people in the street until killed. As he picked up the ensorcelled sword. Conan was accosted by Hordo, a one-eyed thief and smuggler whom he had known as Karela's lieutenant.

Conan sold the magical sword, hired his own free company, and taught his men mounted archery. Then he persuaded King Garian to hire him. But Albanus had made a man of clay and by his sorcery given it the exact appearance of the king. Then he imprisoned the king, substituted his golem, and framed Conan for murder (*Conan the Defender*).

Conan next brought his free company to Ianthe, capital of Ophir. There the Lady Synelle, a platinum-blond sorceress, wished to bring to life the demon-god Al'Kirr. Conan bought a statuette of this demon-god and soon found that various parties were trying to steal it from him. He and his company took service under Synelle, not knowing her plans.

Then the bandette Karela reappeared and, as usual, tried to murder Conan. Synelle hired her to steal the statuette, which the witch needed for her sorcery. She also planned to sacrifice Karela (*Conan the Triumphant*).

Conan went on to Argos; but since that kingdom was at peace, there were no jobs for mercenaries. A misunderstanding with the law compelled Conan to leap to the deck of a ship as it left the pier. This was the merchant galley *Argus*, bound for the coasts of Kush.

A major epoch in Conan's life was about to begin. The *Argus* was taken by Bêlit, the Shemite captain of the pirate ship *Tigress*, whose ruthless black corsairs had made her mistress of the Kushite littoral. Conan won both Bêlit and a partnership in her bloody trade ("Queen of the Black Coast," Chapter 1).

Years before, Bêlit, daughter of a Shemite trader, had been abducted with her brother Jehanan by Stygian slavers. Now she asked her lover Conan to try to rescue the youth. The barbarian slipped into Khemi, the Stygian seaport, was captured, but escaped to the eastern end of Stygia, the province of Taia, where a revolt against Stygian oppression was brewing (*Conan the Rebel*).

Conan and Bêlit resumed their piratical careers, preying mainly on Stygian vessels. Then an ill fate took them up the black Zarkheba River to the lost city of an ancient winged race ("Queen of the Black Coast," Chapters 2–5).

As Bêlit's burning funeral ship wafted out to sea, a down-hearted Conan turned his back on the sea, which he would not follow again for years. He plunged inland and joined the warlike Bamulas, a black tribe whose power swiftly grew under his leadership.

The chief of a neighboring tribe, the Bakalahs, planned a treacherous attack on another neighbor and invited Conan and his Bamulas to take part in the sack and massacre. Conan accepted but, learning that an Ophirean girl, Livia, was held captive in Bakalah, he out-betrayed the Bakalahs. Livia ran off during the slaughter and wandered into a mysterious valley, where only Conan's timely arrival saved her from being sacrificed to an extraterrestrial being ("The Vale of Lost Women").

Before Conan could build his own black empire, he was thwarted by a succession of natural catastrophes as well as by the intrigues of hostile Bamulas. Forced to flee, he headed north. After a narrow escape from pursuing lions on the veldt, Conan took shelter in a mysterious ruined castle of prehuman origin. He had a brush with Stygian slavers and a malign supernatural entity ("The Castle of Terror").

Continuing on, Conan reached the semicivilized kingdom of Kush. This was the land to which the name "Kush" properly applied; although Conan, like other northerners, tended to use the term loosely to mean any of the black countries south of Stygia. In Meroê, the capital, Conan rescued from a hostile mob the young Queen of Kush, the arrogant, impulsive, fierce, cruel, and voluptuous Tananda.

Conan became embroiled in a labyrinthine intrigue between Tananda and an ambitious nobleman who commanded a piglike demon. The problem was aggravated by the presence of Diana, a Nemedian slave girl to whom Conan, despite the jealous fury of Tananda, took a fancy. Events culminated in a night of insurrection and slaughter ("The Snout in the Dark").

Dissatisfied with his achievements in the black countries, Conan wandered to the meadowlands of Shem and became a soldier of Akkharia, a Shemite city-state. He joined a band of volunteers to liberate a neighboring city-state; but through the treachery of Othbaal, cousin of the mad King Akhîrom of Pelishtia, the volunteers were destroyed—all but Conan, who survived to track the plotter to Asgalun, the Pelishti capital. There Conan became involved in a polygonal power war among the mad Akhîrom, the treacherous Othbaal, a Stygian witch, and a company of black mercenaries. In the final hurly-burly of sorcery, steel, and blood, Conan grabbed Othbaal's red-haired mistress, Rufia, and galloped north ("Hawks Over Shem").

Conan's movements at this time are uncertain. One tale, sometimes assigned to this period, tells of Conan's service as a mercenary in Zingara. A Ptolemaic papyrus in the British Museum alleges that in Kordava, the capital, a captain in the regular army forced a quarrel on Conan. When Conan killed his assailant, he was condemned to hang. A fellow condemnee, Santiddio, belonged to an underground conspiracy, the White Rose, that hoped to topple King Rimanendo. As other conspirators created a disturbance in the crowd that gathered for the hanging, Conan and Santiddio escaped.

Mordermi, head of an outlaw band allied with the White Rose, enlisted Conan in his movement. The conspiracy was carried on in the Pit, a warren of tunnels beneath the city. When the King sent an army to clean out the Pit, the insurrectionists were saved by Callidos, a Stygian sorcerer. King Rimanendo was slain and Mordermi became king. When he proved as tyrannical as his predecessor, Conan raised another revolt; then, refusing the crown for himself, he departed (*Conan: The Road of Kings*).

This tale involves many questions. If authentic, it may belong in Conan's earlier mercenary period, around the time of *Conan the Defender*. But there is no corroboration in other narratives of the idea that Conan ever visited Zingara before his late thirties, the time of *Conan the Buccaneer*. Moreover, none of the rulers of Zingara mentioned in the papyrus appear on the list of kings of Zingara in the Byzantine manuscript *Hoi Anaktes tês Tzingêras*. Hence some students deem the papyrus either spurious or a case of confusion between Conan and some other hero. Everything else known about Conan indicates that, if he had indeed been offered the Zingaran crown, he would have grabbed it with both hands.

We next hear of Conan after he took service under Amalric of Nemedia, the general of Queen-Regent Yasmela of the little border kingdom of Khoraja. While Yasmela's brother, King Khossus, was a prisoner in Ophir, Yasmela's borders were assailed by the forces of the veiled sorcerer Natohk—actually the 3,000-years-dead Thugra Khotan of the ruined city of Kuthchemes.

Obeying an oracle of Mitra, the supreme Hyborian god, Yasmela made Conan captain-general of Khoraja's army. In this rôle he gave battle to Natohk's hosts and rescued the Queen-Regent from the malignant magic of the undead warlock. Conan won the day—and the Queen ("Black Colossus").

Conan, now in his late twenties, settled down as Khorajan commander-in-chief. But the queen, whose lover he had expected to be, was too preoccupied with affairs of state to have time for frolics. He even proposed marriage, but she explained that such a union would not be sanctioned by Khorajan law and custom. Yet, if Conan could somehow rescue her brother from imprisonment, she might persuade Khossus to change the law.

Conan set forth with Rhazes, an astrologer, and Fronto, a

thief who knew a secret passage into the dungeon where Khossus languished. They rescued the King but found themselves trapped by Kothian troops, since Strabonus of Koth had his own reasons for wanting Khossus.

Having surmounted these perils, Conan found that Khossus, a pompous young ass, would not hear of a foreign barbarian's marrying his sister. Instead, he would marry Yasmela off to a nobleman and find a middle-class bride for Conan. Conan said nothing; but in Argos, as their ship cast off, Conan sprang ashore with most of the gold that Khossus had raised and waved the King an ironic farewell ("Shadows in the Dark").

Now nearly thirty, Conan slipped away to revisit his Cimmerian homeland and avenge himself on the Hyperboreans. His blood brothers among the Cimmerians and the Æsir had won wives and sired sons, some as old and almost as big as Conan had been at the sack of Venarium. But his years of blood and battle had stirred his predatory spirit too strongly for him to follow their example. When traders brought word of new wars, Conan galloped off to the Hyborian lands.

A rebel prince of Koth was fighting to overthrow Strabonus, the penurious ruler of that far-stretched nation; and Conan found himself among old companions in the princeling's array, until the rebel made peace with his king. Unemployed again, Conan formed an outlaw band, the Free Companions. This troop gravitated to the steppes west of the Sea of Vilayet, where they joined the ruffianly horde known as the *kozaki*.

Conan soon became the leader of this lawless crew and ravaged the western borders of the Turanian Empire until his old employer, King Yildiz, sent a force under Shah Amurath, who lured the *kozaki* deep into Turan and cut them down.

Slaying Amurath and acquiring the Turanian's captive, Princess Olivia of Ophir, Conan rowed out into the Vilayet Sea in a small boat. He and Olivia took refuge on an island, where they found a ruined greenstone city, in which stood strange iron statues. The shadows cast by the moonlight proved as dangerous as the giant carnivorous ape that ranged the isle, or the pirate crew that landed for rest and recreation ("Shadows in the Moonlight").

Conan seized command of the pirates that ravaged the Sea of Vilayet. As chieftain of this mongrel Red Brotherhood, Conan was more than ever a thorn in King Yildiz's flesh. That mild monarch, instead of strangling his brother Teyaspa in the normal Turanian manner, had cooped him up in a castle in the Colchian Mountains. Yildiz now sent his General Artaban to destroy the pirate stronghold at the mouth of the Zaporoska River; but the general became the harried instead of the harrier. Retreating inland, Artaban stumbled upon Teyaspa's whereabouts; and the final conflict involved Conan's outlaws, Artaban's Turanians, and a brood of vampires ("The Road of the Eagles").

Deserted by his sea rovers, Conan appropriated a stallion and headed back to the steppes. Yezdigerd, now on the throne of Turan, proved a far more astute and energetic ruler than his sire. He embarked on a program of imperial conquest.

Conan went to the small border kingdom of Khauran, where he won command of the royal guard of Queen Taramis. This queen had a twin sister, Salome, born a witch and reared by the yellow sorcerers of Khitai. She allied herself with the adventurer Constantius of Koth and planned by imprisoning the Queen to rule in her stead. Conan, who perceived the deception, was trapped and crucified. Cut down by the chieftain Olgerd Vladislav, the Cimmerian was carried off to a Zuagir camp in the desert. Conan waited for his wounds to heal, then applied his daring and ruthlessness to win his place as Olgerd's lieutenant.

When Salome and Constantius began a reign of terror in Khauran, Conan led his Zuagirs against the Khauranian capital. Soon Constantius hung from the cross to which he had nailed Conan, and Conan rode off smiling, to lead his Zuagirs on raids against the Turanians ("A Witch Shall Be Born").

Conan, about thirty and at the height of his physical powers, spent nearly two years with the desert Shemites, first as Olgerd's lieutenant and then, having ousted Olgerd, as sole chief. The circumstances of his leaving the Zuagirs were recently disclosed by a silken scroll in Old Tibetan, spirited out of Tibet by a refugee. This document is now with the Oriental Institute in Chicago.

The energetic King Yezdigerd sent soldiers to trap Conan and his troop. Because of a Zamorian traitor in Conan's ranks, the ambush nearly succeeded. To avenge the betrayal, Conan led his band in pursuit of the Zamorian. When his men deserted, Conan pressed on alone until, near death, he was rescued by Enosh, a chieftain of the isolated desert town of Akhlat.

Akhlat suffered under the rule of a demon in the form of a woman, who fed on the life force of living things. Conan, Enosh informed him, was their prophesied liberator. After it was over, Conan was invited to settle in Akhlat; but, knowing himself ill-suited to a life of humdrum respectability, he instead headed southwest to Zamboula with the horse and money of Vardanes the Zamorian ("Black Tears").

In one colossal debauch, Conan dissipated the fortune he had brought to Zamboula, a Turanian outpost. There lurked the sinister priest of Hanuman, Totrasmek, who sought a famous jewel, the Star of Khorala, for which the Queen of Ophir was said to have offered a roomful of gold. In the ensuing imbroglio, Conan acquired the Star of Khorala and rode westward ("Shadows of Zamboula").

The medieval monkish manuscript *De sidere choralae*, rescued from the bombed ruins of Monte Cassino, continues the tale. Conan reached the capital of Ophir to find that the effeminate Moranthes II, himself under the thumb of the sinister Count Rigello, kept his queen, Marala, under lock and key. Conan scaled the wall of Moranthes's castle and fetched Marala out. Rigello pursued the fugitives nearly to the Aquilonian border, where the Star of Khorala showed its power in an unexpected way ("The Star of Khorala").

Hearing that the *kozaki* had regained their vigor, Conan returned with horse and sword to the harrying of Turan. Although the now-famous northlander arrived all but empty-handed, contingents of the *kozaki* and the Vilayet pirates soon began operating under his command.

Yezdigerd sent Jehungir Agha to entrap the barbarian on the island of Xapur. Coming early to the ambush, Conan found the island's ancient fortress-palace of Dagon restored by magic, and in it the city's malevolent god, in the form of a giant of living iron ("The Devil in Iron").

After escaping from Xapur, Conan built his *kozaki* and pirate raiders into such a formidable threat that King Yezdigerd devoted all his forces to their destruction. After a devastating defeat, the *kozaki* scattered, and Conan retreated southward to take service in the light cavalry of Kobad Shah, King of Iranistan.

Conan got himself into Kobad Shah's bad graces and had to ride for the hills. He found a conspiracy brewing in Yanaidar, the fortress-city of the Hidden Ones. The Sons of Yezm were trying to revive an ancient cult and unite the surviving devotees of the old gods in order to rule the world. The adventure ended with the rout of the contending forces by the gray ghouls of Yanaidar, and Conan rode eastward ("The Flame Knife").

Conan reappeared in the Himelian Mountains, on the northwest frontier of Vendhya, as a war chief of the savage Afghuli tribesmen. Now in his early thirties, the warlike barbarian was known and feared throughout the world of the Hyborian Age.

No man to be bothered with niceties, Yezdigerd employed the magic of the wizard Khemsa, an adept of the dreaded

Black Circle, to remove the Vendhyan king from his path. The dead king's sister, the Devi Yasmina, set out to avenge him but was captured by Conan. Conan and his captive pursued the sorcerous Khemsa, only to see him slain by the magic of the Seers of Yimsha, who also abducted Yasmina ("The People of the Black Circle").

When Conan's plans for welding the hill tribes into a single power failed, Conan, hearing of wars in the West, rode thither. Almuric, a prince of Koth, had rebelled against the hated Strabonus. While Conan joined Almuric's bristling host, Strabonus's fellow kings came to that monarch's aid. Almuric's motley horde was driven south, to be annihilated at last by combined Stygian and Kushite forces.

Escaping into the desert, Conan and the camp follower Natala came to age-old Xuthal, a phantom city of living dead men and their creeping shadow-god, Thog. The Stygian woman Thalis, the effective ruler of Xuthal, double-crossed Conan once too often ("The Slithering Shadow").

Conan beat his way back to the Hyborian lands. Seeking further employment, he joined the mercenary army that a Zingaran, Prince Zapayo da Kova, was raising for Argos. It was planned that Koth should invade Stygia from the north, while the Argosseans approached the realm from the south by sea. Koth, however, made a separate peace with Stygia, leaving Conan's army of mercenaries trapped in the Stygian deserts.

Conan fled with Amalric, a young Aquilonian soldier. Soon Conan was captured by nomads, while Amalric escaped. When Amalric caught up again with Conan, Amalric had with him the girl Lissa, whom he had saved from the cannibal god of her native city. Conan had meanwhile become commander of the cavalry of the city of Tombalku. Two kings ruled Tombalku: the Negro Sakumbe and the mixed-blood Zehbeh. When Zehbeh and his faction were driven out, Sakumbe made Conan his co-king. But then the wizard Askia slew Sakumbe by magic. Conan, having avenged his black friend, escaped with Amalric and Lissa ("Drums of Tombalku").

Conan beat his way to the coast, where he joined the Barachan pirates. He was now about thirty-five. As second mate of the *Hawk*, he landed on the island of the Stygian sorcerer Siptah, said to have a magical jewel of fabulous properties.

Siptah dwelt in a cylindrical tower without doors or windows, attended by a winged demon. Conan smoked the unearthly being out but was carried off in its talons to the top of the tower. Inside the tower Conan found the wizard long dead; but the magical gem proved of unexpected help in coping with the demon ("The Gem in the Tower").

Conan remained about two years with the Barachans, according to a set of clay tablets in pre-Sumerian cuneiform. Used to the tightly organized armies of the Hyborian kingdoms, Conan found the organization of the Barachan bands too loose and anarchic to afford an opportunity to rise to leadership. Slipping out of a tight spot at the pirate rendezvous at Tortage, he found that the only alternative to a cut throat was braving the Western Ocean in a leaky skiff. When the *Wastrel*, the ship of the buccaneer Zaporavo, came in sight, Conan climbed aboard.

The Cimmerian soon won the respect of the crew and the enmity of its captain, whose Kordavan mistress, the sleek Sancha, cast too friendly an eye on the black-maned giant. Zaporavo drove his ship westward to an uncharted island, where Conan forced a duel on the captain and killed him, while Sancha was carried off by strange black beings to a living pool worshipped by these entities ("The Pool of the Black Ones").

Conan persuaded the officals at Kordava to transfer Zaporavo's privateering license to him, whereupon he spent about two years in this authorized piracy. As usual, plots were brewing against the Zingaran monarchy. King Ferdrugo was old and apparently failing, with no successor but his nubile daughter Chabela. Duke Villagro enlisted the Stygian super-sorcerer Thoth-Amon, the High Priest of Set, in a plot to obtain Chabela as his bride. Suspicious, the princess took the royal yacht down the coast to consult her uncle. A privateer in league with Villagro captured the yacht and abducted the girl. Chabela escaped and met Conan, who obtained the magical Cobra Crown, also sought by Thoth-Amon.

A storm drove Conan's ship to the coast of Kush, where Conan was confronted by black warriors headed by his old comrade-in-arms, Juma. While the chief welcomed the priva-teers, a tribesman stole the Cobra Crown. Conan set off in pursuit, with Princess Chabela following him. Both were captured by slavers and sold to the black Queen of the Amazons. The Queen made Chabela her slave and Conan her fancy man. Then, jealous of Chabela, she flogged the girl, imprisoned Conan, and condemned both to be devoured by a man-eating tree (*Conan the Buccaneer*).

Having rescued the Zingaran princess, Conan shrugged off hints of marriage and returned to privateering. But other Zingarans, jealous, brought him down off the coast of Shem. Escaping inland, Conan joined the Free Companions, a mer-cenary company. Instead of rich plunder, however, he found himself in dull guard duty on the black frontier of Stygia, where the wine was sour and the pickings poor.

Conan's boredom ended with the appearance of the pirette, Valeria of the Red Brotherhood. When she left the camp, he followed her south. The pair took refuge in a city occupied by the feuding clans of Xotalanc and Tecuhltli. Siding with the latter, the two northerners soon found themselves in trouble with that clan's leader, the ageless witch Tascela ("Red Nails").

Conan's amour with Valeria, however hot at the start, did not last long. Valeria returned to the sea; Conan tried his luck once more in the black kingdoms. Hearing of the "Teeth of Gwahlur," a cache of priceless jewels hidden in Keshan, he sold his services to its irascible king to train the Keshani army.

Thutmekri, the Stygian emissary of the twin kings of Zembabwei, also had designs on the jewels. The Cimmerian, outmatched in intrigue, made tracks for the valley where the ruins of Alkmeenon and its treasure lay hidden. In a wild adventure with the undead goddess Yelaya, the Corinthian girl Muriela, the black priests headed by Gorulga, and the grim gray servants of the long-dead Bît-Yakin, Conan kept his head but lost his loot ("Jewels of Gwahlur").

Heading for Punt with Muriela, Conan embarked on a scheme to relieve the worshipers of an ivory goddess of their abundant gold. Learning that Thutmekri had preceded him and had already poisoned King Lalibeha's mind against him, Conan and his companion took refuge in the temple of the goddess Nebethet.

When the king, Thutmekri, and High Priest Zaramba arrived at the temple, Conan staged a charade wherein Muriela spoke with the voice of the goddess. The results surprised all, including Conan ("The Ivory Goddess").

In Zembabwei, the city of the twin kings, Conan joined a trading caravan which he squired northward along the desert borders, bringing it safely into Shem. Now in his late thirties, the restless adventurer heard that the Aquilonians were spreading westward into the Pictish wilderness. So thither, seeking work for his sword, went Conan. He enrolled as a scout at Fort Tuscelan, where a fierce war raged with the Picts.

In the forests across the river, the wizard Zogar Sag was gathering his swamp demons to aid the Picts. While Conan failed to prevent the destruction of Fort Tuscelan, he managed to warn settlers around Velitrium and to cause the death of Zogar Sag ("Beyond the Black River").

Conan rose rapidly in the Aquilonian service. As captain,

his company was once defeated by the machinations of a traitorous superior. Learning that this officer, Viscount Lucian, was about to betray the province to the Picts, Conan exposed the traitor and routed the Picts ("Moon of Blood").

Promoted to general, Conan defeated the Picts in a great battle at Velitrium and was called back to the capital, Tarantia, to receive the nation's accolades. Then, having roused the suspicions of the depraved and foolish King Numedides, he was drugged and chained in the Iron Tower under sentence of death.

The barbarian, however, had friends as well as foes. Soon he was spirited out of prison and turned loose with horse and sword. He struck out across the dank forests of Pictland toward the distant sea. In the forest, the Cimmerian came upon a cavern in which lay the corpse and the demon-guarded treasure of the pirate Tranicos. From the west, others—a Zingaran count and two bands of pirates—were hunting the same fortune, while the Stygian sorcerer Thoth-Amon took a hand in the game ("The Treasure of Tranicos").

Rescued by an Aquilonian galley, Conan was chosen to lead a revolt against Numedides. While the revolution stormed along, civil war raged on the Pictish frontier. Lord Valerian, a partisan of Numedides, schemed to bring the Picts down on the town of Schohira. A scout, Gault Hagar's sons, undertook to upset this scheme by killing the Pictish wizard ("Wolves Beyond the Border").

Storming the capital city and slaying Numedides on the steps of his throne—which he promptly took for his own—Conan, now in his early forties, found himself ruler of the greatest Hyborian nation (*Conan the Liberator*).

A king's life, however, proved no bed of houris. Within a year, an exiled count had gathered a group of plotters to oust the barbarian from the throne. Conan might have lost crown and head but for the timely intervention of the long-dead sage Epimitreus ("The Phoenix of the Sword").

No sooner had the mutterings of revolt died down than Conan was treacherously captured by the kings of Ophir and Koth. He was imprisoned in the tower of the wizard Tsotha-lanti in the Kothian capital. Conan escaped with the help of a fellow prisoner, who was Tsotha-lanti's wizardly rival Pelias. By Pelias's magic, Conan was whisked to Tarantia in time to slay a pretender and to lead an army against his treacherous fellow kings ("The Scarlet Citadel").

For nearly two years, Aquilonia thrived under Conan's firm but tolerant rule. The lawless, hard-bitten adventurer of former years had, through force of circumstance, matured into an able and responsible statesman. But a plot was brewing in neighboring Nemedia to destroy the King of Aquilonia by sorcery from an elder day.

Conan, about forty-five, showed few signs of age save a network of scars on his mighty frame and a more cautious approach to wine, women and bloodshed. Although he kept a harem of luscious concubines, he had never taken an official queen; hence he had no legitimate son to inherit the throne, a fact whereof his enemies sought to take advantage.

The plotters resurrected Xaltotun, the greatest sorcerer of the ancient empire of Acheron, which fell before the Hyborian savages 3,000 years earlier. By Xaltotun's magic, the King of Nemedia was slain and replaced by his brother Tarascus. Black sorcery defeated Conan's army; Conan was imprisoned, and the exile Valerius took his throne.

Escaping from a dungeon with the aid of the harem girl Zenobia, Conan returned to Aquilonia to rally his loyal forces against Valerius. From the priests of Asura, he learned that Xaltotun's power could be broken only by means of a strange jewel, the "Heart of Ahriman." The trail of the jewel led to a pyramid in the Stygian desert outside black-walled Khemi. Winning the Heart of Ahriman, Conan returned to face his foes (*Conan the Conqueror*, originally published as *The Hour of the Dragon*).

After regaining his kingdom, Conan made Zenobia his queen. But, at the ball celebrating her elevation, the queen was borne off by a demon sent by the Khitan sorcerer Yah Chieng. Conan's quest for his bride carried him across the known world, meeting old friends and foes. In purple-towered Paikang, with the help of a magical ring, he freed Zenobia and slew the wizard (*Conan the Avenger*, originally published as *The Return of Conan*).

Home again, the way grew smoother. Zenobi gave him heirs: a son named Conan but commonly called Conn, another son called Taurus, and a daughter. When Conn was twelve, his father took him on a hunting trip to Gunderland. Conan was now in his late fifties. His sword arm was a little slower than in his youth, and his black mane and the fierce mustache of his later years were traced with gray; but his strength still surpassed that of two ordinary men.

When Conn was lured away by the Witchmen of Hyperborea, who demanded that Conan come to their stronghold alone, Conan went. He found Louhi, the High Priestess of the Witchmen, in conference with three others of the world's leading sorcerers: Thoth-Amon of Stygia; the god-king of Kambuja; and the black lord of Zembabwei. In the ensuing holocaust, Louhi and the Kambujan perished, while Thoth-Amon and the other sorcerer vanished by magic ("The Witch of the Mists").

Old King Ferdrugo of Zingara had died, and his throne remained vacant as the nobles intrigued over the succession. Duke Pantho of Guarralid invaded Poitain, in southern Aquilonia. Conan, suspecting sorcery, crushed the invaders. Learning that Thoth-Amon was behind Pantho's madness, Conan set out with his army to settle matters with the Stygian. He pursued his foe to Thoth-Amon's stronghold in Stygia ("Black Sphinx of Nebthu"), to Zembabwei ("Red Moon of Zembabwei"), and to the last realm of the serpent folk in the far south ("Shadows in the Skull").

For several years, Conan's rule was peaceful. But time did that which no combination of foes had been able to do. The Cimmerian's skin became wrinkled and his hair gray; old wounds ached in damp weather. Conan's beloved consort Zenobia died giving birth to their second daughter.

Then catastrophe shattered King Conan's mood of half-resigned discontent. Supernatural entities, the Red Shadows, began seizing and carrying off his subjects. Conan was baffled until in a dream he again visited the sage Epimitreus. He was told to abdicate in favor of Prince Conn and set out across the Western Ocean.

Conan discovered that the Red Shadows had been sent by the priest-wizards of Antillia, a chain of islands in the western part of the ocean, whither the survivors of Atlantis had fled 8,000 years before. These priests offered human sacrifices to their devil-god Xotli on such a scale that their own population faced extermination.

In Antillia, Conan's ship was taken, but he escaped into the city Ptahuacan. After conflicts with giant rats and dragons, he emerged atop the sacrificial pyramid just as his crewmen were about to be sacrificed. Supernatural conflict, revolution, and seismic catastrophe ensued. In the end, Conan sailed off to explore the continents to the west (*Conan of the Isles*).

Whether he died there, or whether there is truth in the tale that he strode out of the West to stand at his son's side in a final battle against Aquilonia's foes, will be revealed only to him who looks, as Kull of Valusia once did, into the mystic mirrors of Tuzun Thune.

L. Sprague de Camp
Villanova, Pennsylvania
May 1984